01/21

DEATH COMES HOT

DEATH COMES HOT

Michael Jecks

CRÈME de la CRIME

This first world edition published 2020
in Great Britain and the USA by
Crème de la Crime an imprint of
SEVERN HOUSE PUBLISHERS LTD of
Eardley House, 4 Uxbridge Street, London W8 7SY.
Trade paperback edition first published
in Great Britain and the USA 2021 by
SEVERN HOUSE PUBLISHERS LTD.

British Library Cataloguing in Publication Data
A CIP catalogue record for this title is available from the British Library.

ISBN-13: 978-1-78029-131-4 (cased)
ISBN-13: 978-1-78029-735-4 (trade paper)
ISBN-13: 978-1-4483-0457-8 (e-book)

This is a work of fiction. Names, characters, places and incidents
are either the product of the author's imagination or are used fictitiously.
Except where actual historical events and characters are being described
for the storyline of this novel, all situations in this publication are
fictitious and any resemblance to actual persons, living or dead,
business establishments, events or locales is purely coincidental.

All Severn House titles are printed on acid-free paper.

Severn House Publishers support the Forest Stewardship Council™ [FSC™],
the leading international forest certification organisation.
All our titles that are printed on FSC certified paper carry the FSC logo.

Typeset by Palimpsest Book Production Ltd.,
Falkirk, Stirlingshire, Scotland.
Printed and bound in Great Britain by
TJ International, Padstow, Cornwall.

For Jane, Katie and Billy for their patience during the writing of this latest. With all my love.

ONE

There are times when life seems to drift along placidly, like a twig floating on the Thames, happy and carefree, just ambling downriver with nothing but an occasional area of turbulence to disturb the calm.

That morning, I knew, was not one of those times.

On those glorious days, a man wakes up and just *knows* the sun will continue shining all day, that the pie he eats will contain at least mostly beef, and that when he trips, a friendly hand will appear and keep him upright. But there are other days, days when the sky is leaden, when his first mouthful of pie demonstrates the cook's imaginative use of sawdust, gristle and dogs' tails, and when every unwary step is apparently placed on a sheet of ice. And no one is there to catch him.

This, I knew, was to be one of *those* days.

I have had my share of days of excitement, and I can assure you that I greatly prefer the days of tedium, when the most exciting thing is stepping in a dog's turd on the way home. I can cope with boredom. Today, when I heard the knocking at the door, I knew immediately that this would be one of those days on which it was better not to remain in my bed. No, this was a day to be up and about – *urgently*!

'*Blackjack!* You black-hearted, black-souled, black . . .' At this point my visitor appeared to run out of relevant epithets and instead bawled his command: 'Open this door!'

The banging was like the thunder of Satan's hammers, great leaden mauls striking at sinners' flesh to torment them, and I was awake in an instant.

'Sweet merciful . . .' I began.

Yes, this was not a day to lie abed. This was a day to make use of my carefully thought-through escape.

Why had I a well-thought-through escape plan?

Well, you see, I had experienced a swift rise in popularity

in recent years. Since the appalling shock of the rebellion of
Wyatt and his merry men of Kent, I had become a professional
man, a fellow of some authority and importance. I served my
master, John Blount, which meant that I had been elevated
from the ranks of the poor and dispossessed into a position
of wealth. All was based on the mistaken assumption that I
was a cold-hearted assassin whose skills might assist Master
Blount's master, the sleek Welshman Thomas Parry. I would
have disabused them of the notion, were it not for one fact
that struck me: if they were looking for an assassin, and
had told a man (me) that they wanted to hire him, for him
(me) to refuse them might lead to his (my) becoming their
first victim. If you take my meaning.

No. If I had learned one thing over the last years living in
London, it was that life was cheapest at the bottom, and at
that time, as a failed cut-purse who was already implicated in
a murder or two, being adopted as an assassin might well be
an advantage. After all, if I was put in a difficult situation, I
reasoned, I could always run away. And in the meantime,
I was being offered a fresh suit of clothes every year, a good
income and a house in a fashionable part of London. There
were significant advantages.

However, there was also one disadvantage. While the
money and house were appealing, there was always the risk
that others might get to hear of my new career. The profession of assassin has its detractors, after all – especially
among those who choose to deplore my function. Those,
say, who feel I might have made an attempt on their life,
or believe I might at any moment be persuaded to do so, or
those who believed I had been paid to remove a relative.
Or others who believed I had been instructed to remove a
relative and I had not complied – there were several wives
who would have appreciated a new husband, for example.
These ingrates could appear at any moment, and it now
sounded, from the thunder at my front door – which would
be seriously marking my new oaken timbers, I feared – that
such a moment had arrived.

It was time to leave.

*   *   *

Leaping from the bedclothes, I pulled on my hosen, slipped a shirt over my head, grabbed at my jack, caught hold of my belt and rushed to the window, donning the jack and tugging on boots.

My chamber was in the top floor of my house. It was jettied, as were all the other properties there, and from my window I could see the upper chamber of the house opposite. At the noise below, and the shouting of 'Open in the name of the Queen!' from beneath me, I saw my neighbour and his wife suddenly jerk awake and sit upright, he looking comical with his nightshirt and hair all bristled beneath his sleeping coif, staring about him blearily like a stunned sheep. She was less amusing, but thoroughly interesting, for in the warmth of the summery evening she was wearing only a thin chemise that gaped at the front. Seeing my attentive leer, she grabbed at it instinctively, and then shot a look of pure venom at her husband and let it gape once more, looking at me in what I could only describe as a speculative manner.

But I had no time. I smiled and saluted them, tying up the points attaching my hosen to my jack before grabbing my wheel-lock pistol, a bag of balls and flask of powder, slipping their straps over my head, pulling on my baldric, thrusting the pistol's long barrel into my belt, and then carefully pulling on my hat. I studied my appearance in the mirror. There was no denying, I looked rakish but superb.

My preparations complete, I clambered out on to my window's ledge.

It is no secret that I have no head for heights. Not for me the excitement of the fool who disdains to grip a rope at thirty feet of loitering death. If death is waiting for me in a hard-packed roadway, I would prefer the security of a hempen rope. The distance to the ground from this vantage point was enough to make the sweat pour. I clung to the window's frame and tried not to think about the ground and how very hard it was. Visions of my body, broken and bloody, flooded my mind, and it was a cautious and thoughtful Jack who reached up, over the roof of the jettied chamber, to the rope hanging overhead.

Rope? Well, yes. From the moment I had taken on my new

position under the instruction of Master John Blount, I had determined that I would ensure that, no matter what, I would always have an escape route planned. Last year, a loose tile from my roof had slid down and almost struck a woman in the street. It was deeply irritating, since she had struck up such a fuss that I had felt bound to pay her to silence her howls, and at the same time I knew that losing such a tile must mean I had a leak in the roof, so I instructed a fellow to come and replace it. Apart from anything else, I didn't want to have to open my door to another complaining harpy like her. I had thought she would scratch my eyes out, so demented did she appear. It had not even struck her.

Thus, I had a man come. He pitched his ladder against my wall at the rear, and clambered on to the roof, probably breaking more tiles than he replaced, in the natural manner of a London workman. However, while he was there, he gave me his considered opinion that many more tiles would have to be replaced soon.

Then it was that I had my moment of genius. 'Good fellow,' I called. 'I cannot have this work done at present, but soon. Why don't you leave a coil of rope fixed to the chimney, so that next time you come, it will be easier to ascend?'

In short order, a good hempen rope was attached and I had my escape route. All I had to do was grab the rope, use it to pull myself to the roof, and then run lightly across to the next building, or the one after that, and make good my escape.

It was simple, I reasoned. *What could possibly go wrong?*

I was about to discover.

The rope dangled just to one side of the window, and I carefully climbed from the window, grasping the hemp. It uncoiled easily enough, and with a little effort I swung out over the roadway, with many a clatter of gun and sword and dagger. A glance around, and I saw that my neighbour was glaring short-sightedly at the noise. It was well enough for him, I considered, with his buxom wife at his side. She was peering at me with a look that was much more interested, and I was loath to depart from that view so soon, but a renewed battering on my door beneath was enough to persuade me. I hauled on the rope and made my way to the roof. She would have to wait until later.

Below me, I could hear the bellows of the fool at my door, and I cast a glance down with amusement as I coiled the rope and left it beside the chimney breast. Then, gaily enough, being assured of my safety, I followed the ridge of the roof to the next building.

My useless manservant, Raphe, who knew more ways to avoid work than there were days in a twelvemonth, would not rise for such a row. The lazy fool was never an early riser, and would deprecate leaving his warm bed for any man, let alone one who bellowed so loudly. He would think, and rightly, that the first person to open a door to such as was making his temper so clear would be a fool. A man so choleric was surely either consumed by a rage so intense that a flashing glance from his eyes would likely blast a Queen's navy ship to splinters and fragments of kindling, or in the grip of an excess of rum. Whichever was the case, the man opening the door would likely receive a buffet on his pate that would rattle his brains till the next Easter. Raphe would stay in his cot behind the chimney in the kitchen, warm and snug with his hound curled up beside him. Except . . .

A sudden sharp barking removed whatever shreds of peace might have endured the savage thundering on my door, and I heard voices from other houses raised in remonstration.

'What in the name of the Saints . . .'

'Keep the noise down, you whoresons . . .'

'If you don't stop this row, I'll come and knock you so hard you'll . . .'

Alas, I would have enjoyed remaining and listening to some of the more inventive comments made by my neighbours, but it occurred to me that I would be better employed putting as much distance between the owner of those fists and myself as quickly as possible. Still, I heard doors slam wide and men protesting strongly, their voices raised in angry demonstration of the true Londoners' respect for their own rights. Such a dispute could have continued for many a long hour, but already I could hear blows exchanged.

Thus reassured that pursuit was unlikely, I strolled along

the pitch of my roof to the next, which was a full foot lower, so no great challenge to a man with my skills, and made my way by degrees over the various angles of a number of roofs, until I came to a long, sloping pitch of tiles. Here I half slid, half trotted to the lowest point, and from there sprang down lightly. It was only a short drop, and I landed with the agility of a cat.

Although I am not one to boast, I must admit that it was a leap to make a tumbler jealous.

However, as I stood and began to saunter towards the gate which stood wide, there were two matters that struck me as odd.

The first was the fact that the gate was open this early in the morning. I had leapt from a low roof into a neighbour's rear yard. This place, like any other, should have been kept enclosed. No one would want strangers wandering about their yard in the dead of night, so since curfew the gate should have been held shut and locked until the household was awake. It was peculiar, I thought.

This, I admit, was soon forced from my mind by the second consideration: the sudden feeling of cold, sharp steel against my neck.

I don't know whether you have ever experienced such a sensation. There is something particularly unpleasant about being brought up short by a length of steel at the Adam's apple. I was once, when young, shown how to skate on a frozen pool. It was a wonderful experience, and I thoroughly enjoyed the feeling, right up to the moment when a skate came loose and I was sent whirling into an area of weaker ice that suddenly broke up under my weight. That feeling – of joy swiftly turned to despair as the ice shattered and I was propelled beneath into the fiercely chill waters – was rather similar to my current experience. It was a bafflingly horrible situation, made all the worse by the fact that I did not know who wielded the steel.

Yes, there is something quite hideously repellent about a razor-sharp sword held at one's throat. Somehow, no matter what the actual environment, a sharp edge will always feel truly cold, like a shard of ice. This blade felt sharp enough to cut the air in two. I had a conviction that it could cleave waters. If Moses had wished to part the Red Sea with ease, he could have flourished this sword and the waters would have retreated from that horrible blade with speed, giving soggy apologies for any delays. This was a highly unpleasant-feeling weapon.

There was a voice at my ear, and it was little improvement on the blade. 'Master Blackjack. Now, this is a strange thing, ain't it? What would you be doing running down the roof like that, eh? Not trying to test your tiles, was you? See if there was any broken ones, like?'

He put a hand on my shoulder and persuaded me to turn and face him, the weapon resting at the side of my neck. My artery seemed to shrivel like a salted slug as I felt the keen edge rest there.

The brute holding it was a repellent fellow with thick, lank, dark hair. His eyes gazed at me from below his cap, and his mouth was a wound in the beating heart of the English language. He was not as well made as me, with my upright carriage and honest face, but he made up for that in animal cunning and sheer cruelty. His was not a face to inspire confidence or a sense of fellow feeling.

'You have injured my reputation,' he added with a snarl.

Which was a hard accusation to accept.

After all, how does a man injure the reputation of an executioner?

Hal Westmecott was a man in his middle years, I would have guessed. It was said that he had been a butcher, and that he offered his services after his predecessor finally revolted at the task of tearing the hearts from living men, cutting off their limbs or private parts, or making them dance a hempen jig – but I doubted that. I have known several butchers, and even the worst of them would have made a better job of killing their victims than Hal Westmecott. To call him a butcher was to slander all those who hacked at dead animals for a living.

His headsman's axe may have been blunt, but this blade was not from the same mould. Perhaps it was because he needed to defend himself often that he kept his sword blade true; whatever the reason, this was a weapon in much better condition.

'Oh, hello, Hal,' I said.

'Don't squeak. I s'pose you thought I'd be at your door, waiting for you to open it, eh?' he said, and grinned.

It was an appalling sight. Blackened stumps were displayed like ancient gravestones in a haunted cemetery. I almost thought I could see tiny ravens flying about them, but then a gust of his foul breath struck me, and I was forced to avert my head quickly before I retched. An unfortunate reaction, I realized, when I felt a line of fire burn my throat.

'You've cut me!' I exclaimed.

'You cut yerself,' he said unsympathetically. 'Get used to it, because when I do it, you'll feel it more.'

'Why do you want to hurt me?' I said, trying an offended tone of voice.

'You know why, else you wouldn't have tried to slide away over your roof, would ye?' He shoved me back until I was against the wall, and now the blade was at my windpipe. I swallowed – carefully.

'Hal, how do you expect a fellow to behave when you come and beat down his door? I have some people who are not friendly towards me.'

'Aye, I can believe that,' he said uncharitably. The blade was still at my throat, and I tried to keep my Adam's apple from moving too much as I swallowed.

'Have I upset you?'

His face lurched towards me, and I tried to avoid the spittle as he shouted, 'Have you upset me? What do you think? You sold me that powder, and it was no good, was it?'

'Well, I did say that it was a little . . .'

'You said it was fine, and you charged me for it! And now it's all over London that I can't even kill a priest!'

And there you have it. A nasty case, certainly, and I could see that he might have grown annoyed with my little trade, but that was no reason to try to shave my head from my body.

I suppose I should explain.

Hal Westmecott was a renowned fellow in London. His

rough, unkempt appearance was largely due to his business as an executioner, but when I say that, I don't mean it was a career choice to look scruffy. It was not that he was a rough, tough fellow who prided himself on looking the part. No. Hal Westmecott looked unkempt and a mess because he was invariably drunk. When he took a slash at a victim, his blade often went awry, and his efforts tended to be met with ribald comments or horror-struck intakes of breath. Everyone had heard of him, although very few people knew what he looked like, of course. He had a face that was instantly recognizable to me now, but all that most people saw of him was his hood and mask, with two madly staring, bloodshot eyes.

As to his poor victims – well, they must have been prey to extreme dismay on hearing who would put them out of their woes. I once heard that a nobleman, sentenced to beheading, had walked to his headsman before his ending and felt the axe's edge with a dubious expression. No doubt he was justified. Many told of Westmecott having to take a second or third swing before he managed to take the head from its body. One had roundly condemned him after the third blow had removed his ear but missed his neck.

It was hard on those about to die, but no easier on Westmecott, I felt. I could all too easily imagine the self-loathing and horror, every night waking screaming at the memory of the anguished souls he had forced to suffer. Even a brute like him must grow to despise himself and his office. No man can end lives daily without being affected. They must seek to escape it, and all too often the easiest escape and means of losing unwanted memories was in a bottle. A brutalized man sought oblivion so he didn't have to look at himself in the mirror.

Yes, his competence was questionable. When he brought down his axe, his blade oft missed his target; when he performed a hanging, even when he tried to reduce the suffering of his victims, he often missed his cue and forgot to call the family forward to jump on the body and end things more swiftly. But he wanted to do a good job, I daresay.

The previous week he had knocked at my door, and while I tried to escape the deadly fumes emanating from his foul mouth, he told me that he had heard that I possessed a quantity of black powder, the explosive powder used to launch missiles from cannons or bullets from handguns. Someone had told this noddle-pate that I was the proud owner of a wheel-lock pistol and had a supply of powder. He wanted to buy some.

Well, I was not happy with the idea of the fatuous brute having access to powder. What, was he going to enter the sixteenth century at last and dispatch his next unfortunate with a more humane, modern device? No, I didn't think so either. It was not that the fellow was so deep sunk in depravity that he wished to inflict as much pain and fear as possible; it was more that he was constantly drunk, and, besides, he had no understanding of modern firearms. He could have slaughtered the by-standers.

'Why do you want powder?' I asked.

Admittedly, many children enjoy playing with a little powder. They would use it in miniature cannons to create the setting for a battlefield when playing with toy soldiers; others played with it, setting alight long trails of the stuff. I had done that myself with my first small barrel. After drinking rather too much strong wine, I thought it would be amusing to ignite a line of powder. It lit and fizzed and sparked delightfully along my hearthstone. It was so enjoyable (and made my companion squeak and giggle so voluptuously) that I instantly created a line that swerved like a snake's track in sand. I set one end on fire, and the trail was instantly a mass of flames and hissing as it ran along the snake-like track most satisfyingly. Indeed, it was so appealing that I made a circular spiral of powder and lit the end. There was a short sizzle, and then a loud report as the powder exploded, taking my eyebrows and moustache with it.

I didn't try to make pretty patterns from powder again.

But Hal Westmecott was no child, and nor was he the sort to seek intellectual diversions with powder. If he wanted powder, it was no doubt for a specific requirement.

'Do you have it or not?' he grunted, his brows dropping alarmingly. When he did that, he reminded me of some of the apes I had seen in the bestiary, but they looked like cuddly poppets compared to this.

I was about to deny any knowledge of powders when he pulled coins from his purse. 'I have money,' he said simply.

'Well, of course,' I said. 'I only wondered why you wanted it, but if you want it, I'd be happy to help.'

And that was that, or so I thought at the time. Because at that moment I didn't realize what he wanted it for.

He wanted to burn a priest to death.

Well, each of us has our own pastimes, I suppose. Personally, there was a ginger-haired little minx who worked at the Cardinal's Hat, down at Southwark in the Bishop of Winchester's parish, with whom I would have enjoyed a few diversions. She would have been an enthusiastic entertainment according to all I had heard from Piers, the man who stood as apple-squire to the doxies inside. He said that she . . . but in any case, Hal Westmecott was not the sort of man who could afford her, let alone aspire to possess such a beauty. No, his tastes ran to an entirely different level.

I admit candidly that, had I known what he wanted my powder for at the time, I would have been more cautious. As it was, I supplied him with a pound or so and took his money. I could afford to give him that much, because it came from a barrel I had owned for some while, and the powder had grown a little damp in my cellar. Damp powder can produce misfires or cause the firing hole to rust over, so I didn't want to use it in my gun. I sold it to him and thought nothing more of it.

The news came to me a little later when I was sitting in the Blue Bear with some companions.

'There's another priest to be executed,' said one whose name was Matt, laying down a domino with the air of a man who would shortly be able to buy a barrel of ale with his winnings.

'Who?' demanded another, morosely surveying his tiles in the hope that a beneficial Creator had changed the numbers for him.

'The vicar of some small church in the city. He refused to recant some sermon or other, and the authorities came down hard. He's to be burned at the stake . . . Can you go?'

'I'm just thinking! Give me a little time. What was he talking about?'

'Who knows what these fools talk about? Something to do with idolatry, or the use of texts that no one can understand except priests, or some such or other.'

'Hmm. He should have thought before he used inflammatory language,' murmured a third. This was a tall, horse-faced man in his late twenties who affected a superior manner, although he was no better born than I was, I'd swear. He chuckled to himself, but none of us could see why.

'Are you going to take your go?' Matt said again. He was a shortish, plump fellow with a face like a fresh apple. At different times, he could look like an apple as autumn struck, rosy-cheeked as a young maid, and other times, usually in the morning, he could look as green as a young apple that was sour as a sloe.

His opponent, a scrawny wretch named Picksniff, grumbled and complained, but eventually threw down a piece and picked up his black leather mug and drank deeply. He had the look of a man who would as happily draw his knife and stab young Matt as continue with this game.

Matt glanced at me and then over to the aristocratic figure slumped elegantly on a bench. 'We should go and watch. It should be entertaining, after all.'

I had no wish to watch another man's final moments. It was common enough in those days for the better elements to go and view a burning or a hanging. After all, everyone needs a diversion, and from the look on Picksniff's face, this game was not proving to be so appealing. He and Matt might enjoy the walk, but I had no wish to see it. In all truth, the mere thought had the gorge rising in my throat. 'You fellows go,' I said. 'I'll wait here.'

Thus it was that I heard about Hal's disaster only later, when the men returned to the tavern and told me.

'It was the most amusing thing you ever saw,' Matt gurgled. 'The expression on the executioner's face was a picture!'

I have to rely on Matt and Picksniff for the following account. I don't think many people could bear the thought of being burned to death at the stake without a shudder of horror. Not easily. And in some ways, of course, it would be worse to watch such an execution as a relative of the victim. Hearing their cries and screams, I mean. You know, a fellow could watch someone dangling from a hanging tree for a few minutes before running and jumping on the wriggling body to put them out of their misery. But a burning? There is little a fellow can do to stop the suffering. There is one way, and only one: bribe the executioner, so that he puts bags of powder at the groin, armpits or breast. As the heat grows, the powder ignites and *pouf*! End of suffering.

That day I had better things to do than witness two or three men being slowly roasted over a pyre of faggots. I've heard that it takes a couple of London carts full of wood to entirely destroy a human body. It goes to show, I suppose, that the folk of London are prepared to pay for their entertainment. Personally, I find a meal at a good inn, washed down with plenty of ale and followed by a short walk to the nearest brothel, suits my temperament far better. After all, I have seen my fair share of bodies.

But others are not so inclined. They go to Smithfield in their hordes whenever the burnings are announced, and stand at the barriers, peering excitedly as they wait for the arrival of the victims. The vendors of ancient pies and supposed sausages would wander among them, as would the hopeful harlots, offering something rather more comforting than the gristle-stuffed lumps of intestine, and the cut-purses who would invariably come away with the greatest profits of the day. There were times when I wished I was back there, watching the people and dipping into other men's purses. I had been poor, but my troubles seemed minor compared with my more recent difficulties.

But more of my problems later.

That day the victims were not long in appearing. They had already been supplied with a large bowl of ale to send them on their way with a full belly that would hopefully soothe their fears as they approached their posts. Three large wagons brought the faggots, one per person. These arrived first, and the executioner's assistants began throwing them about the two posts which were set waiting. Their job was only half done when the victims arrived.

They didn't walk, these fellows, but were brought to the place of execution on a wagon. All were in clerical costume and were praying. Two were older, but the third was a younger man who was, so I am told, a good-looking example, not that I ever met him, poor devil. I doubt he looked good that day. He was tall, with thin dark hair, and a way of leaning his head forward as though stretching his neck in the urgent desire to hear another's words. His brows were constantly creased as if anxiously desiring to help others, as a priest should be. Not that it helped him.

I did not know his brother Geoffrey at that stage, but later I heard that Geoffrey was in the crowd, as well as my friends from the inn. I imagine he was weeping and praying for some form of amnesty even at that late hour. Miracles could happen; miracles *should* happen, and he could not understand why his brother was there, about to die. What had he done, other than preach a sermon? He was a deeply religious man, who had never done harm to another. But in this topsy-turvy kingdom, the religion that had been imposed by the old King Henry some years before, was now to be evicted, and the Roman faith was to return by order of the Queen. No one argued with a Queen, or any other monarch. For to argue was a short path to the execution grounds. Queen Mary disliked dissent. She had been anointed Queen, and that meant she was God's chosen ruler, in receipt of His authority. No one could argue with her, for to argue with her was to argue with God. That was heretical. Or something.

There was to be no miraculous intervention that day.

Matt laughed, he told me, as the wagon was brought forward, the hooded executioner walking behind with an assistant. The horses were halted, and the three priests slowly disembarked, standing in a huddle. The guards who had walked with them from the prison spread out inside the fenced ring, their polearms in their hands, some leaning on the fence, others standing in a moderately military manner. None appeared to pay much attention. They had all seen such sights before.

Geoffrey had, too – but not like this. Later, he told me, he had tears in his eyes and a tightness at his brow as the men went about their business. It felt as if his head was in a clamp and an executioner was tightening it. He watched as the three were chained to their posts, his brother James on his own, the other two back to back on the other, the little bags hung about their necks, other bags tied between their legs, more faggots arranged about them, and then the oil sprinkled liberally over the wood. A Catholic priest intoned the last rites, making the sign of the cross, and then a burning torch was brought and thrust into the faggots by the executioner, the flames rising, the noise of crackling, the sudden flare as clothing caught, the screams and anguish, and then the reports, loud and forgiving, as powder exploded, killing two of the priests before they could be forced to suffer too much or too long.

But one priest did not receive that same generous death. He remained in the flames, squirming, as the heat grew, coughing and calling for an end to his suffering. They say he was calling for a half hour.

No, I didn't go. But I heard about it from Matt and Picksniff, and that was bad enough.

'Why? What went wrong?'

The aristocrat, who was named George, took up his seat once more. 'The fellow had hung a bag of gunpowder about the priest's neck, so that, as the flames rose, his suffering would be put at an end. However, the powder was not good, or the fool had used the wrong powder. Perhaps he had mistaken ground pepper corns for explosive? In any event, the bag did not explode.'

'It didn't?' I said.

'No. There was a sad kind of fizzing, and then some did detonate, but he was long dead before that.'

'The flames got to him?'

'No!' Matt laughed, interrupting to take up the story again. 'He began berating the executioner for failing to serve him after he had paid for a speedy conclusion, and even as he said that, the platform he stood on collapsed, and a beam holding up the post he was bound to fell and broke his neck. It was delightfully ironic. He met a swift end as he wished, the hangman succeeded in his ambition to execute the priest, but neither achieved their aims in the manner they had anticipated.'

George chuckled again, but it struck me that there was little humour in his face.

And you may not believe this, but at the time it did not occur to me that this might come back to haunt me, or that there might be a child involved, or the rivalry between the Queen and her half-sister, or a runaway wife and her child. I did not think about the man lighting the fire to kill the priest. Why should I? There was more than one executioner in London. Queen Mary was determined to ensure that, no matter what, her reign would see to it that the apprenticeships for that single profession would rise, if no other did.

I had no idea that the hideous Hal Westmecott was the priest's executioner. No, and my powder surely was not so damp as to be useless. It was just unreliable in my pistol. I had sold it in good faith – well, moderately good faith. In any case, Matt and I set to with a fresh game of dominoes, and put the dead priest from our minds.

It was only later, when Westmecott caught me, that I learned that the Queen's executioner was looking for me because something had gone horribly wrong, and he blamed me.

So you will understand why, when Hal Westmecott had me cornered after I had fled across the roof of my house and the next two besides, I was not entirely comfortable. His mouth opened, and I was forced to stare into that gaping maw once more. I winced at the odours.

'You made me look a fool in front o' the crowd,' he said.

'Me? What have I done?'

'You gave me the wrong powder, didn't you? You thought I was too stupid to realize.'

'I don't know what you mean. You wanted gunpowder, and I sold you some.'

'The powder you sold me didn't work!' he shouted, head jutting.

I am known for my courage, I think it is fair to say, but this man was alarming. I thought he might headbutt me in a moment, and tried to jerk away, but that only brought a stinging sensation at my throat. I winced. That blasted edge was keen.

When I continued, I attempted a more soothing tone. 'Perhaps you didn't use it right?'

He growled at that. 'You think me a fool?'

Suddenly, the blade at my throat pressed more heavily. You may find this hard to believe, but I had thought it could not press harder. Now it felt as if it must pass through and lodge in my spine. I gave a quiet moan of fear, trying to draw my neck away from danger. That sword really was astonishingly sharp. I tried to breathe more carefully. I wasn't going to argue any further, but I confess the idea that the powder was all that sodden seemed unlikely.

He leaned closer until I could barely breathe with the reek from his mouth. It was suffocating. 'You made me look foolish, and I don't like that. You made an officer of the law look ridiculous in front of the crowds, and the city officials won't be happy with that either. The family paid for the powder, too, and they won't be pleased you made the priest suffer.'

'I'm sorry,' I managed in a rather high-pitched, strangulated voice.

'Not enough.'

There was little I could say to that. I mumbled something about how truly sorry I was, and while that blade was at my throat, I was indeed, but there was a gleam in his eye. I didn't like the look of it.

'Not sorry enough, I'll warrant,' he said. 'I want money!'

That was, at least, some relief. He didn't intend merely to cut off various parts of me; he was hoping to make a profitable exchange.

'Of course, if you're sure, I'll be happy to reimburse your money. I'm just very sorry that the powder didn't work for you. I'll go and fetch the money right a—'

'Wait 'ere!' he said, and pushed with his blade until my skull cracked against the wall behind me. 'I'll 'ave my money, but I wan' more than that. I'll need your 'elp with a little matter.'

'What sort of little matter?' I asked suspiciously. I had been caught before.

'I've 'eard you have contacts in the city,' he said, and there was a strange, new tone in his voice. It sounded plaintive. Yes,

I know, it's hard to think of a headsman trying to make an appeal, but as he spoke, I felt the blade withdraw slightly, and he almost seemed to smile ingratiatingly. I preferred his glower.

'I may have some,' I said warily. 'What sort of contacts?'

'Men who can make enquiries.'

'About what?' I said.

He took the sword away, and scuffed his boots in the dirt for a moment or two. 'I 'ave a son. But his mother, the bitch, took 'im away from me, and I don't know where they are.'

'You want me to find them?'

'Not 'er! No, I don't want to see her again, unless she's laid on top of my faggots for witchcraft! But I'd like to see my boy again. He must be close to eight years now. It's time 'e knew his father.'

'So he can be prenticed to you?'

The sword whipped up and rested on my throat again. I tried to apologize, but only a wheezing squeak came from my throat. It felt like my eyeballs must pop from their moorings, they opened so wide.

'Don't joke about my job! It's not one just anyone could do, and I wouldn't 'ave my boy set on my path, damn your soul, I wouldn't! But I would' – and the sword dropped again – 'I would see him again. Try to set 'im on 'is own road. Maybe apprentice him to an innkeeper or . . .'

He rambled on a bit about coachmen and grooms, but all I could think of was that the old sot wanted a son who would be in a position to fill him with a gallon of ale of an evening.

I was not keen to remain long in his company, and it was a relief when, a short while later, the owner of the yard arrived in his doorway bearing a stout cudgel and made it clear that he had two hungry hounds who would look on us as prime breakfast material for trespassing.

It was a persuasive little speech, and Hal and I departed for the more accommodating environment of a hostelry which was keen to serve ale by the pint, and present us with a burned offering of blackened bacon and an egg that had suffered a worse immolation than Hal's priest the day before. On the way, Hal waved to a man who walked towards us from my house. He was square-shouldered, with that stance that tells you he knows how to handle himself in a fight. Hal walked to him and spoke briefly – I guessed he was the man who knocked at my front door while Hal waited in the yard for me – and I gained the impression of a pair of glittering eyes. I didn't like the look of him and was glad when Hal left him and returned to me.

Hal was still worrying at the shame he had suffered at the death of the priest like a toothless hound mumbling a marrow-bone. 'He insulted me, in front of all the people crowded round! Me! There were no need for that! And then 'e jerked, like 'e was tryin' to shake his fist at me, or something, and the platform collapsed, and 'e fell down in among the faggots, and that made all those watchin' start shoutin' more an' more, an', I told 'em, they could kiss my arse, I couldn't give a fart for any of them, and 'e was bawling about the fire and the powder, and then the blasted pole itself came loose, God's *hounds*, and fell over 'is neck and broke it, and that was 'im done. He couldn't complain then. But then the bag of powder fizzed up and some sparked, and made an ungodly smell, like the devil's own had arrived to snatch his soul, as they must, for he was an unreligious 'eretic, so they say, but the people, I swear, I thought they would come and pull me limb from limb. I 'ad to get the soldiers to guard me.'

He stared morosely at the bacon on his plate. Looking at it, I was reminded of burned bodies I had seen during Wyatt's rebellion, and pushed my own plate aside. I hadn't touched my egg. It didn't look as if it would appreciate being chewed. I suspected that it would return in my gullet to take its revenge.

'Why do you need me to find your boy?' I said.

'You 'ave contacts. People you know, what can find 'er and 'im.'

'Don't you?'

He looked up at me. 'My kind o' job don't lead to long-term friendship.'

That was probably true. A man would be unlikely to want to spend time with a fellow who had that morning put to death a trio of thieves, cut-purses or murderers. It tended to put a blight on a man's appetite even for beer, when the hand that shook yours had earlier been inside another fellow's breast to pull out his still-beating heart. I found I was wiping my hand on my jack and quickly stopped. 'I don't know whether I can find him,' I said. 'What can you tell me about him? If I'm to seek him, I will need to know what I am looking for.'

'Aye. Well.' He threw me a hunted look. 'He was about so 'igh,' he said, holding his palm some three feet from the ground. 'And 'e 'ad dark 'air like mine, and brown eyes.'

'So he's only a yard tall? And with—'

'I daresay 'e's grown since. That were some years ago.'

'How long?'

'Well, 'e were four summers then.'

'And now?'

He gave a rueful grimace. 'That were three, four year ago – 'e'll have grown.'

I stared at him open-mouthed. 'You mean you haven't seen him in three or four years? How will you recognize him if I find him?'

'Find 'is mother, the poxed whore. She'll bring 'im to you. Probably sell 'im to you for the cost of a pint of ale or old sack. She were never a good mother to him. She were a bawd. Always were.'

I tried to reason with him. 'Look, even if I do find the boy, there is no saying he'll want to know you. He is only young, and if he hasn't seen you in five years, he probably won't even remember you.'

'No, 'e'll know me – 'e were my boy then, and 'e still is now. Blood will out.'

An unfortunate phrase for an executioner, I thought, but I downed my ale and considered as he kept talking. The boy could possibly be found. His mother's name was, apparently, Molly, but she had been known to go by a series of different names. When he called her a whore, it was little more than the truth, as far as he was concerned. He was convinced that she was hawking her body about the stews. If so, I wondered how well the boy would have fared for himself.

'Oh, 'e'll be fine. Strong, good lad, my boy.'

'Why did she leave you?'

He looked at me, but his eyes slid away in shame. 'I'm a

good man, me. I work hard for my money. But she grew to think there was somethin' shameful in me . . . doin' my work. She di'n't like it. I said to her, "What else can I do?" But she di'n't want to listen. And then one day, it was after I had three men on the tree in one dance, I came home that night and she was gone. Just taken everything and my boy, the bitch!'

'You think I can find him, but I am unlikely to have any more luck than you. I don't think . . .'

He fixed a glower on me. 'The family o' that priest, they were right angry their man di'n't die right. They wanted to know why the powder didn't go off as it should.'

He need say no more. I could quite understand his hint. If I were to help him, he would keep my name secret. Fail, and the priest's family would learn who had supplied the defective powder. It was not an ideal arrangement, but better to do a little work hunting down the boy in the hope that I could present him to the executioner.

I had no choice. I persuaded him to describe his wife and their boy in more detail, downed my ale, and left him glumly staring deep into the depths of his own. He gave the distinct impression of a man who was determined to remain in his seat until they swept him out with the rest of the trash into the gutter.

His wife was a woman of some four-and-twenty, with a large bust, red-gold hair, and a thin, pinched, shrewish face. But that could have been the ale and his hurt feelings speaking. A woman who went by the name of Moll or Molly Cripplegate. Hal was fairly sure that she would not be using his name. His boy was a lad named Ben, but he would not say whether Ben had any distinguishing marks.

He was just a boy, apparently.

I rubbed my throat as I walked home. There was a fine thread of blood about my neck where his blasted sword had parted my skin, and I felt like a man who had been all but hanged, reprieved at the last moment by a kindly pardon. But as far as I was concerned, this injury was unnecessary and unjustified.

'Raphe, where are you, you bull's pizzle!' I shouted as I

entered my house. After all, the fellow should have risen and barred the door, or stood there to hold any miscreant from entering. All my bellow received by way of acknowledgement was a sudden barking from his benighted hound.

'Raphe? What are you doing? Are you still abed?'

I stalked out to the kitchen and peered up the steps that led to the little bedchamber snug behind the warm chimney, but he was not there. His brute was, sitting, expectantly staring at me, while his tail swept a clear fan in the dust and reeds of the floor.

Feeling irritable, I took a plate and sliced some ham and cheese and bread, before filling a pot with ale and taking them through to my parlour. I spent some time lighting the fire and soon had a flame from my tinder. I placed fresh twigs and kindling over it and waited until they too had caught, before I set some split logs about them, and some light pieces resting on them, and thicker limbs on top where they would catch all the heat.

I was about to sit and eat when I frowned to myself. That powder should not have been so uncooperative. I have never known black powder to be reluctant to misbehave at the drop of a hat. Thoughtfully, I took up my flask and tipped a little into the palm of my hand. I threw it on to the fire, and it sizzled and sparked as I had expected. Yet the executioner was utterly convincing. And I had heard from Matt and Picksniff that the powder had done nothing until the poor priest was already removed from this world, so his words must have been true.

For a moment or two I wondered what he had preached about to so enrage the Church's officials, but in this present confused time, with two religious groups vying for authority, and the Queen having set her heart on the most stringent demands of the old Catholic Church, rather than her father's newer English Church, it could have been any one of a number of points. There were regular demands for cartloads of faggots to remove argumentative religious clerks and others. Even men like Latimer and Ridley, who had burned the previous year, who had been well-respected men of the cloth. If they were not safe, nobody was.

I looked at my hand, then at the flask. It was from the same

barrel as the one from which I had taken the powder to give
to Hal Westmecott. On a whim, I went down to my cellar and
lifted the lid on my powder store. It felt dry enough. I took a
handful, replaced the lid and went back up. Throwing it on
the fire, there was a sudden flash and gout of smoke that roiled
about the mantel before slowly slipping back inside the
chimney breast and up into the flue. There was nothing wrong
with my powder. It may not be safe in my pistol, but in a
large bag it should have gone off without problem. The fool
must have stored it in a damp place, and that was what
prevented the ecclesiastical termination.

Satisfied, I sat back in my chair and brought the plate to
my lap. And that was when I realized that there was no ham
and no cheese, and Raphe's monster was looking at me all
slantindicular with an occasional lick of his lips.

After aiming a satisfying kick at the dog, who scampered away
full of remorse for his theft, I cut another slice of ham and
chewed on that as I left the house. Where was Raphe? If he
went shopping, he usually took the ruffian, whom he had
named Hector, supposedly for his courage, with him. It was
rare that he would leave the rascal in the house alone, for the
obvious reason that, as a street dog, he would steal any spare
food left lying about. The damned monster would have to start
to earn his keep. He was no good as a guard, letting all in
who wished to enter, and only barking at those who knocked
at the door. Which was rather pointless.

I put him out of my mind. Just now I wanted to make sure
that I was seen to be helping Westmecott. I had my usual garb
on and walked out into the lane, glancing up at my neighbour's
window, remembering the sight of her in her bed. It was a
happy thought, and I held on to it as I made my way to Rose
Street. I stopped at a small-fronted building that stood a little
back from the lane. There was a deep gutter which ran with
noisome water, and a slab of rock served as a bridge.

Two years before I had made the acquaintance of a fellow,
the intellectual friend of Piers, a man called Mark Thomasson.

Some men can impress by sheer force of personality. They
enter a room, and all others immediately submit, not that the

great men condescend to notice. Others can impress by their
volubility. They overwhelm lesser spirits by the words they
spew like arrows flying from a bow. A man who knows that
number of words, someone might assume, must have a brain
the size of an ocean. And yet there are others, men to whom
a passer-by would not give a second glance, men who might
stand in the middle of a street and stare at the sky as if puzzled
by the rain, men who would examine with close attention the
mark made by a walking stick on a painted post, or who would
watch avidly while a dog sniffed about a courtyard in search
of a treat; such men would be watched with amusement, or a
man might tap his temple meaningfully while jerking his head
at the poor fool.

They would be wrong, because the poor dolt may actually
be considering an abstruse mathematical concept in his head,
or persuading himself that a man with a stick of a certain
dimension had caused the paint's dent, and that same stick
had been used in a murder, or watching the dog to see whether
there was a piece of a corpse lying beneath the mud.

A man like that, a man with a brain like a steel trap, was
a hard man to get to know, and harder to keep as a friend,
because, on personal experience, the damned genius had the
common sense of a sparrow, and less engaging manners. That
was Mark Thomasson.

Mark Thomasson was a man with a permanently baffled
expression. He found everything confusing because, unlike
other men, he never accepted what was presented to him
without questioning it. When I had met him, he was a slim
man, with aquiline features and a nose that could have split
logs. His mouth was a mere gash, his hair a mass of tawny
locks. While he was moderately tall (taller than I), he always
carried his head at a slight stoop, as if he hoped always to see
something before anyone else. He had a habit of mumbling
to himself with a frown, and then, every so often, a beam of
brilliance would enliven his features, and he would speak with
clarity and precision. But then he would return to his mumbling
and frowning.

His house was an utter mess. The first time I had visited
him, the presence of tables was a matter of faith. The sheer

volume of books, coats, scrolls and papers had to be resting on something, and I assumed there must be tables. But I had no proof of this, because the legs were themselves concealed behind towering ledgers, piles of paper or assorted mechanical devices and sections of armour. Since my last visit, his house had become used more by a scavenger who patrolled the streets at night gathering every piece of metalwork and deposited them in Mark's parlour – or so it seemed. At my last visit, I had remarked upon a helm with a great dint in it, next to a breastplate with two large holes. Now there were three other cuirasses and a second helmet, which sat upon a wooden bust. A crossbow bolt projected from it, and there was a second hole beneath the bolt that spoke of a sudden death for any man occupying that metal hat.

There was one thing that always unnerved me about the house. It was Peterkin, Mark's 'little' hound.

Peterkin was the sort of brute that would make an elephant think twice about charging. He was the size of a donkey, a vast hound with amber eyes and deep grey coat. As I walked in, Peterkin rose, stretched like a cat and padded towards me. I am not scared of hounds, and did not want to be, so I made a fuss of him for a while, all the time speaking to Mark about my conundrum.

'You say that this affair could affect a lady and her reputation?' I was not going to tell him who exactly the lady in question was. After all, Mark was also a servant of Elizabeth. I didn't want him to go blabbing the story to anyone. 'Well, in that case something must be done. We cannot have a lady of good birth suffering the slings and arrows of mean-spirited gossip.'

'What should I do?'

'Tell me again.'

So I did. I told him of the executioner's story and emphasized that I must somehow find the man's wife and child. As I spoke, Mark's servant, a grim-faced, weaselly fellow, appeared every so often, refilling my wine goblet whenever it looked in danger of becoming empty. The wine warmed me to my toes, and I began to lose my reticence and spoke more openly.

'My difficulty is that I cannot hope to find a woman like that in all the brothels of London,' I said. 'How many women would fit his description?'

Mark nodded. I had first met him because he had gone to the Cardinal's Hat, the brothel where my friend Piers worked, with a view to an energetic bout with a pair of the doxies. Mark occasionally needed rest from his mental labours, and he had a fine eye for a buxom wench with a welcoming gleam in her eye.

He looked up now. 'Why don't you tell John Blount?'

I shivered. 'I don't think that would be a good idea.'

'Why?'

'I doubt he would like to hear that I was consorting with a mere executioner.'

'Then don't tell him. However, Blount must know dozens of men about the town who could help. His agents are everywhere. One of them must know where this lad has been hidden away.'

He suddenly stopped and peered closer at me. 'Wait! You can't tell him, can you?'

'What do you mean?'

'Your reluctance. It is all of a part. And when I ask about your master, you look away every time, as though that thought cannot be countenanced. See? You do it again.'

'You are mistaken.'

He leaned back in his seat and studied me complacently. 'With a matter such as this, you would usually have hurried to John Blount, and the fact you have not indicates clearly to me that you do not think he would help you. Worse, he might hinder you, or so you fear. I am right, am I not?'

I couldn't answer directly. As I opened my mouth, I realized that his monster was standing at my side. His drooping jowls oozed drool, and his amber eyes stared at me intently, as though wondering what flavour my marrow might have.

Mark had spoken again, and I shook my head. 'Sorry?'

'You think that John Blount might feel unhappy to be involved in such a matter and, most likely, very unimpressed with you being involved. He has higher aspirations for you, after all.'

'Yes. That's why I can't tell him.'

'Ah. In that case, I can suggest an easy solution for you. I shall ask him on behalf of a fellow I know. I can tell him it's a matter of interest to me and no one else.'

I gaped. It was the perfect solution. Blount need never know I had any part to play in the matter, I need not explain anything about Ben, and his evacuation to a safer place could be effected with nobody any the wiser.

'Would you do that?'

Mark beamed. 'Of course. And in the meanwhile, we could do worse than looking at some of the brothels near here, just to see if she might be there.'

I should not have been surprised. I knew him well enough. Still, I was relieved to hear he would help me and gave a short gasp of joy, and perhaps it sounded menacing, because suddenly I was pinned to the seat when an over-enthusiastic Peterkin jumped on to my breast, causing not a little pain. Not that I cared at the time, because I was much more concerned about the massive jaws that held my throat in a gentle but very wet embrace.

'Peterkin, get down, boy! Down! There are many brothels,' he said with a beaming smile. 'We could go about the nearer ones and try to find her.'

It was a thought. 'How many brothels are there in London? There must be many thousands of them.'

'Then we should set off,' he said. He stood, staring about him with an air of sudden dejection.

'What is it?'

'Where is my hat?' he said, mournfully gazing about him like a child who has lost his favourite toy.

We started at a small brothel Mark knew near Ludgate. From there, we walked westwards towards Westminster, stopping off at a place near the Mews opposite Whitehall. Here Mark seemed well known. Having gone to three different houses of variable virtue, he took me to another place nearer to Westminster. There, he told me, were more expensive whorehouses, where knights and nobles were keen to relax after a hard day's hunting, drinking and gluttony.

At each, as soon as we entered, Mark would stand and stare openly at the wenches. It was all he could do not to dribble. After the first, when we were still near Whitehall, he took me into a cheaper residence suitable for the servants of nobles. There, while Mark stared adoringly at a couple of smiling hussies who showed a little leg to get his attention, I spoke to the dark-haired woman of the house, who gave me to understand that men with questions like mine could get out of her parlour, since time was the shape of a silver penny, and she had little enough of both.

'I only want to know if you have a woman called Moll here, with a son called Ben.'

'I have plenty of women. What do you want her to look like?'

'A good figure, with weight to her top, and a thin face,' I said, trying to remember Westmecott's precise description.

'I could have. Fair-haired?'

'No, red.'

'What did you want her name to be?'

'No, no, I am looking for a lady with the name of Moll, who has a son called Ben. I don't want you to make one up.'

We were soon out of that one. She hustled us out like two vagrants found in her doorway.

Outside, we continued on our search, but although two madams reckoned they had just the girl for me, it was clear that they were merely seeking to sell me one of their stable. We stood outside the fifth, and I looked up and down the roadway. There was a tall, thin, haggard woman in the roadway. She walked like a duchess on hard times. I could see her face was ravaged by harsh living. It always astonished me that women like her would keep on travelling to London to try to make a living. Even peasants must surely know that life in the city was not easy. It was cruel and hard even to those with youth and vigour on their side. But even those must sink at some point.

This woman had neither looks nor health, as far as I could see. But then, when a man looked at the women about the houses of ill repute, there were often women like this. Poor souls who, perhaps, had once made a reasonable living inside the houses, but who were so over-used that they were evicted from their rooms and now plied their trade as best they might in the roads outside the brothels. The next stage was to be moved away from these haunts to try to sell themselves to the drunks in a tavern or inn, or to fall to the worst stage, at the alehouses where the sailors congregated. It was a short walk from there to death in the river or a stab for her purse.

I grunted. 'This is a waste of time.'

'Then go and tell him you can't find her.'

'I don't think that would be a good idea,' I said, and rubbed my throat thoughtfully. 'He may not wish to hear it.'

'Well, there are several more houses I can think of,' he said.

'What is the point? There are so many of them, the chance of finding her in any of them is remote!'

'Well, if you feel like that, I might as well go back inside,' he said hopefully.

'What else can we do?'

'Perhaps go to the Cardinal's Hat? At least there Piers won't push you from the door.'

He had a point. It was a tempting thought. Piers would also provide me with an ale or two, if I was in luck.

I left him as he entered the nearest brothel, and directed my steps to an alley leading to the river. Before I entered it, I was struck by the sight of the haggard woman again. She was at the side of the brothel, watching Mark. I thought I could detect wistfulness in her stance, as if she was thinking that once he would have gone to see her. I felt a surge of sympathy for her.

It must be hard – I mean, to be a gormless peasant left without support in a city like London. So long as she didn't expect me to slip her a coin for a knee-trembler in an alley. I wouldn't waste my pennies on a raddled tart like her when there were fresh strumpets waiting on the other side of the river.

I waited at the river bank, but the wherries were all downriver. Rather than wait and waste the day, I chose to stroll over the bridge to the Southwark bank, and made my way to the bear pits and thence the area known for its Winchester Geese, the whores that thronged the banks and helped keep the Bishop of Winchester's coffers so well filled. There, with a splendid view of the pits, stood the Cardinal's Hat, where my friend Piers resided.

It was a kindness to call him 'friend', really, because he was more of an acquaintance. Once he had been a barber, and had been a good one – but then he got to enjoy his drink too much. It was expensive: it cost him his wife, his children and, finally, his business, but because he was a large man, with fists the size of a child's head, he was welcomed at the Cardinal's Hat as an apple-squire, a man to guard the doors, to be there to throw out unwanted guests, and to take on such other duties as the madam saw fit to pass to him. In his more sober moments, he would cut the hair of the bawds, and he was still very capable of doing so – as long as he had not already taken a quart or two of strong ale.

'Do you know how many wenches there are in this city?' Piers demanded, incredulous, as he poured a fresh pot of sack from a leather flask. We were sitting in the brothel's entrance hall, and a fresh barrel had been set up ready. I was drinking a smooth ale that was strong enough to guarantee that most visitors would soon lose all their inhibitions – and financial sense. 'There are more whores in London than you have lice! There are more than the fleas on a mastiff! This city has . . . thousands! How do you expect to find one with a boy in a city this size?'

'That was why I came here,' I said. 'I have little doubt that you are right, but I have to try.'

'Why?'

I pulled my shirt aside and pointed to the thin line left by Hal's sword on my neck.

He peered. 'A scratch like that? He wasn't serious.'

'He will be next time, and if he isn't, other people will be!' I said hotly. It was my throat, after all. I felt I had a right to be protective.

'What would you think we can do? Ask every street-walker whether she was married to Westmecott? Wander round all the brothels and ask the tarts? Go into them and try to see how many boys they have working there with their mothers, clearing up and cooking, holding horses, taking torches to lead men home . . . Do you have any idea how many whores have bastards with them?'

I nodded, feeling as glum as Westmecott when I'd left him earlier. As he suggested, it was remarkably unlikely that I would find the mother, let alone the boy.

Sipping my ale, I sighed. 'There must be some way of finding the woman, this Moll.'

'A woman of four-and-twenty, big breasts, red hair? All I can think of is looking for a place that caters for men who like women of that type,' Piers said. His eyes widened with the effort of alcohol-infused concentration. 'If she has a pleasing manner, she could be installed in a place that is well positioned for the wealthy, I suppose, especially if her boy is willing and helpful. Some better houses might agree to take her on.'

'Where should I start?' I asked.

'There is a brothel I have heard of, which is up near the Bishop's Gate. They talk about their whores being there to tempt the travellers from the north, but it's just a sales gimmick, I think. They're just ordinary wenches, same as we get here.'

'Oi, we ain't all ordinary,' a voice called.

'You certainly aren't,' he said without a glance.

'That's a nice way to talk to a lady,' she said.

She was a slim little thing, with fair hair and pale skin. Very appealing in a sort of waif-like manner, but not to my taste. She looked more the kind of woman who would tire a fellow out, whereas I preferred a more peaceable sort.

'Why're you lookin' for this wench, anyway?' She had approached us and now stood before me with her arms akimbo, her eye wandering over me with interest.

I have been told that my face is very pleasing, marred only by a slight scar. Women tend to see trustworthiness in me, and they want to mother me. This one looked more like a feral cat eyeing up a shrew.

'I have been asked to find her by her husband. He is sore distressed at the thought of his son and not having seen him in three years or more.'

'Means he probably beat the boy and her until she decided to go.'

'Quite possibly,' I agreed, thinking of the grim visage Westmecott showed the world.

'Who is this husband?'

'He's not the sort of man she'd want to live with,' I guessed. 'It's Hal Westmecott, the executioner.'

She paled. 'Why'd she want to go back to him, then?'

'I don't think she will. I doubt he wants her.'

'So it's only that he wants his son? Waited until his boy had been fed and watered and protected, and now he's of an age to become a useful worker, the man wants him back, eh? And at the same time, he'll deprive his wife of the only companion she's been able to rely on? That don't sound friendly to me!' the harpy announced.

'I am no child-stealer! If either of them don't agree, I'll just leave them in peace.'

'Oh, really. Why? How much is he paying you?'

'Nothing.'

Piers looked at me pityingly. My inquisitor laughed aloud.

'Ho, yes. You're prepared to spend months just wandering the streets and speaking to the wenches, and all you'll get is the man's thanks at the end of it, eh? I should just think so,' she finished with withering scorn.

'Well, thank you for your help,' I said to Piers, rising from my stool.

'Where are you going?' the woman said.

'To see whether she might be at the house Piers mentioned,' I said loftily.

'Her name's Moll, you reckon?' she said with a sharp little look at me, her eyes full of a strange suspicion.

'Yes. Moll or Molly.'

She gave me that odd glance again. 'I know Moll. You'll be goin' to the wrong place. I can take you where you'll find her.'

It is rare indeed that I find someone quite so accommodating, but as I have said before, I do have the good fortune to possess an honest, open face which has led to many women wanting to trust me and mother me. It is good to know that a fellow can make his way based on his charm and intellect.

I know that it may surprise some to see me placing my trust in a common trull, but the fact was I knew perfectly well that such women were often looking for a clean-living fellow who could protect them. This was no different. True, she was a little sharp of tone, and she was capable of trying to fondle my significant parts – by which I mean my purse – but she was clearly more enthusiastic about helping a fellow in need than in trying to fleece me blind at that moment. It was all to the good.

We took the bridge. The weather was growing less than clement for May time. I was more used to balmy, sunny days, but today it was definitely cool, and a fine drizzle was blowing in our faces. It was one of those days when the river looked grey as old steel, and there was a spray being thrown up from the ships and wherries that plied their trade. Not many were going out. A man trying to shoot the bridge in this weather would be brave indeed.

'How do you know of this woman?' I asked as we walked.

'There are some girls I know. She's one.'

'What, you mean you have a circle of companions?'

She cast me a glance of frowning suspicion. 'We shouldn't have friends?'

'No, no, I just meant . . .'

'We get to know others of our age and profession, same as you do, I suppose. I've known Moll for a while.'

'And she's running from her husband?'

'Many women do. And they need support of their friends.'

I mulled over that. 'You mean you know of others, no matter where they are in the city?' That was an interesting idea: that any of the wenches could send a message to their peers had never occurred to me. It was sensible, certainly, for it meant that many of them could warn others of the more dangerous clients. But only the higher level of bawd would have access to such a network, surely. The lowest street-walker no doubt had to make her own judgement.

She walked with a deliberate swiftness, barely glancing from one side to the other, which was a surprise. She was evidently keen to get on with this introduction, and I had to admire that in the woman. Most whores would be spending their time shooting coquettish little looks at the men about, eyeing up the next gull. I've never known one to ignore all the men about her like this one. I had to hurry a little to keep up with her. Especially when we came to a cart on the bridge, with a man swearing and gesticulating at a fellow with a barrow who had allowed a load of cabbages to roll free, and who was hurtling about the road gathering them up before they could be trampled. He, for his part, was responding in a low monotone of vile language.

The way between the two vehicles was narrow, and she slipped through like a tumbler on a stage. I tried to follow, but my sword's scabbard got caught in the spokes of the cart, and I was forced to dicker about, trying to retrieve it. By the time I had, the woman had passed on through the crowds.

I cried out, 'Hoi!' and hurried after her, but only caught a glimpse of her hat and coif as she passed up Bridge Street. Really, she should have realized that I was falling behind. I had to hurry, one hand on my sword's hilt, the other on my pistol, to catch up with her.

She was turning off to the left as I came close.

'Woman, hold hard,' I said. 'Wait! I don't even know your name to call to you!'

She threw me a look over her shoulder, in which disdain and annoyance were close bedfellows. 'You can call me Peg, if you must.'

I was almost at her side now as we walked up Crooked Lane, a narrower street where only the ubiquitous London cars could travel. The longer carts were fourteen feet by four, and could only be manoeuvred along the broader ways, while cars, being only twelve by three, could cope with narrower ways. Even so, when one came past, Peg and I were forced to take refuge in a doorway while the driver snarled and swore at us for slowing him. Peg shouted out, 'You polled knave!' The man turned and tried to cut at her with his whip, but he missed, and instead caught me on the shoulder. I roared with pain, and the man took one look at my sword, pistol and face, which surely was as red as a choleric publican's, and urged

his knackered beast on with more urgency as he saw my hand
on my pistol. I wasn't attempting to pull it and fire at him – I
was merely holding it so it did not slip from its moorings –
but I suppose he caught sight of a man with his hand on a
steel handgun, and drew a sensible conclusion.

Peg swore under her breath and flicked a finger at the man,
and I snapped at her with exasperation. 'You have already
caused me enough pain, woman! What, do you want him to
whip me again? Calling him a castrated peasant and then
flicking your finger at him – are you mad?'

'He could have hurt us,' she said, 'driving his car like that
in this narrow way.'

'He *did* hurt me – when you insulted him,' I said. My earlier
view of her as an appealing mount for a bedtime gallop had
dissipated somewhat with the sting of the lash. 'By all means
slander men, but do so when I am not in the area to be hurt!'

'It was hardly a powerful blow,' she said, glancing at me,
and then her eyes widened a little. When I glanced down, I
saw a sight to make my stomach roil. There was a slash in
my jack as if a knife had drawn across it, and where it had
hit, there was a stain of blood forming. I felt queasy.

'Come along, if you're coming,' she said.

The house was new, with bright, fresh timbers newly lime-
washed and the daub clean and unmarked, as yet, from men
and dogs pissing against it. A jetty that can only just have
passed the city rules on how high it must be, and how far it
could jut out over the lane, was close to braining any man of
moderate height, I thought. The rules are explicit about the
height of each building's jetty, but so often the rules are twisted
by corruption. A purse of coins can persuade the hardest-
hearted city official to mismeasure a house's dimensions, after
all. At least the place looked well built. Its fresh limewash
made the lane brighter. It almost hurt the eyes, even on a
gloomy day like this.

'Wait here,' Peg said as she knocked on the door.

'Why?'

She gave me a look that clearly as words stated, 'Do you
ever use your brain?' before saying, 'Because, lummox, she

is not expecting you. Look at you! A man with a gun and sword? What do you expect her to think? I heard you talking to Piers. When she hears you are come from her husband, a man who kills others for a living, a man who snips off ears or noses, who beheads, hangs and burns to death, who quarters his victims and castrates them in public, do you think she will welcome you with open arms?'

Well, putting it like that, it was a cause for thought, I realized.

'I'm going in there to ask her to give you a fair hearing. She will listen to you, and tell you whether she is prepared to give up her boy or not. Does that not sound fair?'

I could hardly argue with her logic. Nodding, I leaned against the wall, rubbing my sore shoulder as she slipped inside. My shoulder was painful, I have to say. There was a throbbing, and while I didn't believe the injury to be too severe, I was most loath to open my jack and look. I had a strong reluctance to witness the depth of the injury. As matters stood, I was in a position to believe that it was only a scratch. After all, it is the smallest of splinters in the palm of the hand that hurt the most, is it not?

The door opened, and Peg appeared. 'Come in,' she said, standing aside.

I entered with gladness. After the lightness outside, it was very dim and gloomy inside. I could barely see my hands before my face.

Stepping forward, I smiled at Peg as I passed her, and as I did so, I became aware of shadows; little more than shadows, but there were three of them, and then all at once there was a hand on my arm, pulling it away from sword and pistol, while two men stood before me. I squeaked in alarm. Then a man kicked at my knees, and I was on the floor, one man on my chest, while I was divested of all my weapons.

'What is this?' I demanded.

'We know you, Jack Blackjack. We know who you are, and whom you serve. Did you think us so stupid as to let you kill him?'

Now, I have been in worse scrapes. Waking on the piss-laden ground of a privy beside a dead body was unpleasant; then there was the time when I was dangling over a cesspit, and a great bear of a man was trying to force me in to drown in . . . well, in *that*; and I will not forget waking from a sore head in the chamber of one of the kingdom's most senior, devious, untrustworthy, dishonest politicians – that was even more terrifying than the others.

Having said that, there was something about lying on the floor with at least three men about me in the dimness of that chamber that caused me to forget the insult to my person and the pain of my shoulder. Instead, I had to concentrate on containing my bladder. These men sounded determined; they were determined to hurt me. That seemed most obvious. And they appeared to know of my employment. Oh, and one large fellow was holding a sword's point at my bowels. That concentrated my mind most effectively. Especially when he grinned at me. It was as reassuring as seeing a wolf bare its teeth at me.

'I don't think we have quite the right understanding,' I said, keeping my voice calm and reasonable.

'Who ordered you to come here?'

'Hal Westmecott, the executioner. He asked me to find his wife because he wants his boy back. I suppose you know that—'

'A reasonable invention,' the voice said again. Gradually, as my eyesight began to discern the figures in the chamber, I could make out faces. The speaker was a tall man, with a most pointed face, his chin a sharp angle, as though his features were a triangle. If he were to give up knocking innocent fellows to the ground, he could have gained employment as an awl in a leatherworker's workplace. He had a thin beard and moustache, and the jack about his shoulders looked to be of good quality, perhaps satin or silk. His voice was smooth and careless, which was worrying. It made him sound like a nobleman, and noblemen tend to be unconcerned about injuries suffered by fellows such as me.

He continued, 'Who really sent you? We are not persuaded that you could have been sent by some oafish knave like him. He's too sotten with ale to care about his wife or son.'

'You may think so, but he was most persuasive.'

The man smiled. It was not a reassuring look. 'You think he is the sort of man to care about his wife and son?'

'Ask her! She will tell the truth, I am sure,' I said, but my belly was cringing at the nearness of that sword's blade, and suddenly I was assailed by the thought that if they asked this benighted woman, and she didn't agree with what I said, that sword might plunge down in an instant.

'Don't whine,' the man said. He peered at me closely. 'What sort of man is this executioner? Is he the sort to treat a wife like a chattel? Beat her, whip her, use her abominably?'

'I don't know!'

'Oh, really? And I suppose you aren't being paid to find her?'

'No.'

He looked at me as though I was a cockroach, but a cockroach that could whistle a shanty. 'In that case, why did you agree to look for her and his son?'

'Ask Peg there – she told me she knew his wife, and was taking me to her,' I said, looking at her sorrowfully. 'Why don't you let me speak to her, and I'll be on my way if she wants nothing to do with her husband?'

'Are you so dull-witted that you need to ask?'

This was from the heavyset man with the sword. He seemed irritable, as though he thought I was making fun of them all.

The last man was over by the wall with Peg. He was even broader than the man with the sword, with square shoulders and the look of a man who would be handy with his fists. Or a knife. Or a sword. Or . . . You get the idea. He was vaguely familiar, as heathen, murderous, brutes often are. 'I've heard enough. He was here to kill the child. Just run him through now and let us be on our way, in God's name.'

'No! Wait!' I protested, and made a brief move to rise. The sword's point was instantly more noticeable, and I sank back again. 'I don't understand! I was sent to find the boy, nothing more, not to hurt him, and now . . .'

'We know who you are, Blackjack,' the nobleman said. 'We know you serve that black-hearted son of a fox, John Blount, so don't try to persuade us you're just an innocent abroad. What did he tell you?'

'It has nothing to do with him!' I said with surprise, and my voice and face must have been convincing, because even Peg said, 'I believe him.'

'All the more reason to kill him,' said my friend who was standing beside her. 'If he is lying, he's too believable. If he's telling the truth, he's heard too much from us. I say kill him now and be done.'

There was a shivering in my bowels on hearing that flat tone. 'You would kill a man because he knows nothing? You would murder me just for trying to do a good deed for a man who asked it of me? You would kill a man—'

'For not being silent and continuing to whine like a kicked whelp? Yes,' the nobleman said.

I suddenly had a feeling of remorse for kicking Hector after his theft of my breakfast. 'But I only wanted to bring back—'

'The boy, yes. The deeply caring executioner wants his son back. Why would that be, do you think?'

'He feels the loss of the lad? How would I know? He told me that he wanted the boy back, and that was all.'

'Why does he want the fellow now?'

'I don't know!'

'Perhaps because he thinks there is something to his advantage?'

'From the son of a bawd? He thought to make money from her or their son?'

Sadly, there was an answer which he supplied himself. 'If he wants the woman, perhaps he has heard she had an arrangement with a man far superior to her class and her husband's? Perhaps he thinks he can use this child? He might seek to capture the boy and demand ransom for his safety?'

That was not something that had occurred to me in my wildest moments. 'He . . . she . . . you mean . . .'

'Exactly.'

'No, surely not. Westmecott wouldn't be happy to raise the child of another man.'

'If he knew.'

'Of course, he must have known,' I said, and then I was silent. Westmecott, who was drunk every night so he

could forget his work; Westmecott, who would barely have
recognized his own face in a mirror, and would never
have recognized the face of another man in his son; Westmecott,
who probably routinely beat his wife . . . It was all too believable that he wouldn't realize he was raising another's boy. But
by the same token, 'How could you know that the boy was
not his? If his wife was so incontinent as to be flying about
the city and offering herself to your nobleman, how would he
know it was not Westmecott's?'

'Perhaps because Westmecott didn't know his woman had
given birth? Perhaps because she left him when the beatings
grew too violent, and she had not yet had a child? Perhaps
because she was placed in a safe home, and became concu-
bine to her lover? Perhaps because ten months later, she
gave birth to a boy?'

'Hah, but that would mean she left Westmecott before
she had her son!'

'Yes. At last I believe you begin to understand.'

'But if the lad wasn't born, how could he have told
me about his boy?'

The man with Peg sighed. 'As I say, run him through. We
don't have time for this.'

'He has heard that Moll has a child with her, since he has
asked you to find them, I suppose?' the nobleman said. 'And
now he seeks to capture the boy and demand money – or he
has another plan. Something even less to my taste. Whichever
it may be, it is not acceptable. The question is, were you sent
to kill the boy or to kidnap him?'

'Me?' I squeaked, and at that moment several things
happened.

First, the nobleman looked across to the man with the sword,
and I saw a wordless communication pass between them;
second, reading in that message a significant threat to my
health, I gave a shrill squeal, slapped the sword away before
it could puncture my belly, and rolled away; third, a loud
hammering came at the door, and a cry of 'Open in the name
of the Queen!'

There was instant pandemonium. I continued rolling, then
scampered to the far wall, where I cowered with my arms over

my head. The nobleman gave a sharp command and strode through a door at the rear of the chamber, closely followed by his companions, and Peg ran to the door, drawing the bolts, and then threw herself at my side, her arms about me. I cringed at the feel of them and tried to pull away, but she was like one of those things that clasps to the timbers of ships – a barnacle – and I could not shake her off.

The door was flung wide, and a heavyset trio marched in, the leader a city tipstaff. He held his staff towards me and snarled. 'Is that him?'

'Aye!'

It was the carter, and he spat in my direction. 'Threatened me with a gun, he did.'

'All right, that's enough.'

'What is this?' Peg demanded. I was still shivering from the thought of the sword held at my belly.

'This man says you two had foul words with him, and your man tried to shoot him.'

'That's a lie! The carter almost ran us down in the lane outside here, and when we protested, he lashed us!'

'Your man fired his gun.'

'No, I didn't!' I said hotly. 'There's my gun, on the floor over there. Smell it and see. If it had been discharged, you would be able to smell it. I have not fired it.'

'It is easy enough to clean a pistol.'

'With what? Tell me if you can find a piece of rag or anything else that I have used to clean it,' I said. I was growing angry now. The threat to my life of the last few minutes, the pain (which I was once more aware of) in my shoulder, the sight of the man who had caused the injury standing there and accusing me of threatening *him*, all built until I was filled with a righteous exasperation. 'What is the meaning of this? That fellow tried to run us down, and when we remonstrated, he cut me with his whip – here, look!' I said, and pulled my jack open.

Peg gave a small 'Ooh' and looked away. I glanced at her and then down. And as I did so, I was aware of a sudden hissing and boiling noise. It sounded as though the Thames was rising to flood the entire city. It truly sounded to me as if we were about to be inundated. But then the noise abated.

My shirt was a mass of blood. The sight made me go from boiling hot to freezing cold in an instant.

I heard no more. I fainted.

I have had worse awakenings. To be brought to my senses with my head resting on the soft, warm thighs of a woman while she stroked my cheeks and brow with a clean cloth, that was all perfectly acceptable. She was drinking strong wine from a goblet, and she tipped the rim to my lips. I sipped. It was a good Sherris sack, one of those fortified wines from Spain. When she spoke, I could smell the warm odour on her breath. It made her still more lovely to my eye. Women with a cargo of strong wine on board are always more likely to fall for the Blackjack charm.

'Who are you?' I asked.

Of course, I should have guessed. This was a day of surprises for me, but the red-gold hair, the eyes that held a reserved gaiety, while not concealing the pain that lay behind them, and the positively bouncing bosom that moved so wondrously as she inhaled – these surely would have told me in an instant who owned such bounties, were my brains not addled from questionings and beatings.

'You were looking for me, Peggy says.'

I sat up and winced. My shirt was gone, and instead I now wore a curious tracery of bandages about my chest and shoulder. 'Where am I?' I said, looking around. It was a large chamber, with a large, good-quality bed on the right, windows that gave a splendid view of an ancient building opposite, and a door before me. I was lying on Moll's lap, on a truckle bed that was too short for a man of my height. Clearly, then, a bed for a child.

'Where are the tipstaff and the carter?'

'When the tipstaff saw your injury, he took the carter away. I think he has some explaining to do.'

'Good,' I said, trying to rotate my shoulder. It was very sore. 'Who did this?'

'I was taught how to bind a wound when I was a child. How are you feeling? You fainted quite away.'

'You cannot be Moll. You wouldn't be Westmecott's woman,'

I said, and I meant it. She was lovely. Small-boned, she was a pretty, lithe little thing, with the kind of vivacity that comes from owning a certain position in the world; I could not see her being the wife of a drunken oaf like him.

'Why?'

I tried to give her the old Blackjack charm. 'You are far too beautiful, my lovely.'

Shutters dropped behind her eyes. I had overplayed my hand. She hadn't consumed enough wine yet. 'Yes, you are better.'

She pushed me from her lap and stood, wiping her hands down her skirts to smooth the material. 'Peggy told me about you.'

'Then you know I am not here to hurt you. Please, more wine?'

'No, you only came to steal the boy from me.'

'No! I was asked to find you and see whether you would let your boy go to him. He wants to see his son.'

'It's not his, and he knows it.'

'How could he tell?' I scoffed.

She gave me a very direct stare which included a certain degree of puzzlement. 'Because I am not his wife. I don't know him.'

Of course many women can lie most effectively, especially the ladies of her profession, but I was struck by the conviction in her tone. I am graced with a good ear for dissembling. This sounded like the truth.

'The boy is nothing to do with the man you speak of,' she said. 'I will not give him up.'

'You aren't married to Hal Westmecott?' I tried again.

'I don't know him. I was married to Hugh Tanner, but he died. Then I met a pleasant nobleman. And . . . well.'

'Of course, some ladies might decide to forget marriage with a man like Westmecott,' I said with an attempt at an understanding smile.

'You think I've forgotten getting married?'

'Some people can forget,' I said. 'Some may choose to forget an unhappy marriage.'

'Some might. I haven't.'

That was a hard one to counter, but it was not my place to wonder. 'So, you will not allow your boy to be taken back to his father.'

'He is with his father often enough,' she said tartly. 'I told you: Westmecott is not his father.'

'I will tell him.'

'And what else will you tell him?'

'Me?' I shrugged. 'Nothing. I have no wish to be involved in anything further to do with you or him. This is all the result of a misunderstanding between him and me, and now I learn he misunderstood the situation between himself and you. And the boy. I have no desire to be caught between you all.'

And I did not. I pulled on my shirt – stained and befouled with my blood, and with a new slash in the shoulder where the lash had cut – with some difficulty, tucking the tails under my buttocks, and pulling the jack on, binding the points to my hosen. The lady was kind enough to tie those at the rear for me, and soon I was dressed once more. I searched about the room for my sword and baldric, the pistol and my pouch of powder and balls, but I was told that they were not here. I could see that.

'Where are they? I cannot walk the streets without protection!'

'My friends did not want you to wake here in my house with weapons.'

'This is intolerable! I want my pistol,' I said. Without the damned thing, I felt quite naked.

She clapped her hands, and a man walked in. It was the same brute who had stood at the wall with Peggy. 'Walter, please fetch this fellow's weapons. When he leaves the house, you may give them back to him. I don't want him inside with them.'

'Yes, Mistress.'

'And, Walter, make sure that he leaves.'

I bowed to the woman, because while she might have been a prostitute, she had more class than a number of well-born women I could think of. While the man called Walter waited, I took my leave and strode from the room with a haughtily uplifted chin that, I think, demonstrated my status compared with his own. I heard, I think, a snigger as I passed him, but I treated that with the contempt it deserved, and continued out through the door and down a steep flight of steps. There, I stood and waited while Walter followed after me.

A door opened a little way ahead of me, and I saw a tousled head appear. A boy with a distinctive face peered out at me, a face that was perfectly symmetrical and triangular in shape, with dark eyes that took in my appearance without any great demonstration of pleasure or of being overly impressed by my appearance. He merely took in the sight of me and then withdrew, closing the door quietly behind him.

Well, that answered one question. If the woman had given birth to her lover's child, the father was the nobleman who had interrogated me. His face was remarkably similar to that of the boy.

'Outside,' Walter said brusquely.

I would have cavilled, but the man was young and healthy, and I was injured and unarmed. When he pointed to the door to the front parlour, I walked on, but with a reserved calmness, ignoring him as arrogantly as any duke. At the door to the street, he reintroduced me to my weaponry, and I pulled my baldric over my head with an effort, then hefted my bag of balls and powder to my good shoulder, and last of all thrust my pistol into my belt.

'Don't come back,' he said.

The comment was unnecessary as far as I was concerned. I had been knocked down, whipped and insulted.

It was between Westmecott and this woman, and I wanted nothing more to do with the affair or with them.

The rooms where Westmecott had his lodgings were in a poorer part of Ludgate, south of the cathedral, in the maze of alleys. On all sides were thriving businesses of every kind, with the constant shouts of people selling pamphlets, printers hawking their wares, tradesmen trundling handcarts with flapping sheets of paper to the printers. It was between a low alehouse and a printer's that I found the dark, noisome passage that led to his house.

I may be from the underworld of London's rougher parts,

but that doesn't make me immune to the dangers of a place like this. The darker the alleyway, the more my hackles rise, and I could not remember such a dim, unpleasant corridor as this. Usually, some vestige of light would tentatively creep down from the sky overhead to give a glimmer to the cobbles underfoot, but here there was nothing, only a twenty-foot black maw into which I must step. I can say now that I didn't like to enter.

It was like slipping into treacle. The light was sucked from the place, and without a candle or spark of light to show the way, I had to rely on the vague patches of paleness which showed where a clean cobble stood. Those that didn't show themselves were hidden beneath other things which I preferred not to speculate on. The concealing articles were unlikely to be pleasant.

His lodging, as I was told, was the last door in this grim passageway. I moved on down to the last door, which was more a rough accumulation of planks of wood haphazardly nailed together, and knocked. There was a hollow ring to the place, and no answer. I knocked again, and this time I noticed that the door moved.

It struck me that it was likely that the man was in a stupor, or still in a tavern somewhere, but in case he was inside, I pushed the door wide and called for him.

Inside, it was as dark as the passageway, and my eyes could make out little. I stumbled over something, and then barged into a stool and struck the corner of a table with my thigh, which made my leg go dead, and I all but fell. There was a faint lightness in a wall, and I made my way to it. Over a grimy window was a scrap of cloth serving as a curtain. I drew it aside and rubbed at a pane or two of glass with the material. It felt greasy and rank in my hand, but gradually it began to clear a path through the grime of the window, and when I turned around, I could make out the furniture in the room.

And the body on the floor.

Many people, I suppose, on finding themselves in the presence of death, would perform one of two or three functions.

They might instantly search for money or valuables – but

that was hardly worthwhile in a chamber so bereft of decoration. Anything this executioner managed to filch from his victims he sent to a pawn shop instantly, and drank the proceeds the same night. A man might also search about for someone to blame for the death – but in the case of an executioner, what would be the point? The man had slain so many people, trying to find one specific person with the desire to murder him would be pointless. And finally, of course, many people would hurry from the chamber to find a bailiff or other officer, to begin the process of the law, fetching a coroner to record the death and establish the fines for deodand and all the other little details that could cost the parish dear.

Not I. No, I walked to the stool, picked it up from where I had knocked it over, set it straight and sat upon it.

I suppose, in the months since Wyatt's rebellion, I have seen death in so many forms that to see an executioner lying in a pool of blood was less of a shock, and more of an irritant that must be dealt with. If there was one thing I had learned in the last twelvemonth, it was that hurrying from a place of murder would be unlikely to do anything other than cause people to comment. Better by far to walk away from here quietly, without rushing, with a cheery whistle. No one would notice me in such a manner.

Someone had entered here and slain the man while he was at his table, perhaps, or waited until he opened the door, then struck him down as he turned away. It was plain that the man had bled a great deal. Blood was all over the floor, and now I could smell it, too. I swallowed as my gorge rose, keeping it at bay. As my eyes grew more used to the light, I could see that the man's head had been struck with a weapon and was crushed. There was a great dint in the back of his skull, which was facing me now. His left shoulder lay on the floor, his back to me, and his legs were at the wall. One hand was reaching forward towards his bed, as if to grab a post and pull himself up – but it was too late for him to do that.

I could imagine the scene. Westmecott, hearing a knock, went to open his door. He would invite his guest inside, standing aside and waving the fellow in . . . but no. This figure was lying so close. Perhaps he was less courteous and merely

turned around, expecting the guest to close the door, and as
soon as he showed his back, his killer struck him on the head
with a stout cudgel, or a hammer. Something heavy would be
needed to make that kind of injury.

There was nothing for me here. The only thing I was aware
of was that at least I didn't have to worry about explaining
that his son didn't want to return to him because, well, it
wasn't his son. And, of course, I wouldn't have to worry about
reimbursing him for the cost of the powder.

All in all, I considered as I stood, settling my sword and
pistol and wincing at the pain still in my shoulder, although
it was sad that the fellow had died, his death did remove
several difficulties for me. I could not mourn him. Any responsibility for finding his 'wife' and 'son' died along with him.
Yes, it was a relieved Jack who prepared to leave that
unpleasant environment.

I was about to cross to the door when I heard paces in the
passageway outside. They were slow, burdened paces,
the paces of a heavy man who was stumbling. Suddenly, it
occurred to me that the man before me could, possibly, have
struck out at a man, turned to fetch a fresh weapon and then
himself been struck. Perhaps the killer was on his way back
now, even as I stood there. Perhaps he had seen me enter the
alley and was ready to assassinate me to keep his bloody
murder secret?

It was intolerable. I listened to the slow scrap and shuffle
on the cobbles, and then a shape appeared in the doorway, as
gross as a bear, enormous in the darkness, with a great lump
on his shoulder. With a squeak of terror, I pulled out my pistol
and held it up. 'Don't come in!' I said in a falsetto that would
have done service to a eunuch.

'Go and piss yourself!' came the response. 'What are you
doing here?'

And I gaped and lowered my pistol, for all my problems
had just returned, renewed and invigorated, to haunt me.
Because in the doorway stood Westmecott.

Which rather begged the urgent question of *who* lay on the
ground before me?

*   *   *

'Christ's cods! Damme eyes! What 'ave you done?'

His words were not those I wished to hear. He was carrying a rug over his shoulder, and he slung this on the floor at my feet.

'What have *I* done? What have *you* done?' I spluttered. 'I came here to find you to tell you about the boy, and found this fellow here, as you see him. Who is he? Why did you kill him?'

'Me? Kill 'im?' he demanded with vigour.

That was the beginning of one of those 'I didn't do it, you must have' and 'No, I didn't do it, you must have' conversations which are always essentially fruitless, and tedious to repeat. Suffice it to say that when we had run out of mutual accusations, we both set to staring at the corpse with confusion in our hearts.

'Is he someone you know?' I asked.

'I don't think so,' he said. He went to the body and rolled him over. It made me catch my breath, because the man had wide, staring eyes and an expression of hideous pain.

He was – well, had been – a man of about five feet eight inches, and broad in the shoulder. He'd been a labouring fellow, or a street rough, from the look of him. His knuckles were all calloused and thickened, like a man who was used to using his fists. His face was simian, with a scar that ran under his left eye and away towards his ear, and I could imagine that someone had taken a knife to him and had the weapon knocked away. I pitied the man who had dared to draw a blade against him. Apart from that, he had a shock of thinning, sandy hair, and was missing the last joint of his left forefinger. He was not a man I would have liked as an acquaintance.

'You know him?' Westmecott said, hearing my intake of breath.

'No. Never seen him before,' I said.

He was gazing at me in what I could only think was a suspicious manner, but on hearing the evident sincerity in my voice, he nodded, and his manner appeared to grow more emollient. 'What are you doing 'ere, anyway?'

'Me?' For a moment I was at a loss. 'Oh, I came to tell you, I have spoken to Moll,' I said without thinking.

'You found 'im, then? You found my boy? Good. When will you bring 'im to me?'

'Eh?' I hesitated. Moll's denial of his claim upon her was ringing in my ears still, but I reckoned that informing the executioner that his wife denied their marriage could lead to a buffet about my ears that would set them ringing like the bells at St Paul's. 'No, I spoke to his mother, and she . . . well, she said no. But what about this fellow?'

Westmecott shrugged unconcernedly. 'I dispose of bodies every day. One more or less won't make a lot of difference. I can remove him. But my boy – what do you mean, she won't let 'im come?'

This was tricky. I could see that his suspicions were aroused, but then again so were my own. Moll had been quite definite that she was not this man's wife, and that the boy was not his. Perhaps she had been lying to persuade me to leave her alone? But why, then, would Westmecott want the boy? Purely for a ransom, as the nobleman had suggested? It was possible, I supposed. All I was sure of right now was that Westmecott was a large, strong fellow who could unscrew my head with ease to peer inside, and the nobleman with Mistress Moll was more than capable of ordering my death as well. I wanted no further part to play in this nasty little dispute. Leave it to the parties involved, was my view.

'I have spoken to her, as you asked,' I said with some hauteur, and then a spark of resentment flared. Why should I worry about him and his reaction, when he had asked me to perform a task, I had done so and she refused to comply? It was all one to me.

I stiffened my back. This may hurt, but it was better that he came to terms with things sooner rather than later. 'I am sorry, but she said she would not return. Nor would she send your boy to you. She . . .' I swallowed. 'She said he was not your son anyway. She said she was not your wife, and she didn't know you.'

'Did she?' he said, and a terrible calmness came over him. 'She said that?'

'Yes. She said that she left you and conceived the boy after leaving you. She said you never had the boy living here with you.'

Looking about the place, there was scarce space for a man, woman and child.

'Did she?' he said again, and I was suddenly aware of just how large the man truly was. He loomed over me, even though our heights must have been roughly similar. Still, from where I was standing, he loomed. He definitely loomed. And I felt myself shrinking.

'She weren't lying,' he said, and sighed.

I confess, for an assumed assassin, a mercenary who was happy to kill those who stood in his path, or who stood in the way of his master's enemies, I always disliked the smell and sight of a dead body. It took little effort to persuade my companion that we should perhaps remove ourselves to a more comfortable house where a fire was already alight, and where there was a possibility of warmth and ale. Yes, it was May, but that chamber felt cold with the soul of the corpse sucking the life and vitality from the room.

We walked up the foul little alley to the top of the road, and there Hal Westmecott led me to the back room of the alehouse I had seen before.

It was a cheery enough little place. There was a good fire in the hearth, and the smoke rose to the middle of the bay – this was a house built before the advent of chimneys – and the place felt cheery and warm.

We walked with our ales to a rear table, where we seated ourselves on a bench. I accosted him with all the seriousness I could muster. 'Come, Hal. No more prevarication and dissembling. What is happening?'

'I told you.'

'No. You told me your wife was a runaway with your son. Now she tells me she was not your wife, and you admit she isn't lying!'

'Perhaps our marriage weren't formal,' he said, abashed.

'So you weren't married to her. You beat her, she ran away, and, while away, she conceived and gave birth. So this is not your son, is it? It is the son of another man. So what do you want with the boy, and what do you intend with her?'

He glowered and seemed to inflate to twice his normal size,

leaning towards me and glaring like a bear who has seen his favourite berries stolen, but then he subsided. He sank back in his seat and leaned against the wall behind the bench. 'Very well. Yes, I admit it. She weren't my legal wife, but her and me, we lived like husband and wife. That man took her from me. I don't know 'ow.'

'When was this?'

'She left me for him in 1548 or so, I suppose.'

'That is eight years ago!'

'You think I don't realize?' he snapped.

'Yes, yes, I'm sorry.'

'She was got with child, so I hear. When she came back to London—'

'She had left?'

'Do you want me to finish?'

'Yes, yes, I am sorry. Continue.'

'She came back, yes. I don't know 'ow long she were away, nor where she were gone to, but she weren't here. She came back with her pimp, and lived with him, I think.'

'You mean the nobleman who lived with her?'

'No, I mean the man who'd tooken her from me. He was selling her body all over London.'

'You have proof of this?'

He looked at me from beetling brows and sank a good half pint of ale in a draught. 'I'm her husband. Do I need proof?'

He was not her husband, and he had no proof, I noted. 'So she returned with a baby?'

'Yes.'

'And you know it was not your boy?'

'It might not have been,' he said, his eyes sidling away from mine.

No. The boy wasn't his, and he knew it. 'And then she set herself up in a new home, and you didn't see her.'

'Not until a week ago. I was 'angin' two thieves – 'ad them up on the dancing tree for their last jig – and as the younger was kicking his heels up, I saw her between his legs. She was walking as bold as a knight on his mount through the crowds. I saw her, though; oh, yes, I saw her. She was looking over at me as though she wanted to run and hide, but I saw her, and I knew then that I would never have a moment's peace until I had her back.'

'But you said you wanted her boy?'

'I didn't think she would come to me. I thought, well, if I 'ad her son, she'd surely follow the bastard.'

He had said he had seen her, not the boy. How did he know there was a boy with her? I asked him.

He reddened. 'I ran after her, saw the boy with her.'

'In the crowd?'

'Yes. But she lost me in 'mong the people. I lost her.'

'So you decided to try to take her son, knowing that she could not leave him behind?'

'Yes.'

He sank another half pint, and I sat back in contemplation. There was a lot that I didn't understand, that didn't make sense. If he had wanted his wife back, threatening her with the theft of her son, a son that was nothing to do with him, was surely only going to lead to disputes and quarrels. But this was a man who saw to the end of arguments by use of a long rope and a sharp axe. Perhaps the finer aspects of married life had passed him by. Then again, he must know that whoever the man was who had fathered the boy would be wealthy, and could hire men to steal his boy and wife back. As the brute on the floor of Westmecott's hovel seemed to indicate.

I mentioned this aspect tentatively.

'I know, I know. That had occurred to me.'

'And even now there is proof of it on your floor,' I said.

'Yes. Who would 'ave tried to do that?'

'What, tried to kill you? Or killed the man who attempted it?'

And that, we agreed, was the real question.

TWO

I left Hal in the tavern, no more reassured about the appearance of the corpse than he was.

It was one of those incomprehensible events. There seemed to be no rational explanation as to why the fellow had made his way to Westmecott's, and I had no idea why someone should have taken it into their head to crumple the man's pate like an egg, but my main feeling was one of relief that it was not me lying on the floor in there. After all, if I had arrived there a little earlier, I would wager a good sum that the man lying on the floor would have found me and killed me in his place.

One thing was certain, and that was that I wanted nothing further to do with Westmecott, the woman he called his wife, her son, nor the malevolent wench who had persuaded me to follow her to the house where I could be captured and injured. My shoulder still hurt; my blood had drenched my shirt, and it felt sticky and unwholesome now. The mere thought of that was enough to make my head begin to swim, and I was forced to pause on my way homewards and take a detour into a small tavern where they served a vile brandy that threatened to dissolve the tongue in my mouth. Yet, for all its harshness, I felt considerably happier as I continued.

No. I didn't like Westmecott. His initial outburst, when I first met him, against his wife had been a little too extreme, and then his motivation for my bringing Ben back to him had seemed less in Ben's interests than his own. Ben was not a mere possession to be traded between those who sought ever more personal advantage, I felt. I could remember what it was like to be a young boy in a house without love and affection. I didn't want to see Ben thrown into a similar situation, with a bullying father who spent every evening in a drunken stupor. No, I didn't trust Westmecott.

My door was ajar, and I took a deep breath to bellow at the

vacuous, feckless excuse for a servant as I stepped inside. If I had told him once, I had told him a thousand times to make sure that the door was locked. But today, even as I crossed my threshold, I was taken by the sight of young Hector. He almost cringed to the ground, and I snapped my fingers at him. 'Oh, get up, fool! I'm not angry with you still. You are a good boy, and I'll forgive you. Come here.'

He made no move towards me, and it was clear enough that the chastisement – and yes, it was deserved – for stealing my breakfast had made him fearful. Well, that was all very well, but I had given the brute a command and expected him to obey. 'Come here, I said.'

It was as I gave him the order that I saw his eyes roll, as though he was peering behind me. It was a most curious look, as if a ghost had appeared. And in truth, it made me feel that a cold wind had passed through the hall. I felt my hackles rise. It was terrifying to think that there could be something behind me. But I am known, obviously, for my courage. I cast a quick look around, and when I did, I almost sprang from my skin in terror.

There, behind me, stood a tall man, clad entirely in dark velvet, a hat on his head at a jaunty angle, one hand resting casually on his hip, while the other held, in a rather negligent manner, a pistol pointing at my head.

'Good day, Master Blackjack,' he said.

In my long experience of being waylaid and attacked, I have rarely had a more unexpected and unwelcome appearance. I gave a loud cry and leapt about two yards into the air before falling back and almost crushing Hector, who gave a loud yelp and scurried back out into the kitchen. Meanwhile, my sword's scabbard had become entangled with my legs, and when I landed, the thing caught my left leg, and as I said, 'Damn your eyes, what the devil do you mean by . . .' I discovered that my legs were unbalanced. I tried to shove my left leg out to regain my posture, but all I could do was push my knee out, and with an anguished sense of disaster, I toppled over.

'Very good. I think I'll remove these for you,' my elegant

friend murmured, divesting me of sword, pistol and dagger. 'We wouldn't want another accident, would we?'

'Who are you? What are you doing in my house? And what have you done with my servant and his beast?'

'My dear fellow, please. There is no need for alarm. I only wished to come and speak to you.'

'Where is my servant?'

Having not seen Raphe all day, I was keen to know where the boy had got to. Yes, he was notoriously unreliable at the very best of times, but for him to disappear overnight struck a new low even for him. And I did not want to have to explain to my master, John Blount, that I had mislaid the fellow. I suspected that Blount was his uncle, and I felt sure that the man would deprecate his nephew's disappearance.

'You have a servant?' the man enquired mildly, raising an eyebrow.

'Yes. I admit he may not be the best in London,' I added as he glanced at the heaps of dirty rushes, the cobwebs on the ceiling and furniture, the mud lying in a heap by the door, where it had been swept by the door itself. 'But that does not mean that he deserves to be beaten or injured by a stranger. Where have you put him?'

Of course, a moment's thought would tell you that I was being a little unreasonable here, since Raphe had not been in the house when I had taken my unorthodox exit, but I was not to know that this fellow had not been Westmecott's accomplice, and that he had not in fact beaten Raphe when the door had been opened to him. Besides, I was not feeling unduly reasonable. I was not having a good day.

'There was no one here when I arrived,' the man said. 'The door was open, and I entered without hindrance.'

'Really?' I sneered. It is not easy to sneer when trying to clamber to your feet, but I did my best. 'And you have spent some while looking about you to see what you might acquire of mine, I suppose?'

'My friend,' the fellow said, carelessly thrusting his pistol through his belt. Then, taking a grip of my sword, he twirled it about his wrist, ending with it only an inch from my throat. I could feel the muscles constrict as it came to a grey, flashing halt. 'Please, my fellow, don't make the mistake of considering me some mere simple ruffian whom you can abuse or accuse at will. I have a gentleman's temper for accusations of that sort.'

I nodded very earnestly, keen to assure him that I was utterly convinced of his integrity and honesty.

'Now, why don't we sit in your parlour? I have lit a fire for you – your servant appears to have forgotten to do that as well – and it would be pleasant to sit before the flames, would it not? And while we sit, we can warm some ale, and then perhaps chat about different matters of importance.'

'What sort of matters?' I asked.

'Oh, the little things: the state of the realm, the new laws against our Church of England, the madness of burning priests at the stake, and perhaps the foolishness of providing powder to an executioner that is not up to the job of killing his victim?'

'Supplying powder—'

'Yes. You sold powder to Master Westmecott, did you not? Which could well have been an act of kindness, one demonstrating that you felt sure the flames would not touch him. Perhaps you were motivated to see my brother rise from the funeral pyre in one piece. You may have intended to leap into the flames to rescue him. But then again, providing sodden powder could be perceived by a less generous soul to have been a cynical act of cruelty, trying to inflict even more pain and anguish on my brother as he writhed in agony. I wonder of which of those two alternatives you will attempt to persuade me?'

He had indeed managed to raise a good fire. As he pointed to my seat before the flames, I rested my buttocks and held my hands to the logs.

'No, my friend,' he said with a smile. 'Place your back to the fire, please.'

I was not happy with this. 'I don't think you—'

'Please.'

I turned about. As I did so, he suddenly grabbed my wrist and bound it with a leather thong. Then he bound it to my other wrist, before lashing my legs together at the ankles. 'What has happened here?' he asked, seeing my shoulder.

'A foul-mouthed carter assaulted me,' I said.

'A man of little distinction, no doubt,' he smiled, and sat back in a fresh seat. 'Now, first, perhaps you should tell me why you chose to try to inflict a slow and painful death on my—'

'I had no idea. Westmecott came asking for some powder, and I sold it to him, but it was fine when he went. I can show you! I still have the barrel downstairs.'

'Perhaps so. That might be an interesting experiment later. I can think of ways to test your powder.'

'Yes! Do! I can show you. I have no powder that is not perfectly functional.'

'So that means you must have decided to dampen it just to hurt my brother. That is not, necessarily, the best defence you could muster.'

'I didn't even know whom Westmecott was intending to kill!'

'In truth? How interesting. Perhaps you should tell me all.'

So I did. From the moment Westmecott had appeared and demanded the powder, to the discussion with him about the ineffectualness of the powder I had sold him. I forbore to mention the body in Westmecott's hovel. After all, with luck the corpse would already have been removed. If I didn't mention it, I could deny any knowledge later.

He sat back in my best chair with a faint smile on his face as I spoke. On his lap he had rested my sword, but there was no threat in it. He had a calm demeanour, as so many of these richer nobles will have. They tend to be the sort of people who can entertain a fellow with pleasing comments and anecdotes, and then leap into murderous action in a trice. I don't know what it is about the English aristocracy, but they all seem to possess this same vile love of violence. 'You say the powder was perfectly functional when you sold it? Then who could have adulterated it?'

'I don't know. All I can say is that it was fine. It's in a barrel down below. If you let me loose, I will fetch you some, and you can—'

'I don't think that will be necessary,' he said, and now there was a cold glitter in his eyes that made my ballocks retreat. It was the look of a killer.

'No, please! You have to believe me!'

'I do believe you, my friend. It is a great shame, but I can see no reason to suspect you in this matter. The powder must have been soaked or otherwise spoiled.' He looked out through my window thoughtfully. 'But who could have wanted to commit such a heinous offence? The powder was only there to make his end more comfortable. Who could possibly have decided to do that to poor James?'

'I don't know.'

'No, you perhaps do not. After all, the powder was only there for your own use, I assume? Yes. So why would you have wrecked an entire barrel, when there was no need. I can see no reason for Westmecott to do so, either. It is a conundrum. Unless, of course, you had some objection to my brother's sermonizing.'

'I have no idea who you are, or your brother! I've never met him to my knowledge,' I protested.

'You have not heard of James? So you are not interested in matters of heresy?'

'No. I just try to keep my head on my shoulders,' I said sourly. My hands were losing all feeling, and my back was growing very warm. 'I am happy to help you, Master, but could you please unbind me? My hands are grown numb.'

'Possibly. I wanted to make sure that you realized how warm James must have become as the flames rose higher and higher.'

'You should speak with the executioner, then, not me.'

'But what of the executioner? He thought he had purchased good powder.'

'Which is what he bought.'

'You say.'

'Someone must have found it and soaked it in water. Wet powder won't burn, of course. You know that as well as I.'

'Perhaps so,' he said, glancing down at the pistol he had hung from his belt.

'Consider this,' I said, growing just a little desperate now. 'When I sold him powder, how would I know he would not test it? If it was so poor, the defect would be obvious to the meanest spirit. If he tried to set a spark to it, it would not burn. Obviously, I had to sell him good-quality powder, or I would myself be in trouble.'

'As you are,' he nodded, with a fresh smile.

I ignored that. 'So someone else must have learned he was going to use powder, and soaked it for him,' I said.

'Someone who must have known where he lived, of course.'

'Yes. Or someone who knew his favourite tavern and threw water on it there,' I said. But the idea that someone would have followed Westmecott all the way to a tavern, there to hurl water over a bag of powder, hoping that enough would soak into it to make it resist flames was too much to think of. Then I had a sudden intuition. 'Or,' I said with conviction, 'the fool went to a tavern and set his powder on to a wet table. You know how tables are in low-standard taverns – they are regularly left swimming in ale. Think, if the fool of an executioner went in, ordered himself an ale, sat at table, set his powder before him on the table and started drinking, how long would it be before his pouch had absorbed enough moisture to make the entire bag useless? I would think it would be less than the time it would take him to drink six or seven pints, and once he reached eight, you can be sure that he would have spilled so much more ale that even a wax-cloth purse would have become sodden.'

The man looked at me. 'There is something in what you say. However, I would like to test your own powder before I release you.'

'Yes, of course. It's in the cellar,' I said. 'If you cut me loose, I can show you.'

He rose, but didn't release me. Instead, he strode towards the hall.

'No, please,' I began, but it was no good. The man had already reached the door. With a mocking bow, he passed through.

There was a sound, rather like that of a large metal dish striking a hammer – a ringing, echoing sound – and I stared at the doorway in time to see him return. He wore a smile, but it was composed of mingled surprise and bemusement. He stared at me, his mouth opened, and he pointed at me, and then his eyes appeared to cross over his nose, and he gave a quiet moan as his legs gave way beneath him.

'I have never been so glad to see you,' I said.

Raphe was sitting on the floor before me. He had cut the bonds that held me and fetched rope to tie our visitor securely to a supporting pillar. Now James's brother sat with his arms behind the pillar, his legs outstretched, his back against it, a thick cord holding him in place.

'Didn't sound like it, the way you were describing me.'

'What did I say about you? I was only concerned that you were not about. I had no idea where you were, and I was naturally worried for you.'

'Said I was the worst servant in London, near as anything.'

'No, no, no, Raphe. That was just to confuse him. I wanted him to think he was safe from you, even were you to appear. What, you would prefer me to tell him you were a fiend for battle, that you would attack him, as any good servant would?' I said heartily. I didn't want news of my insults to return to his uncle – not that Blount would have been worried. He knew what sort of a feckless nephew Raphe was, I was sure. It was likely that which had led to Raphe being installed in my house in the first place. 'So, this fellow. What shall we do with him?'

Raphe eyed the man, and then stood and kicked him between the legs. 'He was cruel to Hector. Hector wouldn't come to see him after he appeared. He must have done something to the poor dog.'

I looked away. This did not seem the best moment to explain that I had been forced to chastise the brute.

With the impact of Raphe's boot, the man had given a low groan and bent over slowly, sucking in his breath. He made a half-hearted effort to bring his legs together for the protection of his sceptre and diamonds, but the mere act of bringing his legs into closer union was enough to make his eyes pop.

'Who are you?' I asked.

The fellow's forehead was growing. A large plum appeared to have been cut in half and thrust on to the right side of his brow. It was only the colour of a greengage just now, but I had faith it would grow and darken. As for himself, the man narrowed his eyes as he glared at Raphe, but that did little to dampen my servant's ardour. He pulled his leg back again.

'You do see your problem, don't you?' I said. 'Raphe here believes you have mishandled his dog, and he is quite prepared to exact the most painful of punishments. Of course, if you wish, and if you are brave, you may decide to test his ability and your own endurance. But I should warn you . . .' His boot slammed forward, and I winced. 'He really is most fond of his dog. As you can no doubt tell.'

'Yes,' he said with earnest conviction. I tutted and waved Raphe away even as he brought his foot back once more. 'No, Raphe. I think our guest would appreciate a glass of sack, and I know I would. Now, if you please.'

Raphe gave our guest a virulent look that should, if the world were to rights, have melted the man there and then, before stalking out of the room and along the passage to the buttery. I, meanwhile, leaned back in my chair and smiled down at the fellow. 'Now, why don't you tell me what this is all about?'

'I am called Geoffrey of Thorney,' the fellow told me. He squirmed a little, and I thought the two kicks must have left him feeling a need to rearrange his pizzle and balls. I could easily imagine that the two were swelling to the size of pigs' bladders after Raphe's enthusiastic treatment of them. When he looked up at me again, arching his back as though to reorder his anatomy and make its contact with the floor more comfortable, I smiled at him.

'I come from near Westminster. My father had a good holding there, bordering on the river, but he lost it in recent years. My family was keen to support the old King, and his son. But now . . .'

He said no more about our Queen, but I could see the direction of his thinking. There was no need for him to emphasize the situation. 'Continue.'

'My father was a loyal subject of King Henry, bless his name. But this latest member of the family – she is little better than a snake. She bites and poisons all whom she meets. Look at how she treats her father's priests! She captures them, insists that they should change their beliefs, and then threatens them with death if they refuse!'

'And one such was your brother?'

'He gave a sermon in which he spoke of the honour and integrity of the new Church. It was a matter of faith, so he believed, and thus he preached. He was a man of honour, my brother James, a man who always spoke his mind and tried to be honest with all. He spoke a sermon, and only a day or two later, the henchmen of the Queen appeared and arrested him. They tortured him, tried to force him to recant, but he wouldn't. He stuck to his faith, and in the end they decided to execute him on the pyre. And then—'

'Someone made certain that his powder was wet,' I said.

Raphe walked in at that point and stood near Geoffrey with a tray in his hands. The injured man looked up at him, and I could see the thought running through his mind that he could snap his leg up and hit the back of Raphe's knee, knocking him to the ground. It was tempting to see it happen, but sadly a fellow cannot live for pleasure alone. I snapped at Raphe to leave the prisoner alone. He grumpily set the tray on the table near me and left. I stood, took up my dagger and used it to slash through the bonds holding Geoffrey to the post. He stood, teetering a little, a hand going to his head, and then made his way to a stool. I poured wine and passed him a goblet. He lifted it in mute salutation and drank. 'Very pleasant.'

'It should be for the price,' I said. 'So your brother was held.'

'Yes, only a couple of days after his sermon.'

'Why a couple of days? Usually they will arrest a heretic in a matter of hours.'

'Perhaps there were too many other heretics to catch that day.'

I shook my head. 'Was he not there to be arrested?'

'I don't know.' He shrugged with bafflement. 'What does it matter? He was found and they killed him.'

'Which is illuminating, but there is the other aspect: what

if he was being watched, and the men captured him at the first opportunity when he was in the church again?'

'Well? What of it?'

I wasn't sure myself, but it did seem odd. Queen Mary's men tended to be along at once when they heard of a priest who had not stuck to her script. They were wont to move in quickly to remove any elements of sedition or heresy, yet they had allowed this priest to remain free. If he had been away, of course, they would not have been able to catch him. I made a mental note of that. 'Where are you living?'

'I live over at Thorney, but I doubt I will be able to remain there for long. Now they have killed James, I do not doubt that they will come for me.'

'Why, you haven't been giving any sermons, have you?'

'Me? Nay! I am no sermonizer. But his blood runs in my veins. You know how the rich think of such things. If a man has the same blood as a traitor, that man must be executed. It is hazardous to be related these days.'

'Well, in future, try to withhold your more violent urges, good fellow. Don't try to attack the innocent. Next time, I may not be so lenient. I will allow Raphe full dispensation to take whatever vengeance he feels he wishes.'

He pulled a face. 'Aye. And now you will let me leave, I suppose?'

'Yes. I have no use for you.'

'What, you will allow me to walk from here?'

'Yes.'

'And your boy will follow me, I expect?'

'I doubt it. I have work for the fool.'

He looked about him as though expecting to see at any moment a band of halberdiers or archers burst in from behind the tapestries, and his expression was so comical that I could not help but chuckle. 'The door is there, and you are welcome to use it.'

'Even after I assaulted you?' he said.

'I think Raphe revenged me.'

He walked to the door and opened it, leaning out to peer up my corridor. Returning, he went to the tray and refilled my goblet and then his own. 'There is one thing that may help me to find the men who ended my brother's life,' he said. 'I believe that it was one of the Seymour family who reported him to the officials.'

That I had little idea who the Seymours were should really not be a surprise. Yes, I had heard the name related to poor Queen Jane, the lady who married King Henry and who gave birth to his son, before succumbing to the ailment so common to mothers shortly after they give birth. Henry had revered her, for she was the only wife who had given him his most fervent desire: a son. When she died, she became the first of his wives to be buried as Queen, and her bones rested alongside his in Windsor, I had heard. But that was all I knew of her and her deadly family.

Oh, in England we have our share of ruffians. There are many who rise through the ranks of the aristocracy and become great men, but make no mistake: for every good gentleman who sits in a lofty palace, there are twenty or a hundred more who are little better than pirates or thieves. If you find yourself confronted by a man who calls himself a lord, best that you duck and run, because he will run you through faster than a drawlatch steeped in brandy. The higher they rise, the poorer the manners, the more vicious the behaviour, the more ruthless the greed, and the more despicable the crimes. I have known murderers who would blench to see the way that a lord or duke might flatter a fellow and then stab him as soon as his back was turned. Even the most cruel and vile dregs of London's lowest sewers would grimace and avert their gaze, were they to witness some of the acts I have seen perpetrated by the highest in the land.

But for sheer, callous ambition, the brothers of Jane Seymour would take considerable beating, I was to learn. One was Edward, Earl of Hertford, who became the Lord Protector to King Edward till the poor lad's death; another was Thomas, Lord Seymour of Sudeley Castle, who had the temerity to marry the last Queen of King Henry, Catherine Parr – who was, by all accounts, a kind, loving lady who deserved better than a husband who was engaged only in increasing his lands and taking as wife a woman who could increase his standing.

Not that it did him any good. Lord Thomas was soon thought to be overreaching himself, and had been arrested and beheaded some years before. It made me wonder briefly whether his executioner was the same Westmecott who had so signally failed to kill Geoffrey's brother with dispatch. It would have been his usual incompetence, if so.

So, yes, I did know of the Seymours, but they tended to be men of the past, men who had been in positions of power eight, nine, ten years before, but who were certainly not prominent now. One was dead already, and his brother, the Lord Protector, had fallen out of favour since the rise of Queen Mary, no doubt. He was one of the old guard, one of those men who had aided her half-brother on his campaign to enforce the new religion. As such, she would have wanted him removed from any position of authority as soon as she took her throne. That was my feeling.

As for other members of the family, why should I have heard of any of them? It was my belief that the family had little in the way of influence, and that which they did hold on to was unlikely to affect a local parish priest. Especially since the Seymours were, or so I guessed, keen supporters of the new Church and not the old. The man who must have reported Father James was surely a Catholic, seeing James punished for being so determined to preach against the return of the Catholic Church.

That was how I reasoned, in any case. Which only goes to show how far adrift a man's reasoning can fly from the target.

I watched Geoffrey as he walked from my parlour. At the front door, he cast a lingering glance at Raphe. Raphe opened the door for him, and the fellow slipped through it and out into the busy street. A boy stood nearby, no doubt waiting for a horse that required a mobile tether, and a pastry boy ran past with a basket filled with pies. At the corner, a man leaned against a wall and sharpened his knife on a whetstone, spitting on it to lubricate it, and a woman, vaguely familiar, crossed the road behind him. London, busy and noisy as always.

Once we were rid of the hobbling Geoffrey, who was still suffering even after three good goblets of wine, I turned to

Raphe and demanded where he had been so early in the morning.

There are some men who can dissemble with the best. Raphe was not one of those. He reddened, turned away, studied the ceiling, bent to fuss his beast and, all in all, refused to give me a sensible answer. His attitude seemed to indicate that he was determined to evade any close questioning of his absence, which was, of course, the one sure guarantee that I would not leave him alone on the matter.

'Where were you?' I demanded again. I had followed him through to the kitchen, where he was attempting to emulate a deaf mute while he cleaned the tray and goblets.

'I went out.' It was hardly helpful, but at least he had broken his Trappist vow.

'I could tell that. Where had you gone so early in the morning?'

'There was a game over at the Dragon,' he muttered, and at last daylight began to shine.

'You were gambling?'

'I didn't mean to! I didn't want to be there! I only went for a little while to enjoy the drinking, but then . . .'

'What was it? Cockfighting? Dogs? Cards?'

'Cocks,' he admitted. His head hung, and I was sure there was more to this than first met my eye.

'How much?'

He mumbled something, and I pressed him to answer.

'Three shillings.'

I gaped at that. A man would be fortunate, were he able to afford to lose so much of an evening; for a lad like Raphe to throw away three shillings spoke of untold riches. And if he possessed riches, it was not from my pocket – at least, not knowingly.

'Where did you get three shillings?' I demanded, and caught hold of the short hairs between his ear and temple. I have learned that if a man pulls these hairs and twists, his victim will be hard pressed to concentrate on anything other than his master. 'Well?'

'A man, Master, a man! I meant no harm by it! He was there in the tavern, and he offered me money for a little information – just information, that is all!'

'What did you tell him?' I was appalled to hear that he had been talking to strangers, and my first thought was, what about?

'I . . . Ow! He wanted to know who visited you the day before the execution of James Thorney – that's all! He wanted to know who it was and why he had visited. I didn't see any harm in it, so I told him it was Westmecott, and he paid me.'

'He paid you three shillings, and you didn't think it was strange?'

'He said it was a wager, and I would earn him three times that when he told his companion who it was. His companion . . . ow! He said it was a friend who always won gambles, and he wanted to get his own back on him, said he thought he recognized the man, and he was surprised the fellow was visiting you, that you were more the type of man to welcome the better sort to your house, he thought.'

I had already relaxed my grip. Now I jerked his hair up again. He yelped, and I snarled, 'You told him who I was?'

'No, no, I swear! He knew who you were already; he said you were a henchman to John Blount, and I couldn't argue with that, could I? Then he asked what Westmecott was doing here, and I told him about the powder, but that was all, and soon after the man left me . . . ow!' he added with a surly grimace as I released him, and he could lift his hand to the injured temple. 'That hurt,' he added.

'Good,' I said. 'What did this interesting gambler look like?'

'Oh, I don't know. Average. About your height, maybe taller. He was dressed in old travelling clothes, but he was a London man. I could hear that in his voice. He was trying to look foreign, but it wouldn't fool a blind scarecrow.'

'Hair?'

'Brown, and his eyes, too.'

'Beard?'

'Yes, a little pointy one that missed his cheeks.'

'What sort of clothes did he wear?'

'An old jack and hosen, but not cheap. When they were new, they would have been worth a year's money.'

'What colour were they?'

'A faded green, with some red piping, and slashes at the

sleeves to show light brown lining. And he had a short cloak of blue.'

'Would you recognize him again?'

'Yes, I expect,' he said, still rubbing. 'That hurt.'

'Yes. I want you to keep an eye open for this man. If you do, I may give you a shilling.'

'He gave me three.'

'And you lost them all. When did you come home?'

'When you were out.'

'So you were out all the night?'

'Well, yes.'

'When you were supposed to be here, attending to me?'

'I didn't go until you were ready for your bed, and it was late when I got back.'

I eyed him with revulsion. 'You are without a doubt the worst—'

'Servant in London. Yes, I know.'

'Decant some wine and bring it to me.'

It was early evening when I closed the door behind me and set off to the Dragon. From all I had heard from Raphe, this den of shame and harlotry was worth a visit.

When I arrived, there was a roaring of excitement, and soon a slumped body was brought out to the street and dropped unceremoniously in a puddle. The fellow was stirred awake when a great ox of a man stood over him and slowly tipped a jug of ale over his face. He jerked to, blowing froth and beer in all directions, sitting up blearily.

'That's the last time you come into the Dragon, understand me? Stay away from here,' the ox said, and urged him to his feet with a none-too-gentle boot. Then, while the figure on the ground crumpled into a ball, retching desperately, the bovine character turned and observed me. 'You here for the view, or something else?'

'I am here for the drinking. And perhaps gambling.'

He looked me up and down and apparently didn't object too strongly to what he saw, because he jerked his head at the door, and, only pausing long enough to kick the man on the ground again, he made his way indoors. I followed.

The tavern was much like any other tavern in the city. It smelled of piss and vomit, with a slight overtone of sour ale and vinegary wine. A fire roared in the hearth, and various gentlemen were standing or sitting nearby, watching a couple gambling over a game of cards. Others were at the far wall, chatting the sort of nonsense that drunken men will talk the world over. One was giggling, with a very high-pitched, squeaky voice, while at his side a tall, stooped man was rumbling with a voice so deep I could feel the stones of the flagged floor tremble. However, all this was suddenly of less interest, because as I walked in, the whole chamber grew silent. It was like a candle-flame: one minute all was bright and dancing with energy; the next it was snuffed out.

There are many taverns and alehouses like this, of course. I have been to many of them in my time. Those nearer the great centres for visitors, such as St Paul's Cathedral, are always cheery and welcoming. It's far better for a Londoner to be effusive in greeting foreigners, because that way a man can dip into a purse or cut it free. Beware the London tavern where everyone is glad to see you!

Other places are more like this. I was known here, and after a moment or two the men inside turned back to their drinks and muttering to each other, but it was enough to make me realize that whoever had been in here with Raphe was not unknown. Perhaps the imbecile was right, and the man he saw in here was a London man.

I bought a pint of wine and sat at a table in a darker corner. Others tried to entice me into a game of cards, but although I can palm with the best, I felt far below the competence of these players. Compared with the dazzling dexterity of the sharps in that room, my attempts would have looked clumsy. There was a roaring at the back of the tavern, which was where I guessed a bowling alley was set against the back of the building. From the sound of it, there was quite a gathering there, but I remained in my seat, watching the door. I wanted to see the man as he came in. If he came in.

Settling with my back to the wall, I prepared myself for a lengthy wait. After all, there was no certainty that the man would appear today. All I knew was that he had been in here last night. Many men would go to a tavern one day and not reappear for a week or more. It could well be that this man would not come back for a month. There were many taverns, alehouses and inns in London. A fellow could walk the streets and visit a different one every day for a year. Two years.

Still, the wine was pleasing, the raucous laughter was proof of the good companionship in the place, and my eyes were heavy after waking to Westmecott's knocking so early in the day. I began to feel my lids drop like shutters over a window.

And then I caught a glimpse, and my heart began to race. A fairly tall man, wearing a blue cloak and a green, faded jack with red piping and slashes in the sleeves, had appeared in the doorway to the bowling alley. He stood there now, his eyes lighting about the room like a spy checking for enemies, before entering slowly and crossing the chamber.

I finished my wine and quickly rose and followed the man to the road.

He walked quickly, and I was forced to hurry my steps. The man must have had the stride of a giant, I thought, and I had to move more swiftly to keep up. He strode up the road towards London Bridge like a man who had an urgent engagement. I followed circumspectly, not wishing him to realize he was the subject of my interest. I slipped around a corner, close to where the Thames slapped up against the Walbrook, and was about to step on a plank laid over the bridge when a voice in my ear said, 'You follow a man like an elephant.'

Yes, when he had seen me in the tavern, he had realized, apparently, that I was there to speak to him. It was galling that he had been so swift to guess my intentions.

'How could you tell?' I said.

'You were staring at me.'

'But I merely glanced.'

'Is that what you thought?' he chuckled, pushing me before him.

Now – and this did surprise me – he had no blade in his hand, nor a gun, and yet I found myself obeying his commands like a sheepdog. He seemed to take away any ability of mine to ignore him, and as he moved forward inexorably, I found myself obediently going where he directed. And soon, with a sense of grim foreboding, I recognized the house. It was where Peggy had brought me earlier.

'No, I don't wish to—' I began, but even as I spoke, I found that he had directed me against the door. His face was near to mine, and there was a sharp intelligence in his eyes, as well as a mildly apologetic look, as though he knew that this must be distasteful, but that it was better to have it over and done with, rather than leaving things to fester. Usually, I would have considered that a relief, but today, after spending so much time with an executioner, I was only too aware that the same expression would be likely to be seen in his eyes. Perhaps in part because it is better for the victim to have to endure less suffering.

No, I don't think that either. More likely it is because the executioner does not wish to see his supper delayed.

'Open it,' he said.

I turned the ring and lifted the latch. The door opened, and I almost fell inside.

'Hoi!' I cried, stumbling. Inside, I almost fell over the boy I had seen earlier, who gave a bleat of alarm and fled from the chamber through a door in the opposite wall. He moved so swiftly that I doubt my companion, behind me, saw him.

Inside the doorway, I found myself pushed to one side by the fellow from the tavern. He didn't seem overly bothered by my presence or the likelihood that I would run away. In fact, he had left the door open behind him, and now he glanced over his shoulder. 'Close that, would you?' he said as he walked to the fireplace. Crouching, he laid some sticks over the embers and soon had a fire crackling and spitting merrily.

'Now, Master Blackjack, let us have a talk,' he said, resting his backside on a stool.

'I was intrigued to see you following me,' the man said. 'I had thought you would be uninterested in my problems.'

I smiled, trying to indicate a calm indifference. 'You have me at a disadvantage, sir.'

'Yes, I do, don't I? In so many ways,' he said.

'I meant, I don't know who you are.'

'I am Anthony Seymour. I am sure you will know my name.'

'The Seymour family is famed,' I agreed.

'Yes, indeed. We have the sort of fame that many a family would wish for. And yet notoriety is nearer the mark, would you not say? Yes, we have been fortunate with our rise to prominence, but then again, every noble family sees its stronger limbs pruned, don't you think? I suppose it is a means of preventing stronger growth in the future, don't you? Who would want a strong family to appear and start threatening the existing order, eh?'

All of this came in a prattling, inconsequential manner, as though we were two old companions who happened to have met for a chat and pot of wine.

'Who are you?' I said.

He cocked an eye at me. 'Well, now, I am a cousin of Lord Seymour of Sudeley Castle, and of the Earl of Somerset.'

'The man who was the Lord Protector?'

'During the infancy of our King Edward, yes. But I am a cousin, not from such illustrious stock, I fear.'

'Whose house is this?'

He cast a look about the chamber as if seeing it for the first time. 'This? My brother's. He was always keen to maintain a property in London. He says that a man who wanted to be at the heart of things must always have a base in the city. This was always his.'

'I suppose your brother looks rather like you, but has a beard that follows the line of his chin, and a pointed face?' I guessed.

'You could describe him so,' he said.

'He captured me earlier.'

'Really? How typical of him. He is rather hot-headed at the best of times. Why would he have done that, I wonder?'

'I was asking about a woman and her son. Her husband asked me to find them.'

'How fascinating. So you came here to ask after them.'

'Well, yes.'

'And, of course, my brother spoke to you at length about them. Did you say who they were?'

'I was told they were Moll and Ben.'

'Yes,' he chuckled. 'And now you have come here. I wonder what I should do with you?'

'Do with me?' I was beginning to feel that my head was whirling. 'No, wait! I was looking for you, because you have been asking about me.'

'I have?'

'You questioned my servant, asking why Hal Westmecott came to my house,' I recalled. 'And then you bribed my servant with three shillings! And . . .' I had been going to mention the fact that Westmecott was the man who had sent me to find his son and wife, but suddenly I was struck with a reserve. It occurred to me that this man had been asking about Westmecott, and had heard he came to my house to purchase some black powder. This man may well have been responsible for the extended death of James the priest, preventing the powder from exploding. It was a thought to make my skin crawl, that this amiable-seeming fellow was nothing more than a cruel villain who . . . while he may not have been a murderer, he had made a man suffer unnecessarily. Who would do a thing like that? And why?

'Oh, that was your servant?'

'Why were you so interested in Westmecott's appearance at my house?'

'It interested me to see you entertain an executioner. Nothing more.'

'Why should it?'

He peered at me and shook his head as if astonished at such foolishness. 'My friend, no one is keen to welcome an executioner to their home. Except, perhaps, someone who has some other reason.'

'What?'

'Ah, you would have to tell me that. But I suppose executioners can get on with each other. If one meets another, it would be pleasant for them to discuss men they have killed, perhaps? Or traitors they were acquainted with? *Men I have hanged, drawn and quartered* – that would be their topic of conversation, wouldn't it?'

'Perhaps.'

'You are a cool fellow, Master Blackjack,' he said with a chuckle. 'I admire your *sangfroid*.'

'I am only a—'

'I think I know exactly what you are, Master Blackjack,' he said, and this time there was steel in his tone. 'A man is easy to recognize by the friends he keeps.'

'Eh?'

'And now you return to this house, where you were earlier.'

'What is your interest in me and my house?' I said.

'Well, every subject of the Queen has the duty of defending the realm against all enemies, from within and without. And murderers are as much an enemy of the state as are foreign agents, are they not? A man who could assassinate others without people noticing him – perhaps he would be a desperately dangerous person? Is that why you are here, Master Blackjack? Because you intend to murder the boy and Moll? You would find yourself in difficulty, you know. Their murder would make a number of serious enemies. You discovered them, so you would be blamed for any harm that came to them.'

'*Discovered* them? I was led here by a daft whore who wanted to show them to me; it was hardly a case of my careful discovery! I want nothing to do with them. Call Moll now, bring her here, and I'll apologize and promise to keep her whereabouts secret.'

'There is little need. Were you to reveal anything, you would soon cease to be a problem,' he said with a cold smile.

'I'm only here now because you brought me!'

He smiled at that. 'And I would not wish to see you held beyond your welcome. Feel free to depart. I wouldn't want to detain you. But know this: the woman is flown. She has left the coop, and now has the protection of my family.'

I stood, bemused, staring at the doorway through which he had just walked. He had made me come here, almost dragged me against my will, and had held me in conversation, indicating that he knew full well that I had a profession that was not so far removed from that of Westmecott. Why would he do that? Was he trying to test me, telling me that my career was known to him, that I could hardly make any accusations about him and his family deciding to make a mere priest suffer, unless I wanted news of my own profession to be bruited about? It was possible. I could not tell what to make of his words.

In the end, I decided to return to my home and leave all reflections on this confusing day to the calming and pacifying effect of a pint or two of strong wine. I turned to the front door and walked into the street. It was full night now, and the denizens of the darkness were all about me. A whore stood at the corner of the alley, while in the distance I could hear a man bellowing the hours, so that all those who had just managed to doze off would be called to full wakefulness in an instant. I often wondered that so few night-watchmen were beaten senseless, since their whole effort appeared to be bent on making life as intolerable as possible for the ordinary folk of the city. Meanwhile, I heard the unmistakeable sound of a door being prised open. I crossed the road, avoiding the woman in case she was one of those persistent types. I have been importuned by enough beggars in my time.

There was much to distract me on my walk: the man Seymour's snatching of me from the street and bringing me to the house. Was it to warn me away, or did he have some other motive? And then he told me that Moll was gone, that he had her somewhere safe. What was that supposed to mean? Why would he care about my knowing that? Surely most people would be happy enough to know that I was still watching an empty house, rather than warning me I had to search else-where. Why would he want to give me notice that I must seek her elsewhere? And the boy was still there, too. I had almost fallen over the little bratchet. Why take the mother and leave the pup?

I was almost at my house when I heard a slight noise behind me. My lane is a quiet area, and desirable for that reason. It meant I could come and go as I wished, but it also meant that thieves and other felons would occasionally appear. This sound was exactly like someone moving swiftly and attempting to be silent. It was enough to make my hackles rise for the second time that day, and I turned just in time to see the woman bringing down a rock. It struck my head to the side of the

crown of my hat, and I managed to say, 'Who . . . why . . .?'
before my legs seemed to turn to aspic and I fell.

I can happily state that I did not lose consciousness. She did
not hit me quite hard enough for that, but I was half mazed
nonetheless. As she went through my purse and thrust her
hands inside my jack, I was perfectly aware of her soft
little hands. And I could see her face. It was the raddled old
whore I had seen while hunting through the whorehouses with
Mark earlier. I recognized her even now in the dark, and then
I realized that I had seen her elsewhere: outside my house
as I watched Geoffrey leave. She must have been following
me all day.

'You leave Alice alone – you hear me? Stop looking for
her and the boy, else next time you'll earn more than a little
nick,' she said, sporting a knife in her hand. She set it against
my cheek, and I nodded, and then jerked when she drew it
against my jawline sharply. 'That's so you don't forget!' she
snapped, and was gone, and I was left with a headache, a
throbbing scratch at my jaw, and a pained confusion in my
heart.

Who on earth was 'Alice'?

I came to a little while later, my head cushioned most
delightfully by the lap of the lady who lived opposite me.

She smiled down at me with an expression of tenderness
that sent a quick flaring of interest to my loins. I tried to return
her smile without appearing lascivious, but her raised eyebrow
seemed to show that I had failed. At least my broad grin did
not result in her evicting me from my present delightful
position.

'You have been attacked,' she said.

'Mistress, I was assaulted by a mob,' I said.

'Nay, a mere slut. She struck you with a cobble.'

'At least she was so weak she couldn't crush my pate,' I
observed, and then felt gingerly where the stone had hit me.
To my relief, the bone felt solid still.

'She wasn't strong enough to kill,' my neighbour said. 'Did
she rob you?'

I hadn't thought so, but now my purse felt a lot lighter, and I cursed her briefly. What, with the lump on my skull and the scar at my jaw, I did not need to be robbed as well, I felt. Still, at least I was alive. It was odd: the woman had looked capable of breaking my pate. Perhaps she was unused to striking people down.

'You should have a little wine. My husband is away just now, but I could provide you a little wine.'

Her smile implied that I would be welcome to further comfort than mere wine, but even as I was about to agree, Raphe appeared at our side, glowering to see my injury.

'I am fine, Raphe, I . . .'

'You must get inside, Master,' he said, hauling me to my feet. 'Thank you, Mistress Haven. I will take him home now.'

'Of course. I hope you are soon recovered and ready for . . . for fresh adventures,' the lady said and lifted a hand in farewell.

I could have punched Raphe.

My servant helped me to my chair and fetched me a quart jug of wine and a towel before leaving me to my grumpy ruminations.

I soaked the towel in wine and set it to my bruised head, mopping the blood from my chin with a corner. With my sore shoulder from the whip's lash, these fresh injuries were difficult to reach. I was little more, apparently, than a punching bag to all whom I met today. I winced as the pain throbbed in my head, and for a long time I was unsure whether it was the cut to my jaw or the growing lump on my pate that was most painful. In the end I gave up. All I knew was that a short bout of mattress-butting with Mistress Haven would have made me feel considerably happier. No matter what I did, my skull felt as though it was broken into a dozen pieces. I pressed the cloth to the cut on my jaw and yelped. It might have been a short nick, but it stung like a wasp-sting every time I put the wine-soaked towel to it. I poured wine into a goblet and stared into the flames, determined to distract myself and make sense of the things I had seen and heard that day.

A dead priest; Westmecott demanding my help; the man

Seymour with his henchmen, the man I found in Westmecott's room with his pate broken; the girl Peggy leading me to my capture, the bitch; the pale, alarmed face of the boy in the doorway; the priest's brother; the second Seymour; the whore in the street knocking me down and talking about 'Alice' . . . was it any surprise my mind whirled like a rose petal in a stream? It was impossible to sleep. As soon as my eyes closed, I saw again the young boy, or, more often, the figure slumped on the floor in Westmecott's chamber.

I poured more wine.

And then the fire was cold, and a grey light was coming through the panelled shutters. I shivered, looking up in astonishment to see that the night had passed. When I tried to pour a little more wine, I found that the jug was empty. I stood, and my legs felt weak and insubstantial, but that was the effect of sleeping on my chair and not going to my bed. It always left a man feeling tired the next morning. Sometimes, like now, it would leave me feeling restless and dull. And then I glanced at the jug and reflected that it might not only have been my resting position alone.

I stood and stretched my back. There was a pain at the back of my neck that made me wince when I glanced to the right – and a pain in both eyes when the sun appeared. It felt as though someone had shoved a ballock knife into my temples, from one side of my skull right through to the other. Yes, this was more a red-wine headache than a sleeping-in-the-chair headache, exacerbated by the wound to my pate. If only Raphe hadn't rescued me, and I had spent my evening with Mistress Haven. I might have acquired more aches and pains, but they would have been worth it.

Who was the woman who knocked me down? She had warned me against searching for Alice and the boy again, rather than Moll, but who was she? Some strumpet who thought herself the friend of Moll and sought to protect her? Surely she would have got her friend's name correct in that case?

There was a clattering and rattling in the kitchen that told me Raphe was awake and determined to see me suffer for my rudeness to him last night. I stood leaning on the mantelshelf, considering whether it would be better to simply murder the foul pestilence, or to leave the house and find peace and soli-tude in the streets. The streets seemed preferable. I walked quietly from the house, hoping that he would continue to beat the crocks and pans, and later discover that it had all been in vain, and made my way to a small inn near the Tower.

It was a dull morning, a morning of greyness. There were no women lurking in doorways or alley entrances, which was a relief. The sky was thick with smoke from a thousand chim-neys, the clouds above were grey, filled with rain preparing to fall, and the roads and houses were all dull and grim. In short, my mood was not of the cheeriest.

However, after a pint of ale and a slice of sausage – a good, thick sausage made with pork and barley – the world began to look a happier place. I could tell when things were improving, because I saw a man in the roadway smiling. If a man was smiling, there must be something to smile about, I reasoned, and I was about to rise and make the fellow's acquaintance when a hand landed on my shoulder.

I did not need to turn and look. In my experience, a lot can be told by a hand on one's shoulder. Sometimes, and for the best of reasons, it can be a joy: a friend long unseen, who appears after a long absence and entices a fellow to join him in a cup or two of wine or ale. But all too often it is the hand of a tipstaff who appears from the murk and grabs a man's shoulder for more ungratifying reasons.

This was not the light, amusing touch of a mistress playing catch-as-catch-can, or a hail-fellow-well-met grip; no, this was the grip of the tipstaff – or perhaps that of an assassin preparing to remove the obstacle to another's fortune. I felt the hand and sensed the trickle of terror run up my spine at the mere contact of the palm and fingers. If they were the devil's own, I would not have felt more horror.

I turned slowly and looked up into Geoffrey's serious face. 'In God's name . . .' I breathed.

'Good day to you, Master Blackjack. My sincere apologies if I caused you alarm,' he said, and I would have snapped at him for his foolish act, and for giving me the shakes, but there was no humour in his face. He was deadly serious. 'We must talk, my friend.'

THREE

'What do you mean by this? Have you been following me?' I said, hoping that my heart would not leap from its moorings.

'I asked at your house, and your servant said you had probably come here. He said something about the tavern here settling your stomach when you have a touch of liver.' He peered closer. 'What happened to your—'

'Shaving,' I said quickly, and then, 'A touch of the liver?' I snorted at that. But the act reminded me of my earlier pain, and I quickly agreed to a fresh pot of strong ale when Geoffrey suggested it. 'Well? You wanted to find me, and so you have.'

'I scarcely know where to start,' he said, and then demonstrated the lie. 'When we spoke yesterday, I told you of my poor brother, and how he was captured and murdered.'

'Burned at the stake, you mean,' I said.

'Murdered,' he repeated firmly. 'It was your words about the time between his sermon and his arrest. The poor fellow was not taken on the day of his so-called offence, because as soon as his sermon was complete, he was seen to leave the church and go to a carriage. He climbed in and was taken away.'

'But not by his captors?'

'No. He was taken somewhere, and then brought back two days later, on the Tuesday. He was arrested on the Wednesday, charged, and soon taken to Smithfield to be burned to death by that drunken sot of an executioner.'

'I see. What has this to do with me?'

'James was taken somewhere. Where?'

'You think I know?'

'No! Of course not! But it is one question I must have answered. Where was he taken, and why?'

He was sitting beside me now, and I felt a flare of irritation. 'Why does it matter? Your brother is dead, and there is little to be done about the fact. What, will this bring him back? No! Will it ease his pain in his final moments? No! Will it do anything to help others?'

And there I had to stop, because the answer was sitting beside me.

There are times when I have seen Hector look ridiculously appealing. Usually, it is when there is food available, but just out of his reach. He will sit and stare at me or Raphe with eyes made wondrously huge with hopeful adoration, and he will try to indicate that if only he were to be given that bone, that cube of pork, or that steak, he would for ever after be the best behaved, most obedient creature known to any man.

Not that it ever worked, of course, but sometimes it did make me consider, just for a moment or two, succumbing to his outrageous lies.

Just now, it would have been easy to believe that, were Hector miraculously turned into human form, he would look exactly like Geoffrey. There was appeal in his eyes, aye, and hope. They glistened like a maiden's after her first kiss. It made me feel queasy to see it.

'It would help me and his family,' he said quietly.

And I knew I was lost.

'What good can it really do?' I said to him.

His answer lay in his eyes. 'If it tells us why he was taken and executed, that will be enough.'

'And what will truly help you?'

'The men who took him – they were in a carriage that had a crest on the side. Two golden wings, joined, on a crimson background.'

I shrugged. Heraldry had never been a vital item of study for me when I was living with my father, the leatherworker and maker of blackjacks.

'It is the arms of the Seymour family,' Geoffrey said, and sat back, staring at me as if that explained everything.

It didn't.

'So?'

'The Seymours must have taken him away. And later, when

James was captured, he was executed for something he did with the Seymours.'

At that, I felt duty-bound to make an obvious comment. After all, this was London, and a man never knew who might be listening and storing comments for later repetition to a court for treason or some such similar accusation. There are many easy ways of dying painfully, and in London one of the easiest was to slander the Queen or one of her nobles.

'Come now! The Seymours are an ancient, respected family. You think they would stoop to grabbing a priest from the streets and then seeing him murdered? Why? If they pulled him from his chapel, did they have to force him into their wagon? It sounded as though they invited him to enter, and he did so willingly. Was he pushed inside at sword point? No. So it sounds much more as though the Seymours invited him to join them, allowed him to stay with them for a pair of nights, and then brought him back. There is nothing here to suggest that they might have forced him against his will, or that he was given any form of injury, is there?'

'The Seymours are not enthusiasts for the Catholic Church. They might have sought to ingratiate themselves with the Queen by throwing suspicion against my brother.'

'But since they are more keen on the new Church, they would be more likely to spirit him away and protect him,' I countered.

'Why would they take him? What did they do to him?'

'Why do you think they did anything? They brought him back, hale and hearty.'

'And then he was accused and died in the flames.'

'Yes, that was unfortunate.'

'It was tragic.'

'I can see you would think that.'

'What else could a man think? An innocent priest was captured and murdered in the flames of an unjust pyre. It is surely the duty of any Englishman to seek the truth and avenge any dishonourable acts. Especially when directed against a mere priest!'

'Well, if you are set on such activities, I wish you Godspeed,' I said.

'And you are an honourable man.'

'I hope so.'

'So you will help me.'

I goggled. 'No, wait, that is something I can't do.'

'It is the only thing a man of honour could do. You must help me.'

'What, go against the Seymours?' I thought again of the cold malevolence in the face of Anthony Seymour's brother. What was his name?

'Perhaps to support the Seymours,' he said.

That was a thought. I had no idea on which side the Seymours were positioned just now. It was so difficult: some were for the Queen, others for Lady Elizabeth; some were for the Catholic Church, others for the new religion created by King Henry; some were for peaceful coexistence with Spaniards, others wanted to throw them all back into the sea . . . but that was not for me to worry about. The main thing for me was that the Seymours could be on one side or the other, or, depending on how the wind stood, on both. Families of such noblemen were like trees. They did not so much bend with the wind, as let the wind blow through their branches, and every generation could be assured that one or another branch of the great tree would survive to the next gale.

'No,' I said.

'Why?'

'I have my head on my shoulders, and I want it to remain there,' I said. It was too dangerous for a simple man like me to get involved in the activities of the rich.

But I was already involved, whether I knew it or not, whether I liked it or not.

I left him there and stood outside in the street. A cart and two cars came past me, and three men on horseback, and all I could think of was the story that Geoffrey had told me. I needed help with this. I should speak to someone, but to whom? If I were to go to John Blount, he would be duty-bound to tell his master, Thomas Parry, and I had not a doubt in my mind that if I were to go to him and tell such a tale, the first thing to occur to him would be that I was potentially an unreliable person, and such information would be far better held secret. I would be quickly presented with a prize of a nice new chain to wrap about me, and thrown into the river. I had no doubt of that whatsoever. After all, they would be able to find many other men who could perform my duties as an assassin. There were many, like Westmecott, who would be delighted to take on my income and rewards.

Although not many of them would be able to escape capture by the use of a glib phrase or cheeky rejoinder as I could. That was the difference between me and so many of the other fellows who tried to eke out a living in London. I could succeed because of my talents, but they would inevitably become mired in the investigations. They would never be bright enough to ensure that they had a working alibi. I could only achieve that myself by the simple fact that I was never near the potential victim because I am no assassin. All such work had to be passed on to my accomplice.

I wanted nothing more to do with any of this. It all felt too hazardous. I left the road and made my way homewards once more, and did not feel secure until I had closed the door behind me and could lean my back on it. 'Raphe, bring me wine!' I bellowed, setting Hector off again. There were times when having that four-legged walking bag of fleas was a pleasure, but more often he was just a nuisance. Barking when I spoke to him was not the behaviour I expected of him. He should know me by now.

Sitting once more in my chair, I glared at the fireplace. When Raphe appeared, I pointed at it. 'You have not built the fire!'

'I've been busy.'

'With what? Drinking my best wines, eating my best hams?'

'With taking messages for you,' he said grimly.

It was a note from my master. I was summoned to John Blount's house.

'Oh, God's hounds!'

If you have not read my chronicles before, this will no doubt appear curious, but my master was a grim-faced, black-hearted son of a maiden of limited moral compass. He was the sort of man who could fall into a cesspit and come up not only smelling of lavender but also blaming someone else for the foolish act of pushing him in, and generally winning over the audience to his own innocence and incorruptibility. He possessed an iron will, steel for muscles and a total lack of conscience. This was the kind of fellow who could see an innocent executed on a whim, and then salve his sense of guilt by setting another to be hanged.

I set off. There was little point in hiding from John Blount. After all, he was my master, and he did have the right to demand my presence when he wanted it. And just now, I was sure that it was not going to be a good meeting. You see, it had been some while since he had last asked me to see him, and then it had been a matter of a spy who had been deemed necessary to . . . well, to be made to disappear. I won't go into that affair more than to say that from the first everything went wrong. The death happened, to my horror, but . . . No, I will not dwell on that.

Suffice it to say, the last weeks had been wonderfully free of commands to murder people. The need for an assassin had never appeared to be so limited. Perhaps I was to be made redundant. Not that I would object to never being told to commit homicide, but there were other aspects to consider: the loss of my house, my income, my self-respect, for three.

'So you got here at last,' he said when I was shown into his little room.

It was one of those rooms in which a man would wonder how the furniture arrived. In pieces, I would guess. The table at which he sat was large enough to seat twelve, but for all that it was a mass of papers and ledgers. As I walked in, he was reading a small note that could have fitted into his palm. The writing on it was tiny, and I thought that my eyes would have surrendered under the strain of trying to decipher the letters in the dim light of the chamber. Seeing me, he folded it into four and set it under another sheet of paper.

He was a black fellow – black of heart and black of feature. His scowl could have been hidden in a coal cellar in broad daylight. It was that black. I walked in and sat before his table on a stool that was six inches too short.

'Mark Thomasson has told me that you have a little local difficulty. He tried to advise me that someone was looking for a woman with a young boy. He made quite the song and dance about the matter, which I thought intriguing. And it was obvious to me that it was you looking for them. You are trying to find the boy who is the son of Westmecott and his woman?'

I would break Mark Thomasson's leg for him next time I saw him. I fixed a sickly grin on my face. 'Yes. I don't know what I can do to—'

'That is most useful.'

'Eh?'

'By the way, I have a new commission for you,' he said. 'There is a boy who needs to be removed.'

'A boy?'

'He is only young, and shouldn't present you with any problems that you cannot overcome,' he said glibly.

'Who is he?'

'He goes by the name of Ben. He's living with his mother. Her name is Moll Cripplegate.'

I started on hearing that and almost gave a gasp of surprise. 'What?' for that, of course, was the name of Hal Westmecott's wife and the boy he had thought was his son.

'It is fortunate that you have already started to look for them. It should save you time.'

'But . . . I was going to ask you to help find them,' I said, floundering. I could not comprehend the order I had just been given.

'I have no information, other than she may be with the Seymours, either Anthony or Edward, or perhaps their father. They have houses near London Bridge and at Whitehall.'

'What has he done?'

'Who?' He looked up at me as though surprised I was still there. 'What do you mean?'

'What has he done? A mere boy? He can't even be eight years old! What sort of a threat is a lad like that?'

'It is not a matter of what he *has* done, but what he *might* do,' Blount said, peering at me over the top of another missive. 'It is very sad, but he could be a danger to people who matter.'

'But he's only a boy!'

'Yes. You will find him and deal with him. If his mother gets in the way, you can consider it a benefit to remove her, too. There will be the usual bonus, with a certain additional sum should you manage both at the same time. How you do so is entirely up to you.'

'Thank you,' I said. He was already returned to his papers, and I might not have been there.

I left.

I confess, my feet took me meandering about London that evening. It was one thing to be walking the streets with a definite destination in mind, but quite another to be marching about the place with the conviction that the city was a place that was despicable, foul, hate-filled and not somewhere to want to remain. I could happily have packed a bag and left that very night.

What was I become? A mere pawn in the service of a man who cared as much for the innocent as he did for a snake. He had no fellow feeling for me, only a determination to do all he could to make the life of his precious mistress as easy as possible. And to support him, I was expected to slaughter a mother and her child. It was disgusting.

Of course, I would have nothing to do with the actual murder myself. John Blount was always very happy to learn that, no matter who the actual intended victim, I was always ready with my excuse, and away at the farthest corner of town when the murder was committed. It was one of my attractions for him at present – although one day that must change. He must come to realize that it was impossible for me to keep satisfying his need for blood and remaining far away from the crime when committed. Even a purblind idiot must realize that I must be innocent, and that someone else was conducting affairs.

Yet that had little importance to me that day as I walked the streets, ignoring the entreaties of the whores, the beggars and the children who tried to cut my purse while they had a starveling stand before me holding out his or her hands in that appealing manner that professional conmen all adopt.

The roads were thick with men and women desperate to

take me to a darkened room, where I might be persuaded to part with a few coins by a woman with a figure to tempt a saint, or a man who stood hidden with a gun or dagger until the door was shut and the woman safe from me. The number of methods of gulling visitors to London had increased and grown infinitely more inventive with every passing year. It was a testament to the imaginative spirits of Londoners.

I caught a fleeting glimpse of a scantily filled bodice and thin face in the distance, and instantly thought of Peggy. She had been so desperate to take me to her friend's house and see me captured. And why? So that the men there might slaughter me? Just like the fellow who had been slaughtered in Westmecott's room. Who was he? Why was he there, and who had killed him?

Searching for something? Why did that spring into my head? I cast my mind back to the room, the body lying on the ground, the head stoven in. At the time, I had thought it was Westmecott, because the figure looked to have opened the door, turned away and then been struck. If it was Westmecott, it would make sense for the man to have let a friend in through his doorway, but it was not Westmecott – so why would he have turned his back on his visitor? Because the visitor was known to him, I suppose. And that led to the thought of why would another fellow walk in? Because both were searching for something. It seemed to make sense. If they were, for example, searching for diamonds or gold, and one found it, he might well have slaughtered his companion to keep all the profit for himself.

Since Westmecott was alive, it must be another man on the floor. And I thought it logical that he was looking for something Westmecott might have kept hidden there.

There was a flash of a slim figure. Suddenly, my attention was focused. I slipped through the crowds like a knife through a sack of flour, head held low, until I was at her side.

'Hello, Peggy,' I said.

'Oh, it's you,' she said. She didn't seem terribly glad to see me.

*   *   *

She stood and eyed me warily, rather like a woman accused of filching a spare apple from a greengrocer. 'What do you want?'

'An apology would be pleasing,' I said hotly. 'You could have had me slaughtered there. I was trussed like a chicken ready for the pot! All I was doing was—'

'We know what you were trying to do. Well, you won't get him, nor her neither, so you can go back to your master and tell him that!'

I was at a loss. It is true that I have the acuity of a man many years older than me, but this was a surprise, I do not mind admitting. After all, my master had only just told me that he wanted this boy dead, and Peggy seemed to think that it had been a long-standing arrangement. But then, perhaps, she was talking about Westmecott wanting the boy and his mother? 'You mean the executioner?'

'Oh, yes, that's likely, isn't it?'

'Who, then?'

'As if you didn't know!'

'I thought you didn't like Westmecott and were trying to keep Molly from him?'

She sneered a bit at that. 'So you thought you could help us by having him killed? You'll have to try harder than that!'

'In truth, Peggy, I have no idea what you are talking about.'

'In *truth*! For *sooth*! You think I'm just a pair of legs and a bust with no brain, don't you?' she said, but this wasn't so much a sneer as a snarl.

'I really do not know . . .'

'She'll protect him to the end of her life,' Peggy said, moving to me quickly and glaring up into my face. 'You think whores only think about one thing, but we *care*, too! You tried to get him from her, but she'll see you in the gutter before she gives the poor mite away.'

'I have no desire to hurt the boy,' I protested with honesty. Which was a surprise to me as well. Generally, I'm not overly bothered by life affecting other people, and this was a boy who had not created a very good impression, squealing when he opened the door and almost making me fall over as he fled the scene. And yet here I was, already commissioned to execute the lad.

'So you say! What will they pay you to get him, eh? A hundred marks? He must be worth at least that.'

'Who? Who would pay for him?'

'So, you want to trap me like that, do you? You think me such a fool that I'd fall for that?' She spat, rather accurately, on to my boot. 'Get away! Go and fondle a man's arse! You'll get nothing from me!'

And then, to my horror, she gave a piercing scream and slapped my face. A number of fellows turned in time to see me lift a hand to a cheek that smarted, and she suddenly screeched, 'He accused me of being a harlot! He wanted to drop his cods in the alley and have me play with his pizzle!'

One man, to whom I felt an instant dislike, hawked and spat. 'You think to come here and insult clean women, you poxed Spaniard?'

Another fellow, whose face I rather liked, and who seemed eminently the more sensible of the two, gave a loud guffaw. 'Don't you recognize her? That's Peggy, known as Peg the penny, since she's so cheap. Come on, Peg, I'll pay you for a knee-trembler in the alley!'

I was suddenly alone. The men had ignored me and were all making their own offers to Peggy, who stood torn and irresolute: after all, she had expected the men to tear me limb from limb for my alleged insults to a well-to-do woman, but since her little attempt had failed, she was left looking from one man to another with an eye to profit. It was a hard moment for her, I have no doubt, but the idea of profit was far too tempting for the mercenary wench, and she gave a rueful grin before beckoning her following into the alley. Soon all that could be heard was the grunts and pleased groans, one by one, of her companions.

It was enough for me. I took my leave.

My route homewards took me up past St Paul's; while there, I could hear shouting from Smithfield. On a whim, I followed the sound.

At the field there had been a wide enclosure set out, ringed with a fence. Men with pikes wandered or stood with their weapons in their hands, watching the onlookers, and with good reason. Even at this distance, I could see angry fists raised, women sobbing into their skirts, men standing with firm, fixed gazes, staring at the two men in the ring.

They were priests. Both had been bound to a post, and now one stood with his hands clasped before his chest, praying, while the other bellowed his innocence to the heavens. About them both faggots were piled high. I think I mentioned that I had once heard it took two cartloads of faggots to utterly destroy a man in a fire, and now I could see the truth of it. These two were at the centre of the bonfire, and as I watched, a man appeared. From his build, I guessed it must be Westmecott, who held a barrel of liquid, which he splashed liberally over the gathered wood. He tossed the barrel aside, and then bent to a little horn lantern. Removing the candle from within, he crouched at the nearer pyre. While priests intoned from a good vantage point, Westmecott set light to the oil he had sprinkled, and flames began to rise. The priest at his post opened his eyes and gazed down in horror.

I could imagine his feelings. The idea that this foul creature was setting fire to the wood was appalling. No man could help his bowels emptying at that thought. Westmecott walked about the fire and touched his candle to the oil at six places, and as I watched, coils of smoke began to rise lazily in the grey light. One of the men – I couldn't see who – was babbling as though he was driven mad by the sight. Meanwhile, I noticed that Westmecott had set small charges in leather pouches at their breasts. With luck, the two would die long before the torment had grown too foul.

The two men warranted pity, and didn't deserve to have their end witnessed by hundreds of men and women seeking an easy and inexpensive entertainment.

I left them and turned back towards my home. As I went, there was a sudden roar from the crowds. I imagined that a purse of powder had exploded in the heat. It struck me as odd that people could cheer the death of a poor priest who could not have done any of them any harm. That was a sad reflection.

But I had things to be doing. Much though I disliked the idea, I knew I must tell my friend, Humfrie, that he had work to do. It was regrettable, but necessary.

* * *

'A boy?' Humfrie said, and shook his head.

We were sitting at a table in a tavern atop Ludgate Hill in full view of St Paul's. Humfrie was a fellow of about two inches taller than me, with the rangy, sinewy build of a man who had worked all his life. His head was set low on his shoulders, and he had a barrel chest, and for all that he was responsible for more deaths than I could count, yet he was fond of me. I had spent some months with his daughter, and he appreciated the fact that I had always tried to behave as a gentleman should towards her. It had little to do with my respect for the harpy, and a lot more to do with the fact that her father terrified me. But there was a mutual respect between us, I like to think. That and the knowledge that both of us knew enough to see the other tortured and executed in short order.

'Yes, a youngster. Only eight or nine years old,' I said. I recalled the face in that chamber in Seymour's house. He had looked so scared when I had arrived with Anthony, and now I was supposed to cure him of fear forever. I felt a little rebellious stirring in my belly at the thought, but not enough to make me offer open mutiny to John Blount.

Humfrie's face was grave. He had deep tracks scored into his cheeks and brow, and they seemed to deepen as he absorbed this. 'I don't like killing young 'uns. Don't seem right when they haven't had a chance to earn themselves the punishment.'

'Perhaps this fellow has,' I said hopefully. 'Look, I don't enjoy this any more than you do, but we've been commissioned. The order says that if the mother gets in the way, there'll be a bonus for removing her, too.'

'Who's she?'

'Wife, of a sort, to the executioner, Hal Westmecott.'

'He got married?'

'Yes, I was surprised, too. Although not fully legally in a church. Perhaps before he started taking people's heads from their shoulders,' I guessed.

'I hadn't heard that. A woman living with a man like him. Any case, this boy: it don't seem right,' he rumbled, and sipped his ale, shaking his head.

'No. And all because of something his mother has done, I

daresay,' I said, and told Humfrie about my encounters of the last days.

'Two Seymours, eh? Anthony and Edward, you say? That could be interesting.'

'Why?'

'Their uncle, the Admiral of the Fleet, married Queen Catherine after King Henry died, and she and he were set to looking after Elizabeth during the Protectorate. That was another of their uncles who was Lord Protector. So the Seymours had good relations with Lady Elizabeth. They were looking after her.'

'Right.' I wasn't following any of this.

'So if the boy is being sought, it's possible that he could be a danger to someone in power. Or someone who doesn't want to be thrust into the light.'

'Someone to do with the Queen, you think?'

He took a long pull at his ale. 'Depends what the boy is supposed to have done,' he said judicially. 'If he knows something about the Queen or her husband, he could be the target of their anger, but how likely is that? Especially since our master works for her half-sister. That must mean that the boy is sought by her or her people. Which means he could do her harm. Perhaps he knows something about her, and the Queen's men want to hear it?'

'You mean the Lady Elizabeth might be involved in some plots again? Surely she could not be so foolish?'

Humfrie looked at me with the sort of look a dog might give his master when a careless effort had thrown a prized toy into a thorn bush. 'She's royalty, Jack. It's all she knows.'

I left him, still mulling over the idea that the boy could be the target of ill-will from Lady Elizabeth. When I had met her, she had been an anxious but stern young woman. I could not imagine why she might want to command the death of a young boy. She had not seemed particularly vindictive.

My feet took me home by the shortest route, and it was a weary and chastened Jack who reached my door and knocked twice.

For once there was no barking and befuddlement from Hector. I wondered whether the brute had been sent away, or perhaps had been run over by one of the regular carts which plied their trade up and down this road. But no, my luck was not running quite that high.

For, when I entered my parlour, the dog was lying on his back before the fire, all his legs in the air. And tickling his stomach was young Ben. I knew it was Ben. I recognized the triangular face, the dark features. More to the point, I recognized Peggy, who was sitting on my best chair and watching the boy with a small, sad smile.

'What are you doing here?' I demanded, not, I think, unreasonably, bearing in mind the injuries that woman had put me to, or tried to.

'We thought it would be good to see you,' Peggy said. She stood, smoothing down her skirts, and I was forced to eye her approvingly. When the wench was not accusing me of unforgivable offences, suggesting that I existed solely to murder this boy or his mother, or leading me to a trap where I could be held, she was capable of looking quite becoming. I had a sudden vision of my head resting on her soft thighs, just as it had with Moll, and the thought made me grin.

She caught sight of my look. 'You can stop leering,' she said firmly. 'I'm only here to ask you to help protect Ben. We can pay you, and when all is done, we'll take him back.'

'Oh, no! No, no, that is not possible,' I said quickly. There was no possibility that I could look after the boy, not now that my master had ordered the fellow's death. A man had to be realistic and understand that there were limits to anyone's abilities to evade disaster. Being found to be harbouring the boy whom I was supposed to be murdering, I reckoned, was disaster enough. I wanted nothing to do with him.

Peggy looked at me, and there was a calculation in her eyes. 'We could make it worth your while.'

'There isn't enough money in London,' I said gamely.

Between us, Ben was watching the interplay with interest. Peggy motioned to him, and he turned his attention back to the dog. He probably thought the dog infinitely more interesting than the debate going on over his head.

'I could make it more enjoyable. And all for no fee.'

'You mean you would . . .'

She cast a look down at the boy with deep meaning.

'Oh, yes, I see. Um. So you would . . . how long for?'

'A night?'

'*A* night? I don't think you understand the scale of the danger I would be put in,' I said firmly.

'Then several nights.'

'Every night.'

'*Every* night? You think you're—'

I held up my hand. 'I think you are desperate for somewhere safe for this boy. Only a short while ago, you were accusing me of—'

She shook her head sharply.

'Well, you accused me, and refused to let me see him or his mother. Why should I suddenly wish to help you now?'

'If you won't do it for a small boy who needs safety and calmness, then do it for the important lady who is his mother,' she said, swift and quiet.

'Who? Moll?' I asked with confusion.

'His *real* mother.'

'I don't understand!'

She looked at me with that calculating, shrewd expression that I was starting to recognize. 'You truly do not, do you?'

I grimaced. 'What made you realize I was not his enemy?'

'The way you behave. You don't behave like a violent man, like someone who would agree to hurt a small boy.'

It was fortunate that she did not know of my conversation with Humfrie. I pulled my face into what I hoped was a sympathetic grin. Then it hardened. 'No,' I said. 'You didn't trust me before. What has happened to make you believe me now?'

She looked down, and now her voice was suddenly quiet. 'I have no choice. Moll's disappeared, and the men who were seeking to protect her and Ben have gone with her.'

'Disappeared?'

'Stolen away, I think.'

'The Seymours?'

'Edward, yes. He was looking after her.'

I said nothing. She was avoiding my gaze, and if there is

one thing I know, it is that someone avoiding you like that is surely up to something. Peggy was trying to conceal something from me.

At last she chewed at her lip and then gave a gasp of despair, throwing her hands into the air. 'Moll has disappeared! I don't know what's happened to her, but I think . . . I think they want to . . .' She looked down at Ben. When she glanced up at me again, I saw her mouth the words *kill him.*

It did not take long to winkle out the rest of the story. She shook her head at first, and then went out into the hallway, gesturing for me to follow her. There she told me the rest of her tale.

After she had finished with the men in the alley, she had set off to make her way back to the Cardinal's Hat, where she had intended to take a rest until evening, when she must be ready to work again. On the way, she became aware that there was someone behind her who appeared to be dogging her steps. She hastened, but the man behind her increased his own to suit, and she cast a look behind her, only to see that the man behind her was Seymour.

'Which Seymour?' I asked.

'Anthony. He's dangerous, Master Blackjack, an evil man. I don't trust him, and when I saw it was him behind me, I panicked. I couldn't get over the river to the Cardinal's Hat if I'd wanted to. Not with him right behind me. I had to escape, and then I realized that if they were trying to catch me, only Molly could speak for me and save me, so I ran all the way to the house where Ben and Moll were staying, and barred the door to him. He started banging on the door, demanding that I let him in, but I wouldn't, and I ran through to find Moll. I shouted for her up the stairs and down into the basement, but she wasn't there. But Ben was, and he looked so scared.'

She had pulled him out into the small garden behind the house, and there she had slipped through a gate into the next-door's yard. It was a cloth merchant's house, and she had pulled Ben with her through the kitchen and into the shop at the front. There, she had peered into the road, but there was no sign of Anthony, so she had pulled Ben with her out into the road, and ran all the way to my house, reasoning that she didn't know any other place to go. It was too dangerous for her to go to any of her usual haunts. The only thing she could think of was getting a message to Piers to come and help her, but when she suggested that Raphe should go to fetch Piers, he was reluctant. I was surprised that the boy had shown such good sense. It's never a good idea to leave a light-fingered whore alone in a house.

'What can I do?' she said plaintively, looking up at me with her eyes grown huge with fear.

I smiled down at her. 'First, we need to get you fed, and the boy, too. You need rest and quiet. And then we can start to plan what to do.'

'Where is Molly?' she said, starting to worry at a loose thread on her skirt. 'I'll never forgive myself if it's something I've done.'

'What could you have done to cause her to disappear?'

'I don't know. Perhaps taking you there spurred them to act in a hurry? I just don't know.'

'I doubt that. Go back in there now and rest in front of the fire. I will have Raphe bring you wine. Go: rest!'

As she went in and sat at the fire, I beckoned Raphe. 'Fetch them some wine, and bread and cheese. Well done for not leaving her alone in the house.'

'I couldn't. Not with her being a hussy and that.'

'Yes, well, that is fine. Your friend from the tavern, the one who paid you, would you remember his face?'

'Yes. Of course.'

Yes. He would remember a man who had paid him three shillings. 'Good. If you see him about here, let me know. And then, when you have served them in the parlour, I want you to go to find Humfrie and bring him here.'

Before you get all maudlin on me, no, I was not asking Humfrie to come and murder the pair of them. However, it did occur to me that he would have to be squared. I didn't want him to come to my house unannounced and cause mayhem on discovering the woman and boy in residence.

I walked through and sat on a stool near Peggy. She gave me a sharp look, as though expecting me to lift her skirts and molest her there and then, but I had other things on my mind. 'Molly didn't say she was going anywhere?'

'No. Far as I knew, she was there for the day.'

'Right. So, how did you meet her?'

She glanced at me, then stared into the fire, occasionally throwing a short look at Ben, who was playing tug-o-war with Hector, using the brute's favourite piece of old rope. 'It was in the Hat. She was already there when I joined. Her man, she said, was keen for her to earn more money, and she was happy to do it. It meant she could keep something by, when she wanted. And then she had a . . .'

'Yes?'

She had slowed to a halt, and now she stared fixedly at the boy on the floor beside her. I was struck again by the conviction that she was concealing something from me, and I felt a frown start to crease my brow. If the silly wench couldn't trust me now, whom could she trust? I was about to snap at her, when she sighed and nodded as though concluding an argument with herself.

'She became pregnant. She had her child.'

'Westmecott's child?'

She looked at me. 'Unlikely. But for a woman in the trade, it would be hard to be sure who a father was, obviously.'

'You mean Ben, do you?'

She threw a look at Ben and smiled at him. 'No.'

I opened my mouth, closed it, frowned and took a deep breath as I tried to come to terms with her words. 'No, let me . . . you mean . . .'

'Her child was a girl. She was born, but died within the week, and poor Moll was distraught, as you'd expect. She didn't know what to do with herself.'

'She couldn't tell Westmecott, of course. He's a foul bully,' I said, 'and he'd have given her no sympathy. Worse, he'd have sneered and jibed at her inability to give him a boy, I suppose. He would have thanked her for removing a daughter before they wasted any money on her. Besides, she would have been driven to madness if she had gone back to him.'

Peggy gave me a sharp little glance. 'Meanwhile,' she continued meaningfully, 'she had her breasts full of milk.'

A light dawned. 'So she became wet-nurse to someone else's child?'

She gave me a look that must have been admiring, although, with her pinched features, she looked more, well, condescending. 'Yes.'

'Whose?'

'A Seymour.'

'Ah, of course.' Ben was a Seymour, clearly. I had seen that instantly when I first saw him in the house with Edward Seymour. They both had the same sharp, triangular features. 'So Moll took up nursing with Ben, and since then has been as much a mother to the boy as his own mother. She was married to Edward? Or perhaps she was a local girl? And died in childbirth, I suppose?'

'You suppose much,' she said tartly. 'Moll was taken on to look after Ben, and was like a mother to him, yes. In fact, I would think that if you asked her, she would say that this fellow is as much her son as anyone else's. She has seen to his needs every day since he was born, feeding him, washing him, playing with him, seeing he sleeps well, everything.'

'But you think that the Seymours want to remove her from him?'

'Someone has taken her away. And I don't know where!'

Ben looked around at that moment, and in his face I saw the same despair reflected from Peggy's. He dropped the rope and threw himself into Peggy's arms, and the two started to sob just as Raphe opened the door with a board of food and drink. Raphe took one look about him and gave an anxious smile, like a man thrown into a room full of children and told to keep them happy. I motioned to the table, and he hurriedly set out the board and scurried away like a rat running from a cat. Soon afterwards, I heard the door slam. With relief, I reflected that Humfrie would soon be here. I would be glad to hear his thoughts on the matter.

I said soothingly, 'Anthony Seymour told me that she was under their protection.'

'You believe him?' she said scornfully. 'I just don't

understand why they should suddenly turn against her. If she was taken on as wet-nurse, and has fulfilled her duties, why would they want to be rid of her now?'

'Something must have changed.'

'Plainly. But what?'

I looked at the boy, who had nuzzled his face into Peggy's bosom. Perhaps he could tell us what had happened, I wondered, but even as I had the thought, Peggy's brows came down, and she shook her head. She was worried that the boy could be disturbed. It was bad enough that he had lost his mother, without being scared about what might have happened to Moll.

'You know nothing more?'

'No, nothing,' she said, her eyes fixed on the boy.

She wouldn't meet my eye again. She was lying.

Humfrie arrived just as Ben had dozed off and been put in a bed. The boy was carried upstairs by Peggy and placed on the truckle bed in my bedchamber, where he immediately rolled over and began to snore. Peggy tucked in the blankets about him, and I was about to suggest that we might also benefit from resting, and that we could share my bed, but even as I was attempting my lascivious grin, the door slammed. I hurried downstairs.

'He said you wanted me?' Humfrie said, jerking a thumb at my useless servant.

'He was right. Come into the parlour,' I said. Once we were sitting before the fire, I told him what had happened.

'The boy and this whore are here now?' he said, dumbfounded. When I say dumbfounded, I mean his mouth fell wide, and he stood gazing at me rather like the village idiot. If I had announced I could fly, he could not have been more surprised. 'How will you explain that to Master Blount? You said you had been told to kill the lad, and now you invite him into your *house*? How will that look when you need an alibi? I cannot kill them here!'

'I didn't invite *anyone*! They appeared here when I was talking to you, man! You think I want this complication?'

'Well, you'll have to throw them out, as soon as possible.

You can't keep them here. At least there is one good aspect to the whole mess,' he said musingly. 'If these Seymours have changed their mind and want to kill the boy now, maybe they will save us the trouble and embarrassment. I don't like the idea of hurting children, as I said to you. If they are going to do it, well, it will be less of a problem for us.'

'I don't think the boy should die,' I said. 'He's done nothing.'

'Isn't that the same for almost everybody who dies?'

'Humfrie, there is something very strange going on. The Seymours raise the boy, but now seem to have changed their minds. Why would that be? If the boy is of their blood, why would they seek to harm him? Just because he is a bastard? Other families raise their bastards as their own. What could the Seymours have against this lad?'

'You think that the lad is the son of this Edward Seymour?'

'His face is astonishingly similar.'

'I have known men who were second or third cousins to have astonishing likenesses,' Humfrie said thoughtfully.

'Yes, but Edward and the boy are so alike that they can only be father and son, I am sure.'

'If you say so. So he had a fling with Moll, and—'

'I don't know that.'

He looked at me with a kind of withering infuriation.

I explained, 'One thing that Peggy did let slip was that she was sure Moll didn't give birth to the boy. Ben was born about the time that Molly gave birth to a daughter who died. She had milk and was hired to be wet-nurse to Ben. I suppose she was available and convenient, so she remained as his nursemaid.'

'So she isn't needed now,' Humfrie said thoughtfully. 'And there's no way to tell who the mother was.'

'Nor which of the Seymours was the father.'

'If either of them. And if the mother was a whore, perhaps—'

I shook my head at that. 'The boy is remarkably similar in looks to Edward. Even if Ben and Edward weren't related, and they were more removed – say, cousins – surely a family would keep all its bloodlines secure. They wouldn't just destroy a boy because he wasn't quite as pure as others.'

'Have you thought about other matters? What if the boy is

from another branch of the family, and his presence means the two Seymour brothers may not inherit something if the lad endures? Perhaps he is set to take over lands and titles which the two covet?'

'As a bastard?'

'Even bastards can be named in wills.'

'What of Moll?'

'If they decided to do away with the boy, they may feel that the wet-nurse could become . . . problematical. If she's been with the boy for seven, eight years, she could be assumed to have become quite attached to him, couldn't she? They might have thought it would be safer to do away with her.'

'So that they could kill him.'

'Yes. So, like I say,' Humfrie said, determined to look upon the brighter side, 'it's all for the best, really. You throw them out, the Seymours will find them and kill them, and we won't have to do it ourselves. Likely, we'll still be paid by Master Blount.'

'Yes,' I said. It did make sense. I was about to comment when the door opened and Peggy walked in. She looked quickly from me to Humfrie and was undecided about whether to enter fully or to leave.

I looked at her. She had those pinched, nervous features, and no womanly curves, but there was something about her that caught my attention. Every time I had looked at her, I had seen the hard, mercenary exterior of a working wench. This was a woman who would know to the nearest clipped ha'penny what she was worth. For her companionship, so much; for a handy fumble in an alley, a little more; for her company for an entire evening, a lot more – but just now I was seeing a different aspect of her. I was seeing the woman, and this was a scared woman, a woman who knew that her life was in danger, as was the life of her charge.

'Come inside,' I said. Whatever the reason was, this was not a woman in control of her life and fully capable of injuring me, no matter what I tried to do; this was now a vulnerable, scared young thing who needed comforting and protection.

She walked in, chaste as a nun, with her hands clasped before her. 'He's asleep.'

'Good. And now we need to discuss what we can do with you to protect you,' I said.

I saw Humfrie roll his eyes heavenwards.

Humfrie was looking at me doubtfully. He often did, to be fair, when he thought I had lost leave of my senses, but today I felt confident.

'Peggy, I don't think you should stay in London. You need to get away, out into the country somewhere, and you need to take Ben with you, if you are certain that you want to protect him?'

'I have to. The poor little mite can't survive on his own, not now Moll's gone.'

'Right, we need to find a safe place for you, then.' I looked at Humfrie.

'I have a sister who lives in a small village called Clapham. It's far enough outside London to be safe, but close enough that we can see how things are,' he said doubtfully.

'That will be fine, then. You must tell people that Ben is your son. Don't let them think that you are looking after him for a friend. And don't mention Moll. That would lead the Seymours to you.'

'Thank you,' she said, looking at Humfrie.

'Yes, well,' he said uncomfortably. I guessed he was thinking about his instructions to kill the boy and the mother. But this woman was neither mother nor any other relation. She was safe enough from Humfrie. I just hoped Ben was, too.

'How soon should we go?' she asked.

'We will depart at first light,' Humfrie said.

She left us to get her head down before leaving, and I remained in the parlour with Humfrie. 'You are sure your sister will allow you to leave a stranger with her?'

'Sal will cope. She always had a soft heart for those in need, and if she sees that boy, she'll defend him to the last.'

'So you, um, won't—'

'I told you. I don't like that kind of work. He doesn't deserve it. He's safe from me.'

He went quiet, staring at the flames for a while, and I was just thinking that I should perhaps be thinking of getting to my bed as well when he spoke again. 'I suppose you are sure that *she's* not going to hurt the boy?'

'Her? *Peggy?*' I said. 'What on earth . . . Humfrie, you are so used to seeing the worst in people that you find it impossible to cope with real, kind, generous people!'

'You tell me that she took you to where the boy and his mother were, and the Seymours trusted her and captured you. Moll appeared, you said, and you were resting your head in her lap. But now, suddenly, Peggy is hunted by the Seymours; she has to grab the boy to run from them. And she comes to you – a man she never trusted before. What if the Seymours are still trying to protect the woman and the boy, but she has taken the boy from them? I'm just trying to see things in a different light, that's all. Trying to see how this could all go wrong. There's something that doesn't make sense.'

'You're seriously suggesting that young maid could have planned to kill the boy? If she did, why didn't she cut his throat while he was in the house where he lived? Or on the way here? Or not come here at all?' I scoffed.

It was very quiet upstairs, I noticed. My eyes rose to the ceiling. There was the usual noise of Raphe banging pots and pans in the kitchen, pretending to prepare a meal or imitating some alternative servant duties, but nothing from upstairs.

No, I refused to contemplate Humfrie's ridiculous suggestions.

'I was just wondering that. If she could have, perhaps she would worry that the boy's body, in the house where he had been held, might be associated with her. Perhaps she had visited often and wanted to make sure that she wasn't associated with his death? If she took him somewhere else to kill him, it would be easier.'

'What about in the streets?'

'There's always someone watching you in the streets.'

My eyes rose again to the ceiling. There was not a sound from the chambers overhead.

Suddenly, there was a crash, and a noise like a heavy body landing on the floor above us. I sprang to my feet, but hesitated carefully, so that Humfrie had time to leap through the doorway before me, and followed him up the stairs. When he reached the next storey, Humfrie darted straight into my bedchamber. There was no sign of the boy, only a frankly terrified Peggy sitting up in my bed with her hand to her bosom.

'Where is he?' I demanded harshly. 'What have you done with him?'

Peggy began to sob, her breath coming in gasps, and Humfrie set his hand to my arm.

Ben sat up from the side where he had rolled from his mattress, and peered at us blearily.

'Oh. I see,' I said, and allowed Humfrie to draw me from the chamber before I upset anyone else.

FOUR

Humfrie stayed with me that evening, and the next morning he was up before the dawn, persuading a yawning Ben and silent Peggy to rise and eat a little bread and cheese to nourish them for their walk. Then, with a full costrel of wine at his hip, he led them from my door. They would make their way to the bridge, and with luck they would be with his sister before noon.

I was glad to see them go. I had thought to go and share my bed with Peggy, but as I opened the door to peer into my bedchamber, I saw her start up and cringe away from me as if I were a rapist. I stood there, gazing at her, for some moments. Her disarrayed hair, her alarmed expression, the abject way she snatched at the blankets and pulled them up to her chin, all spoke of a woman in genuine terror. I shook my head, and then walked to the chest at the bottom of the bed, pulling out a couple of thicker blankets. I took these and left the room quietly, sleeping uncomfortably on the chair in my parlour.

It was peculiar. She was a whore, after all. A common enough trull of a particularly scrawny form. But in there she had looked like a lady frightened for her life. She was not a murderer intent on destroying the boy, that was sure. She was exhausted and lonely. And it made me want to help her. A strange feeling for me.

I made my way to the kitchen and put a griddle over the fire. I was tired after a not-too-good sleep on the chair, and I needed some food. I heated four slices of bacon, and made a mess of eggs, which I shoved on a wooden trencher. I carried my breakfast into the parlour. Raphe had actually succeeded in laying a new fire already, and I sat in front of it with the food on my lap.

I was almost finished when there came a loud knocking at the door. For once the dog did not bark the house down, which was a relief, but as soon as I settled, I heard the knock again.

Raphe must have gone out with Hector. Grunting, I stood and walked to the hall, opening the door.

A fist shot through the gap and struck me firmly below the ribs. I was aware of my eyes popping wide as the breath left me in a whoosh, and then I was on the floor, gripping my belly and rolling about as I tried to get some air in my lungs.

'Ah, sorry about that,' said Anthony Seymour, stepping in and pushing the door shut behind him. 'I wasn't sure you were going to let me in.'

He smiled.

I whimpered.

He stood in my hallway gazing about him with the air of a student of philosophy struck by a new and peculiar tribe. 'I have often wondered what sort of hovel you would inhabit. This is considerably worse than I had imagined, I have to admit. But each to his own.'

I was still trying to breathe in when he walked into my parlour, pulling off his gloves as he went. Soon he was back, wandering down into the kitchen, while I rolled on to all fours, trying to clear my head of the conviction I was going to die from suffocation. He returned, idly kicked my flank with what felt like a steel boot and made his way upstairs, while I collapsed, a big, bright flower of anguish opening up in my side. It felt almost as if he had planted his entire foot in my ribs, and I was still shivering with pain in a foetal position when he returned and crouched at my side.

'This isn't looking good, my friend. I was hoping that I could save you any unnecessary suffering by taking them away, but since you have apparently already secreted him somewhere, I will have to extract the truth from you.'

'I . . . don't know . . . what . . .'

'Come along, now,' he said with that affable tone of voice used by priests just before hurling threats of eternal damnation. 'You know it, and I know it. You had him here. Where has he gone? Was he with that whore? That's a pity if he was, because it means she can't be trusted.'

'Don't know . . . who . . .'

'Oh, dear. You want me to give you the feeling that you

have been brave, do you?' he said, and suddenly his fist lashed out and caught my chin.

Have you ever seen an owl trained by a hawker, watching its master walk around it? It felt as if my head was going to snap round as far as the owl's, and I heard something crackle. It must have been the gristle of my neck, I suppose. A pain lanced up from my shoulder to my skull, and I fell forward, eyes wide with the pain.

There really is nothing like being attacked to make rational thought disappear. I was finding it hard to breathe, my flank was on fire, and now my head was all but immovable. If I could have told him the whereabouts of my mother, I would have sold her gladly – if I knew where she was. But as things were, I could not speak.

'No, there you are. You have been most bold. Where are they?'

His voice was measured, but there was a sharpness to it that I did not like. It was like the little edge in the voice of the village's bully when he realizes he has been made the target of a witticism that he doesn't understand. An edge that said, *I don't know what you're saying, but I'm going to enjoy giving you every element of agony known to man.*

He leaned down to my face, studying my features with a whimsical little smile. He looked like a father trying to teach a wayward son. 'When I have finished with you, you will beg me to kill you and end your pain. I will take off your skin, and remove your fingers, joint by joint. I will castrate you slowly, and then remove all the flesh from your pizzle. And then I will take my little knife to your face. And I will—'

There was a scratching and scrabbling, and he turned from me to stare at the corridor to the kitchen. 'Aha! Is that where they are? Little Ben?' he called, and stood. For my part, all I could do was retch and vomit a little bile on the floor beside my head as I watched him walk lightly down the passage. He entered the kitchen, and suddenly I heard the most magnificent sound: a dull thud and ringing noise, as of a large griddle being dropped on a man's head. Except it wasn't.

It was Raphe wielding my griddle straight into Anthony's face.

* * *

If there is a more satisfying sensation than being punched, kicked and threatened with . . . with all manner of unpleasant torments, and then seeing the repulsive fellow who threatened so much laid low with a solid iron griddle to the nose, I don't know what it could be. Somehow I felt more alive and cheerful than I have for a long time when that foul man Seymour made Raphe's bell ring using his face as the clapper. I watched as he stood stock still, and then suddenly crashed backwards to the ground. There was an interesting crack as his head hit the floor, which led me to hope that he would have a headache from front and back when he came to. Not that I was worried. Just at that moment, I was more intrigued as to how Raphe had entered the house so silently.

'I saw him come in when me an' Hector were at the baker's. I didn't think he was up to any good when he planted his fist in your gut, so I left Hector there, and came in by the back door.'

'Raphe,' I said, and I don't mind admitting that my voice shook somewhat, 'you are a servant in a hundred.'

'Only a hundred?'

'Don't go to extremes,' I warned. I eyed him, still rubbing my flank where Seymour's boot had been planted. 'But I will. You will have four shillings for your work today. This is the man who gave you the three shillings, isn't it?'

'Yes,' Raphe said, giving the body a grim look.

'And I believe that he was the man responsible for making the black powder fail,' I said. I cast my mind back to the sight at Smithfield. The men standing at their posts, the faggots set all about them, the smell of oils soaking the wood. To place such fellows there, to hang a bag of powder about their necks as though to save them the lingering death and offer them some sort of mercy, and then to soak the powder in water to make it ineffective, that struck me as a truly foul way to kill a man. Give him hope and then snatch it away.

'Tie him up,' I said, pointing to Anthony Seymour. 'He deserves all he will get.'

It was to be a while before I could speak to Anthony. He was trussed like a joint for the fire, and set out in my parlour, hands and ankles bound, a cord running from his hands to the pillar, and I took a jug of wine and sipped from a goblet while I waited for him to stir. However, it took too long, so in the end I had Raphe fetch a bucket of water from the well and tip it over the man's head.

He coughed and spluttered, trying to clamber to his feet before realizing that he was fixed in position where he was. A puzzled expression spread over his face, and he lifted his hands and stared at his bonds, before feeling his nose gingerly. Then his hands went to the back of his head, which involved turning his neck. In so doing, he saw me watching him. I lifted my goblet airily and took a long swig.

'How is the head?' I asked suavely.

He winced as he felt the lump at the back of his skull. 'What hit me?'

'A large cooking plate of iron.'

'I see.' He took his hands away and shifted his legs. 'And, um, my . . .'

'My servant did not like to see what you had done to me. Nor, I suspect, that you had deceived him in the tavern. You remember: when you told him about the powder and the visit of Westmecott.'

'Ah, that,' he said, and wriggled a little. I could empathize with his pain. Over the years, I too have been struck forcibly in the ballocks, and it is never a pleasant sensation. Not that I sympathized. That would be a step too far, while my belly was still aching and my jaw and neck and ribs giving me gyp. Besides, it would be hypocritical, since I too had kicked him while his legs were apart.

'You were here trying to find out about Ben. Where he was and so on, I believe?'

'You know,' he said.

'Perhaps you should assume I don't?'

'You are the assassin. You are told everything. Have you already killed him?'

'Who?'

He practically snarled. If he had been a bear, I would have shot him from natural terror. Although he was bound well, I nearly sprang away. It never hurts to be safe, and better by

far than suffering injury. 'You know perfectly well. If you hurt
that boy, you evil—'

I will draw a veil over the worst of his language. Although I
am not prudish, it adds nothing to my tale, and shows him in a
very poor light.

Instead, I waved my goblet airily. 'I have no idea what you
mean.'

'There are many who would seek to have the mother and
child slain just to save embarrassment.'

I nodded as though knowledgeably, although I had little
idea what he was talking about. 'Embarrassment, yes.'

'When my brother learns what you have done, he will be
here in a trice. If you think I was harsh, you should wait until
his appearance.'

'I may just have the local watch called and have them deal
with you.'

'Oh, yes. The *Queen's* men. I can see you calling them to
attend to me!' he sneered.

I wasn't sure why my words should have caused him such
amusement. I poured myself more wine. 'Perhaps I should
simply dispose of you myself, then.' I reached over to the
table, on which my jug and goblet stood. However, just out
of his vision there was one other item, a knife which I had
been using to cut cheese. I picked it up and studied the
blade.

'What are you doing?' he snapped suddenly.

'I was remembering what you said you would do to me,' I
said. 'I think it was skin me alive, sever every finger, joint by
joint, castrate me . . .'

'I was making an amusing pleasantry,' he said.

'It feels like it,' I said. I felt something at my throat, and
when I touched a finger to it, I realized it was blood. He had
pulled the scab from my jaw. I stared at my finger, trying to
keep the horror from my face.

I must have looked terrifying. When I experience a
wound and see my own blood flowing, I become quickly
nauseous, and today I felt a hot flush run into my cheeks. If
you have seen a picture of a truly choleric man suffering from
a fierce rage, you might get a similar image to that of my face.

Clearly, Anthony felt sure that I was about to kill him. 'I thought you knew where Peggy and the boy had gone,' he said quickly.

'Where have you put Moll?' I said.

'She is at our house in Whitehall. She is perfectly safe there. We don't need to hurt her.'

'And what will you do with the boy if you find him?'

'I will take him to meet his relatives,' he said, and there was a curl to his lip as he spoke.

He was not a man I liked.

'Let us see if I can persuade you to be more helpful,' I said.

I glanced at his body, the lithe form beneath the jack and hosen. With the very tip of the knife, I cut away at the first laces holding his jack to his hosen. I allowed the point of the knife to slip down between his clothing. 'Oh, silly me,' I murmured.

'What are you doing?' he demanded, more loudly. 'You can't kill me! I'm the son of a nobleman, you base-born son of a whore!'

'What did you call me?'

I pressed slightly, and felt the knife's tip meet an obstruction. It was his flesh, and he must have realized that my knife must be close to the big, fat artery that runs between the groin and the inner thigh. I knew of it because I had seen an artilleryman struck by a two-foot-long splinter of wood during the rebellion, and the sudden effusion of blood was enough to make me wish for better protection for that part of my body, especially when the poor fellow collapsed soon after and was dead before we could think of a tourniquet. Not that it would have helped, I am told.

'I can kill you this easily,' I said. The knife, I knew, was blunt. I had tried to cut a slice of ham only last week, and it had performed almost as well as a twig. I pressed down. 'So, be polite.'

'Yes, yes. Very well!'

Now, when a fellow makes a mistake, usually there is a period of grace during which he can rectify matters. Believe me when I say that the knife was blunt. I knew it was blunt. I had tried to slice meat, and the blade would not oblige. It was, most certainly, blunt.

And yet now, as I pressed lightly, the minor resistance became no resistance. There was an incoherent cry, which must have come from him, because all I remember was staring at his thigh and wondering what had happened. I can clearly recall that the thought went through my mind that I must have missed his leg entirely, and that I had somehow snagged a fold of his shirt, that the blade had torn through it, and was even now resting in the gap between his legs. A foolish error, I thought. I was about to pull the blade free and have another go, when events conspired to overwhelm me.

He gave a howl, and I chuckled at his agonized face, thinking my knife's point had scratched his pizzle or one of his ballocks. There was certainly reason to believe that he had been injured. His face was drawn and yellowish, as though he had been castrated without the benefit of brandy, and I would not have been sad to think it was so. He had made some very appalling threats to me, you will remember.

His howl became a terrible cry of loss and horror, and I still smiled at him, although with a sense of growing confusion. He was acting, obviously, thinking to tempt me into releasing him, I thought. But as he continued, I began to wonder: I had not expected such a display of madness. Perhaps, I wondered, I had managed to give him a little scratch? But he would not make such a commotion for a small injury.

It was then that I grew aware of something else. His legs had begun to drum on the floor, and with every movement, the knife in my hand was jerked. And that struck me as odd, because, naturally, if the knife had slipped *between* his thighs, there would be nothing but empty space. If that was the case, I reasoned, there should be no movement in the blade. Just now, it was almost as though the knife was caught in some way.

At that point I glanced down, and whipped my hand away from the knife. 'Oh no! Oh, God, no! God's wounds!'

'You have killed me!' he hissed feebly.

A thick, red stain was spreading from his thigh, and even as his contortions reduced, and his legs moved less energetically, and the spasmodic jig was become a country dance, I could see that the man was dying before me.

'Come closer!' he whispered, and I leaned down, thinking he wanted me to listen to his confession, but even as my ear approached his mouth, he gave a grunt and said, 'My brother will cut off your pizzle and use it for a—'

Mercifully, he never completed the sentence. There was a ghastly rattling sound, and a sigh, and he was dead.

There have been a few occasions in my life when I have been truly shocked. Once was when that massive splinter of wood struck my companion at London Bridge. It was less his death and more the fact that it nearly hit me. It was huge, at least a yard long, and flew so close to me that I felt its passage. I swear it shaved some hair from my head as it passed. However, I think that this situation, in which I had slain a fellow by dint of simple accident, must rank as one of the most appalling I have experienced.

I was still at the side of the body when the door opened.

Now, I have to say that in the past Raphe has occasionally shown me great respect, which I believe is proof that he is more aware of my official position than I would expect from a usual servant. I think I mentioned that I believe Raphe to be related to my master, John Blount? It is clear enough to me that Raphe often has been disrespectful, and then – occasionally – has appeared to regret his outbursts as if realizing that they could possibly be construed as insulting to me. And if he was aware that I was a dangerous assassin, such would be a serious consideration. He might believe that I would murder him for some real or imagined slight.

In recent months, he had grown more and more comfortable – or perhaps I should say complacent. But any complacency in his face was driven away by the sight of a highly visible corpse, whose gore was all about him and me on the floor, and in which I was kneeling.

I was still shocked by the horror of what I had done, but I snapped my mouth shut and stared at him. He barely seemed to notice me. His attention was entirely taken up by the body.

'Raphe . . . *Raphe? RAPHE!*'

Startled by my shout, he looked up, his eyes full of a reasonable fear. 'Yes?'

'I should like to go out for a little. Roll this man into a blanket, and tie it securely, and then clean up the mess. I will be back before noon, I think.'

'Y–yes, sir,' he stammered, and I strode out like a man who had not a care in the world.

I had never needed the privy so badly.

I was in the privy for some little while. Even after drinking a gallon and a half of strong ale at a private party, when a friend had suggested a barrel of oysters afterwards, I don't think I had been as sick as I was that day. I had to stand at the side of the hole and heave until I could heave no more, and then sit for a while with my back to the privy's seat. The stench in there was disgusting in the warm weather, but the smell didn't bother me as much as the memory of the body, and the little slithering feeling of the blade sinking into his . . . no, I can't think about it even now.

When I could bring up no more, I had to go to the well and rinse my mouth. It tasted acrid and sour, as if some demon of the night had entered my mouth and defecated. I had to swill my mouth, spitting water at the pathway six times before it became tolerable, and then, when I looked down, I saw that my knees were as red as a pair of ripe plums. I had to soak both knees in water, rubbing at the fabric to remove the last of Anthony Seymour's blood. It was no easy task, and the cold water seemed to seep into my legs, but I had too much to do to worry about that just now. I left the well and made my way to St Paul's, and down the other side to the alleyway where Westmecott lived. He was an easy man to find. There was no answer when I beat against his door, but when I returned to the tavern we had visited before, I soon saw the hulking figure.

'Westmecott,' I said, but he hissed at me.

'Not so loud! In 'ere men know me as Saul Kerridge. I'm nothing to do with the man who executes the city's felons.'

I was tempted to point out that others in the area where he lived must know his name, but it seemed pointless. No doubt the man was half soused and couldn't think straight. 'I need your aid.'

'That sounds like somethin' that'll cost you a pretty shilling.'

'I will pay what is necessary. The simple fact is a man entered my house today and beat me. I managed to fight him off, and he died. Now I must dispose of the body.'

'A man broke into your 'ouse? Tell the watch, call a coroner, and 'ave his death recorded.'

'No, you don't understand. I cannot have an investigation in my house,' I said. 'It would be troublesome for me. Come, you said you could always lose a body. Here's a fresh one for you.'

'I don't know.'

'The clothing would be about your size,' I said. A good hangman will never turn down the possibility of a quality suit of clothes.

He gazed at me. I could see he was tempted.

'All you need do is take him on a handcart and dispose of him. In the river, or in a grave, if you have a spare.'

He looked at his ale, and I could see that the result lay in the balance. I leaned forward. 'And, of course, it will help me to find your wife. She appears to have disappeared. It will be difficult to seek her without impediments, but if I must call a coroner, and endure the long investigation of a dead body, it will take time, and the trail to Moll could go cold and be lost forever.'

'Aye,' he said, pulling a face. 'I'll come.'

'Good man! I will pay you a shilling, too.'

'Two shillin's.'

'Of course. Two it is.'

I rose and took my leave of him. Had he but known, I would have paid more than double that to be rid of Seymour's carcass.

The house was quiet when I returned, and I had to knock with a will on my own front door. There was silence for a while, and then a whine: 'Who is there?'

'Open the door, Raphe. I need to come in. Be quick!'

I could hear the great horizontal bar lifted from its slots, then the two bolts drawn back, and the third, and then the key slowly turned in the lock. At last the door was pulled open a

little way, and my fearful servant's face appeared. I pushed
him back. His face was red where blood had been carelessly
wiped over his features, and he had the look of a man who
had peered over a wall, only to see Hell and all its demons
on the other side.

'Go and wash your face,' I said curtly, and walked to my
parlour.

There, on the right, was a rolled-up bundle. I was relieved
not to have to look into the man's eyes again. That might be
more than I could cope with. The floor was a mess. Water
from the bucket used to waken Seymour had flowed liberally,
but that was probably a help in cleaning up the blood. It meant
that the blood had not clotted and thickened on the floor. When
it came to Raphe's arrival with a bucket and cloths, collecting
the worst of the blood was easier than it might have been. Not
that I thought he would like me to point that out. At least now,
when he reported me to my master, John Blount would have
fresh eye-witness confirmation that I was a sadistic assassin.

But just then I didn't want to think of bodies.

Westmecott arrived at three o'clock. He was dressed as a
labourer, wearing a leather hood with a long, trailing section
that protected his back. He slid in through the door as subtly
as a bullock entering a tavern, slamming the door wide. I could
smell the ale on his breath as he loudly made his way into
the parlour and stood staring down at the rolled figure. He
had a rather green face, and I was alarmed to see how this
additional death had affected him. Not that it was a surprise.
Perhaps there are men who can cope with daily being forced
to mete out violence and death on others, but for most, surely,
such an occupation must start to pall. I myself was not made
for this type of business, as my own shock and sickness had
demonstrated. But a man like Westmecott was cut from a
different cloth entirely. He was supposed to be inured to
the daily rounds of torture and savagery inflicted on others,
and yet here he was, looking sick to his stomach at the thought
of dealing with yet another body. Was it any surprise that men
like him turned to alcohol as the only way to cope with their
foul tasks?

He gulped a bit and gratefully accepted my offer of a strong

ale to settle his bowels. A quart disappeared in what looked
like four swift glugs, and he did appear a little more comfortable after that, but there was still a strained look to him. His
eyes still stared madly, like a newly caught pike wondering
where all the water had gone, and his hands fluttered a little.

'Would you like some help carrying the . . . the thing?' I
said.

He nodded gratefully, and I called Raphe, telling him to
assist the fellow in any way he could, and then sat down. But
it was uncomfortable. My eyes kept being drawn to the soggy
mess on the floor where the appalling Seymour had died. And,
of course, there was the memory of the knife sliding in . . .
all in all, I was not comfortable there, and no matter how I
tried to divert myself, it was soon clear that I would not be.

Raphe returned after some little while, shaking his head.
'He's not right in his head,' was his conclusion. 'I've never
seen an executioner close up before, but you could see he
hates it. He's weak about death, that one.'

'Don't demean others, just because they do things you
disrespect,' I said loftily, and his eyes suddenly shot to me,
as if he was reminding himself that I was the most dangerous
man in London, and that his own life could be snuffed out as
easily as Anthony Seymour's had been.

'I need to go out. Don't let anyone in while I am gone. I will
return late. Meanwhile, make the fire good and hot, and clean
up the last of the dampness in here,' I said, and walked out.

Over the years I have heard tell of men who have been so
appalled by acts they have committed, or even witnessed, at
war that they have become driven by terrible dreams or even
lost their minds completely.

This was not ever an affliction I had expected to suffer from,
but today, as I walked London's busy streets, I was struck with
a sense of dislocation and almost dizziness. It felt as though
I was walking through a thick mire, and my head began to
swim. All the while, in my mind's eye I could see the face
of the man as he felt my knife sink into his flesh. To know
that the blade was slipping into his body must have been
hideous for the poor fellow.

Yes, I was perfectly able to think of him as a 'poor fellow', even though he had been beating me only minutes before. It would not be kind to hold a grudge against a man just because he had been thinking of injuring me. Not now I had killed him.

Killed him. Those words felt peculiarly final, which, of course, they were – for him. It made me feel queasy again, but not as queasy as the next thought, which was that I must be careful not to emulate Anthony by being killed. Because Anthony's brother would want to avenge him, I had no doubt. So I must ensure that no news of the man's death was ever spread by a dolt, for example, who lived in my house and was notable for his utter foolishness and incomparable lack of tact. There were times when I seriously worried whether the boy had a brain between his ears.

I hesitated. Mayhap this would be a good time to put in place the plan that I had been harbouring for some time, a plan which involved fleeing my usual haunts and making my way to a quiet town or village far from London. Somewhere I could hide myself in among the population and be content with my safety.

How far from London would I have to travel? If Edward's talk earlier had been anything to go by, I might well be safest by leaving London completely, and putting at least two hundred miles between us. However, I wasn't certain that two hundred miles would be enough. The man had shown determination in the past. Considering this was an affair that could be considered a matter of honour, seeing violent retribution for the death of his brother, I suspected that a mere two hundred miles would not be adequate.

I was walking along the road as I considered my options, and whether I should be thinking of moving to, say, France or Prussia, when I was forced to halt by the sudden appearance before me of Geoffrey Thorney.

'At last!' he said. 'I've been searching for you!'

Well, I was glad for him. I had clearly fulfilled his most enthusiastic aspiration of the day, but I did not reciprocate his joy. Sadly, I had no desire to spend time with him. I was more

keen on working out my own best approach to evading Edward
Seymour. That and trying to forget the sensation as I pressed
on what I had thought was a blunt knife, only to find it sinking
into the man's leg and killing him. It was such a strange, soft
feeling . . .

'I am in a hurry,' I said.

'Where are you going?' he asked.

'I need to think.'

'Do you have any news?'

His eagerness was almost enough to make me vomit. All
I could think of just then was the body that Westmecott had
removed. Whether someone would connect that to me, and
whether my master would learn of it, or of the boy and Moll
and Peggy. And meanwhile I was feeling the lack of Humfrie.
The thought that the second Seymour might soon be hunting
for me was enough to make me gibber. I had suffered enough
from the more amiable of the two brothers, and now this
second might seek me to learn what had happened to
Anthony.

He continued, 'I think that the Seymours took my brother
to a house in Whitehall,' he said. 'I have heard that they had
a boy and his mother there at the same time. I heard from a
groom that they were keen to keep the boy and his mother for
some reason. They took my brother back to his church just
before he was arrested.'

'Really.'

'I don't know who the mother and child were.'

'That would be Moll and Ben,' I said without thinking.

'Who are they?'

I irritably gestured as if waving away a wasp. 'I believe
Edward Seymour knows the boy and is seeking to protect him.
Moll was the lad's wet-nurse.'

'Why would he need a priest there?'

'To see him baptized? To make sure that he has been
confirmed? He is too young to marry.' *Although Moll isn't*, I
thought. And she was available.

'I think Edward Seymour means to win money and status,'
Geoffrey said. He had moved into my path, blocking my way,
and now he stared into my eyes with the earnest conviction

of a priest sermonizing about heaven. 'He will do anything to achieve that.'

'Eh?'

He looked a little surprised at my incomprehension. 'He is a greedy man, a rich man who wants more. He's prepared to kill others like poor James to have his way. Where is this Moll? We need to speak to her and her son.'

'Moll has been taken by Seymour, I think. I don't know where.'

'She has been taken? No good can come to her from being held captive by him – we must save her!'

I was a little short, I fear. I indicated to him that Moll was perfectly capable of looking after herself, that she was an unimportant figure in the scheme of things, that Seymour would be unlikely to worry about the wet-nurse of the child, and that I had rather more pressing matters to deal with.

'But we have to find her and release her. She should not be tortured for the failings of the Seymour clan.'

'Tortured? Who said anything about torture? Why would someone torture her? And what failings of the clan?'

He shook his head and tutted. 'Master Blackjack, do you not realize the importance of this woman?'

I was tempted to punch him. In the last hours, I had been attacked by Anthony Seymour, beaten, bound, threatened – and even suffered the shock of accidentally killing the man. And now this fellow was patronizing me. Well, I had endured enough, I felt. 'Not realize? By all the saints, she was a paragon of virtue, the wife of a good, honest executioner, a whore who sold her body all over London. Yes, and then sold her own pap as a wet-nurse. What a vital woman! Why would the Queen's people have any interest in a woman like her? You have allowed your imagination to have free rein, Geoffrey, and I understand your anger at the loss of your brother, but in God's name, man! Be sensible!'

I had allowed myself to run on rather, but I did have good reason. This fellow was pointlessly wasting my time when I really needed peace and freedom to think what I should do next.

He looked like a mouse gripped in the talons of an eagle. I thought his eyes would pop from their sockets.

'You did not know? The wet-nurse's charge? You didn't realize who she was feeding?'

'Oh, do tell me! I suppose it was the Queen's illegitimate son?' I said with sarcasm so profound that it was a surprise it did not scorch his ears.

'No. Not hers.'

'There, then.'

'Her half-sister's – Lady Elizabeth's.'

'You see? I told you . . .' I stopped, my mouth gaping. 'Whose?'

We repaired to a tavern, and once safely ensconced on a bench at the back of the place where it was quieter, each of us with a jug of strong ale, he continued his story.

I listened, I have to say, spellbound. But not in a pleasant way.

'When I learned that the Seymours had taken my brother, I went to learn all I could about them,' he said. He wore such a damnably earnest expression that I had an urge to punch him on the nose. 'The Lady Elizabeth was living with Lord Seymour of Sudeley. Lord Sudeley, Thomas Seymour, had married Queen Catherine, King Henry's last wife. Seymour sought to enhance his position by the marriage. His brother Edward had already been made Lord Protector and Duke of Somerset. He was very powerful, and Thomas Seymour wanted to improve his own status. He had himself made Lord Admiral of the Navy, but that wasn't enough for him. He wanted money, lands and power. When Elizabeth was young, she was installed in Queen Catherine's household. The Queen was her stepmother, after all. When Lord Sudeley married the Queen, he realized that the royal princess could aid his ambitions, and sought influence over the lady.'

'His wife would not have been keen.'

'I have been told others think she indulged him because she was fond of Elizabeth, and was happy to see that the two were content in each other's company. When she realized her error, it was too late.'

'You cannot mean this. The Lady Elizabeth? With child?' I cast my memory back to the slim figure I had met briefly at

Woodstock. There was nothing of the blowsy, motherly figure about her. She did not look like a woman who had ever given birth.

'Aye. A Seymour child. Lord Sudeley was arrested for his molesting of a royal princess, taken to the Tower and beheaded. Princess Elizabeth was sent to a new guardian who was more trustworthy.'

'Surely this is wrong! The Queen would not allow her husband to be executed?'

He gave me a confused look which soon turned to pity. 'It was Queen Catherine, the dowager Queen, widow of King Henry. The woman who outlasted him. Do you not remember her?'

I forbore to point out that at the time I was still an apprentice and hardly interested in the goings-on among the great nobles in the kingdom.

'The tale of the affair was bruited about far and wide. Queen Catherine was in the last weeks of her confinement. It was only eight years ago! Princess Elizabeth was sent to a knight called Denny, but the damage was already done. Queen Catherine gave birth but soon after died of childbed disease, poor lady. And then Lord Thomas was arrested.'

He sighed. 'His own brother signed his death warrant. Edward had no choice. The allegations were proved against Lord Sudeley. He had been seen too often in Lady Elizabeth's bedchamber. He was seen to have dallied with her, tickled her, even threatened to jump on her bed. There could be no doubts. Even Thomas Parry, her Comptroller, was questioned, and her chief lady of the bedchamber, Kat Ashley, and they confirmed the truth of it.'

I was stunned. 'You must be wrong!'

'It is all written down. Lord Sudeley's prosecution and execution are well known. His behaviour with the Lady Elizabeth is common knowledge, and the scandal it caused.'

I could not argue with his conviction, and yet I was held bound by my own hideous certainty that he must be wrong. He *had* to be wrong.

Why?

Well, because if he was right, my master, John Blount, and

his own master, Thomas Parry, had willingly ordered me to murder the son of Lady Elizabeth.

I was not sure what the punishment would be for the murder of a royal prince, or even the bastard son of a royal princess, but I had a strong conviction that the end of a man found guilty of such a crime would not be pleasant.

This was not good news. That Moll had been captured and taken to Whitehall was confusing, but spelled little that could be thought of as good. Moll had been taken alone, and her boy left behind. Did that mean it was Moll who was the focus of Edward Seymour's interest? If questioned by officers, she must surely admit to being only a wet-nurse. She might not even know that she had fed and nursed Lady Elizabeth's little boy. But if he was Elizabeth's son, and if that became known, matters must grow horribly difficult for all of us. And Seymour would benefit.

My reasoning ran along simple lines: if the pious Queen Mary were to learn that her sister, whom she had now declared illegitimate (because Queen Mary's mother remained the true Queen even after the King divorced her and remarried in the new Church of England faith – thus, when King Henry became wedded to Anne Boleyn, Elizabeth's mother, that marriage could not have been legal and any children were by definition bastards), had entertained a man in her bed – and not just any man, but the husband of Queen Catherine, the widow of the King – the Queen must fly into an unsisterly rage. To have accepted him, perhaps to have seduced him, would be the most shameful act imaginable. If Elizabeth had done so, and the boy could be produced as evidence against her, all those at court who detested her and distrusted her would clamour for the most exemplary punishment. Since she had already been suspected of plotting to have Mary removed, and of trying to have herself installed on the throne, the condign punishment would be that of death, surely.

But the ramifications of that were appalling. If she were to go, then so would Sir Thomas Parry, because he would very likely be arrested and held on suspicion or executed; John Blount would have no household or master, so he would become a wandering individual, which meant that I would also lose my living, my house, my little luxuries. It was a thing deeply to be appreciated that I had saved up much of my money in the last year, and would at least have access to some funds. But I would have to find a new way of living. I had seen other men with money, who had immediately visited a tavern on realizing that their income was based on unsteady grounds, and who were neatly divested of all their savings in one night's gambling, drinking and whoring. To think that my own money could be lost to a pleasing harpy and her card-playing cove was enough to make the sweat burst from my brow.

The Seymour brothers must have learned that their benighted uncle had bedded Elizabeth, and now they were keen to enhance their own position. Where Thomas had married a princess, Anthony and Edward had hit upon the splendid scheme of merely taking their half-cousin . . . cousin? Half-cousin once removed? I always find these matters thoroughly confusing – anyway, they were taking the son of their uncle and were going to use him and his wet-nurse to advance themselves. The Queen would be happy to reward those who were so loyal that they would bring the child to her. It was not something that impressed me.

Were the Queen to learn of Elizabeth's boy, there was no doubt in my mind that I would be among those who would suffer her displeasure. Guilt by association with Sir Thomas Parry would be enough in her mind, and I would be permitted one last chat with my friend Westmecott. That my executioner would be the man who sent me hunting for this woman in the first place did not strike me as amusing or desirable.

It was odd that he sent me after the woman and the boy when they were not his. That was a thought that made me frown briefly.

Only briefly, because I had work to do.

Whitehall was not one building, but rather a series of palaces of a greater or lesser size, with a series of smaller dwellings for all the workers and hangers-on. I had been inside two years ago, when Wyatt's rebels had come to assault the city, and I disliked the place with a passion. It was here that I had been hunted by a man with a sword who wanted to open my entrails to the weather. The memory of that horrible time was enough to make my queasiness return. And now I was here to see if I could find Moll. And if I could, I must somehow rescue her and take her from here to safety. Perhaps all the way to Humfrie's sister's house.

I stood at the gate to Scotland's Yard and gazed along the length of the road ahead. It was all horribly familiar. On the right was the long building that was used for stabling, still called the Mews, in honour of the building that once stood here for the King's falcons, so I have heard. That burned down at least twenty years ago, and this new block was imposing, built in the new style, with great timbers and freshly limed daub. Behind it was the new park that King Henry had designed. I've heard it's a glorious place for a hunt, not that I'd ever have a chance of trying my hand at it.

Ahead, the road continued on to Westminster, but here all that could be seen were the great houses and tenements of Whitehall. I knew that there were tennis courts, bowling alleys, a cockpit or two, and all the paraphernalia of noble living. I could smell ale being brewed, the scent of freshly baked bread and the odour of cooking meats of all types. Whitehall, so I'd heard, was built by Henry after he took the original house, York Place, from Cardinal Wolsey. He had this new palace built to become a monument to his glory. But it was not a hall or a house – it was a working, living city of its own on the banks of the Thames. There were men dedicated to making food for all those inside, smiths, harness makers, saddle makers, candle makers, brewers, butchers, gunsmiths – in short, every occupation known to man was inside these buildings. I have no doubt that there were whoremasters, too.

I joined with a few other fellows and entered the gate at Scotland's Yard, trying to look as if I belonged. Not that I had any real idea about what I should do. All I knew was, I must look for a place where the Seymours might have secreted a woman like Moll. Had they taken her willingly, they might have given her a job, although what she was capable of, I did not know. Perhaps, if there was a whoremaster, she could have been held on his ledgers? But that seemed unlikely. The Seymours would not want her to be out of their sight; if Geoffrey was right and she knew secrets they would prefer to keep that way, they would be unlikely to allow her to wander the lanes and alleyways.

Of course, they might have taken her in and offered her a simple job, as milkmaid or dairymaid, perhaps. Yet it seemed more likely to me that they would have kept her hidden until they had their hands on her boy and could present both to the Queen. Surely they would have kept her concealed somewhere, until they had recaptured Ben as well.

I walked on through Scotland's Yard and found myself at the bank of the river. Over on the opposite bank, I could see the buildings of Southwark and felt a pang of resentment that I was here, working, while over there men were watching the baiting, or seeing a play, or visiting Piers and the wenches of the Cardinal's Hat, or any one of the other brothels that lined the ways. Yes, I was jealous, and it made me sad to think that here I was, risking my neck to save the life of this woman just so that she couldn't threaten the position of my Lady Elizabeth. Stiffening my back and pulling my shoulders straight, I reminded myself that I was only here to help her, that my mission was honourable. If I could somehow find Moll and get her away, I would have done a good, selfless thing.

And then I could keep my house. And head.

With a fresh resolution, I walked west along the path. It took me to the main courtyard of Whitehall itself, and here the buildings changed subtly. They were very grand and daunting to a fellow brought up in Whitstable. I hurried my steps, feeling as if the buildings were looking down on me. It felt dangerous just to be there.

Beyond, there were more houses, all fronting the lanes. These were for noblemen who had to spend time at court, and after them were smaller properties for the servants and workers of the palace. The whole complex was vast, and I began to realize how hard it would be to find Moll in this ants' nest of alleys, backstreets and roadways. I found myself outside a buttery and begged a pot of ale from the man in the doorway. He passed me some of the latest brew – which was very acceptable – and watched me with interest while I drank.

'I have a message for the Seymours,' I said. 'I was told Edward Seymour would be here within the palace. Do you know of him?'

The man scratched at his round cheek with a dubious expression. Then he became quite vacant. 'Seymour?' he said, his eyes seeming to be fixed on a point some hundred miles away. 'Yes, go down here to the end, turn to'ards the river, and it'll be third house on left.'

I thanked him and was soon on my way again. There was a slight incline going down to the river, and as I went, I saw a fellow who looked familiar.

He was some thirty to forty feet ahead of me, and while there were not that many people in the street, one man with a sumpter horse overloaded with goods and four or five labourers with packs on their backs were bringing goods up from the river, still they made enough of an obstruction for me to be unable to see for certain who it was. But then I saw him turn and stand on the step of the third house on the left. I saw him knock on the door.

Yes, I saw him clearly. It was Westmecott. What was he doing visiting the Seymours? I slid into a doorway and watched as he glanced about him, waiting. The door opened, and he stepped into the house.

There was no fear on his face, no rage or anger as though he was going to kill everyone inside, possibly including himself. This did not look like a furious husband who has discovered where his wayward wife had gone to hide. He looked more like a servant bringing news to his master. But the good point about all this was that at least now I knew where Moll was likely being held. Not that it meant I could do much about rescuing her. With Westmecott inside, as well as the Seymour servants, there were just too many people there for any attempt at entering to be safe.

I had just reached this conclusion when the door opened behind me.

'Well?'

'Eh?'

'What are you doing in my doorway? It's not raining, is it?'

The owner of the voice was an irascible little man at least six inches shorter than me, and a moustache that was bristled like an angry terrier's.

'I was trying to find the lady who . . .'

He gazed past me at the Seymours' house. 'They sent you for her?'

'I . . . what?'

'Are you her boyfriend? Her lover? Her leman?'

'Well, sort—'

'Oh, close your mouth, boy, before you catch a fly. Come inside,' he said irritably, as though I had missed a perfectly aimed witticism.

I glanced over my shoulder. The door to the Seymours' house was opening, and I saw Westmecott walk out. I quickly stepped into the old man's house.

'This way,' he said, leading me through the hall.

I had no idea where he was taking me, but I followed him in the fatalistic belief that wherever it was, it had to be safer than meeting with Edward Seymour again.

'Out there,' he said, pointing through a small kitchen area to a door.

Unthinking, I opened it and was struck dumb.

Yes, I know what you were thinking. You thought that as soon as he opens that door, someone's going to arrest him. This was all an elaborate trick to try to get that poor fool out to somewhere quiet where someone can knock him on the head and put an end to his foolishness once and for all.

I confess, now I think back, the idea of my opening that door strikes me as ridiculous in the extreme. And yet, no. Nothing happened. Your predictions are entirely wrong.

What happened? I pulled the door wide and was confronted with a rather lovely view. It was a garden, with pleasant little raised beds for all types of greenery. There were kale and onions and garlic, and, well, all sorts of vegetable. In the distance a small cow was thoughtfully chewing the cud, and a cat was sitting on top of a barrel nearby, one hind leg pointing almost straight at the sun, while his head was engaged in some ablution or other. I didn't want to see.

The reason I didn't want to see was that Moll was standing a few yards from me. Her back was to me, while she gathered leaves from the nearer of the beds.

She heard the door when I closed it, and stood quickly.

'Don't be afraid,' I said.

'Who are you?'

'Don't you remember me? You bound my whiplash,' I said, pointing to my shoulder.

Her mouth formed a perfect 'O', and then she smiled and nodded. 'What do you want?'

'I came to rescue you,' I said. And as I said it, I frowned. Because, of course, she wasn't being held against her will, and she wasn't being tortured.

'Rescue me from what?' she asked as she bent to her task again.

'From the Seymours,' I said. I didn't think it right to explain that there was one fewer to worry about now.

'Why should I need to be rescued from them?'

'Well—'

'They are very kind. Why would I want to leave?'

'What are you doing here?'

She shrugged. There was a rather fixed expression of happiness on her face, like a cat who has just discovered the pot where the cream is kept. She had a glazed look in her eyes, and now she paused and then reached down. At her feet was a quart pot, and she raised it to her lips and took a deep swig, before stoppering it and smiling at me beatifically. 'What am I doing? Where else should I be?'

'What of the priest?'

'Oh, the nice man who came to give us our little ceremony?' She hiccupped delicately. 'I liked him.'

'What sort of ceremony?'

She gazed blearily at me with a sudden shrewdness in her eyes. 'Um. I don't think I should tell you. That's a secret.'

'Ben is not your child, is he?'

Her head tilted, and she peered at me in what she must have

fondly considered a sly and arch expression. 'Oh, but how do you know that?'

There was a fog in my mind at this stage. I had seen Westmecott, who said he was this woman's husband, the man who said he would kill her, going into the house over the road where the Seymours had their lodging. He had only just today removed the body of one of the Seymours from my house to dispose of him, which made his presence here utterly confusing to me. The woman herself, his wife, was here, in the old man's house. 'Who is the man who showed me to you?' I asked. 'The man who lives here?'

'Him? He's the old Master Seymour. He's very kind,' she said, but in a manner that seemed to indicate some doubt. 'He loves me, so my husband says,' she prattled happily. Then her face hardened. 'Though he shows me little regard,' she added.

At the thought of Westmecott, I felt a cold lump of stone settle in my belly. It was frozen, from the feel of it. I often get this when I am particularly scared. Other people see me and can tell that I am a courageous fellow, with the body of a Heracles and the face of an Adonis, but sometimes, I must confess, when I find myself in a difficult position, like today, I could happily wish myself a hundred miles away, somewhere quiet and peaceful, where there are no politics, stratagems, plots or dangers that seem to be directed mostly at me.

'I think we should go,' I said.

Listening while she protested that she was more than happy here, I was sure that I heard shouting and a door slam. I tried to grab her wrist, but the feather-witted dullard snatched her hand away like a lady approached by a leper.

I had two options. I could draw steel and protect the woman here in the garden from Anthony Seymour's brother, or I could ensure that I would continue to serve my master. And in the process, protect my cods, heart and liver.

The door opened, and I saw Westmecott in the entranceway.

There was no choice. I ran.

I have had many long years to learn about running. It is a skill that was taught to me early in life, when attempting to flee retribution in the form of a neighbour who caught me at his apple orchard, or from my father when he had drunk enough to fill a Bordeaux merchantman, or occasionally from a beadle or officer of the law who saw me, as he thought, trying my luck at cutting a purse or thieving a trinket from a fellow in the street. In my time, I have fled from the fleetest feet and the slower but determined. Generally, the fleetest tend to be easier, I reckon, because all too often they are soon spent, and I can maintain my speed for a little while longer than they. The slower but determined are considerably more problematic. They will grit their teeth and push on, rather like a dog after a cat, chasing harder and harder until there is a stand-off, and the cat can go no further and turns at bay. Then it's just a matter of teeth or teeth and claws as to which will leave the field least injured.

The main thing about running is not to look back. There is no need to see where you have been; the main thing is to see somewhere you can go. If you hear feet behind you, someone is chasing. The key is to keep running until you can no longer hear someone following. That is when you can risk a quick glance, but still, do not stop. The pursuer may have quiet shoes, and your own hearing may be defective because of the sound of the breath in your throat, the thundering of your heart, the regular beat of your feet on the cobbles.

There were more than two men, because I could hear their boots on the stones as we ran, and although I heard a sharp cry (which could have been Westmecott) and a rattle like a chain being tossed into a large cauldron as a man in armour fell over, I could yet hear multiple feet running after me.

One down, I thought.

I continued on. At the rear of the little garden area, there was a gate into a back lane, and here I immediately turned right. I was guessing, but I reckoned that the left would take me to the Thames, and I had no wish to be caught on a jetty with no escape. Instead, this direction meant heading north towards the main road once more, and when I arrived there, I would be safe enough, I hoped. With luck, I could lose myself in the traffic and make my way to Temple Bar, and thence to a place of safety. Not that I could think of one just now. Master John

Blount's house was not too far, but I might be safer entering a bear's cave than going to my master's house with the news that I had. It was too dangerous for us both. I needed time to think things through before I could see him.

A man was pushing a wheelbarrow. I sprang past him and heard a nervous yelp, closely followed by a shower of curses. I could guess why: the carter had accidentally pushed his barrow into the wall after the shock of my passage. He had obstructed the path for my pursuers; then his wagon's wheel would have got caught by a cobble, and he would be forced to rock it back and forth to release it. By then the two – or perhaps three, not more – men with him would have grown even more angry, would have shoved him and the barrow from their path, and then continued after me. But their feet were some distance behind me now. And some of them were slowing. Perhaps the fast chase was too much for them.

Not for one, though. I imagined I could see him in my mind's eye. A swarthy fellow, probably. Greek or Spanish blood in his veins, because those fellows would always take insult and give chase, like a lurcher spying a hare. They were often indefatigable in their pursuit of a poor fellow, determined and bold. They were exactly the sort of fellows a man like me preferred to avoid. Not only because of their commitment to the hunt, but because they also seemed to have the ability to wish to fight when they had captured their prey. Not that I had been caught. Not often, anyway. But today I could have wished that Humfrie was with me. I felt considerably safer when he was near me.

I had reached the roadway, and now I hurtled along with the horses and carts. My companion in the race would no doubt guess that I would be heading towards the city, but he could not guess exactly where I might go after Temple Bar. And I could turn off along a number of the lanes about here. Especially when I was past the Mews, and could see the Bar in sight. Here it was important, I knew, that I should put on a spurt. A pursuer, seeing my heels increase the pace, should by now be grown despondent at the likelihood of being able to catch me. With luck, it would mean that I would escape with ease. So I picked up the pace.

And then there was a strange sensation. My legs were working in fine style, my left lightly striking the ground, the right moving like a machine, then the left releasing contact a moment before the right was to touch down, and so on. Suddenly, though, my left leg lost coordination. It was a most curious feeling, as if I was suddenly on ice, and it threw me. Have you ever seen a horse standing on ice? Horses have a hard enough time of it, trying to work out which leg to move and when, which is why they need such resolute and patient men to teach them, so I understand. When on ice, all of an instant, they realize that their carefully learned coordination is gone, and you can see legs flying in all directions.

That was exactly how I felt. My foot hit the ground, and yet it didn't seem to want to grip or work as normal. I was left with a moment's imbalance, when my left foot was either stationary, but not gripping the ground, if you follow my meaning, or moving, but not in synchronization with the speed of the road flashing past me.

There are roads and roads. Some are easy to negotiate, with well-paved surfaces, or a good dry bed of soil, but this one, which was certainly supplied with large slabs of stone, was also the path taken by many donkeys, ponies and even cattle and swine on the way to the markets and slaughterhouses of London. The road was, in other words, rather polluted with excreta. And my foot had landed perfectly in the centre of a pile of ordure that was of a perfect consistency to undo my headlong rush.

My foot did something. I don't know what. All I know is that my balance was thrown, my motion dissolved, and I was suddenly hurtling headlong in the road.

There are disadvantages to running on a road filled with the deposits of cattle, pigs and horses. One is that a fellow may slip. The second disadvantage is that the same fellow will inevitably fall into something soft and deeply unpleasant. I suspect that there had been a pig farmer along the way only very recently. There is a distinctive, human quality to the odours that encompassed me.

When I was more aware of my surroundings, I was lying on my belly in the road. I looked around, and all I could see were horses' hooves, legs encased in hosen, a few dogs, some running legs – my interest quickened, but they were a child's legs, not a man's. There was a lot of laughter from the unsympathetic peasants who enjoy the sight of a well-dressed young fellow like me landing on his face – but apart from that, nothing. I was safe.

I rolled over, away from the main thoroughfare and the heavier carts, and looked up into the eyes of my pursuer. Oddly enough, I noticed his eyes more than anything else.

I say oddly, because he was staring down the length of a rather sharp-looking sword.

'Oh, hello, Hal,' I said.

I stared up at him. He stared down at me. He was panting somewhat, but so was I.

It didn't seem fair to me that he was there. I mean, I had thought he had fallen earlier, when I heard the rattle of ironmongery. Perhaps it should have occurred to me that Hal tended not to wear too much in the way of armour. Whoever that man had been, he must have sported a breastplate at the very least. Still, it rankled.

'What are you doing here?' I said. 'You went into the Seymours' house.'

He glared at me. 'You stink! Get up!'

'Hardly my fault,' I said. There was a cart beside me, and I took hold of it and hauled myself upright, carefully. I felt as though I'd been thrown to a bear for baiting. The carter swore at me, seeing my disreputable appearance, but then started to laugh. I gave him a sneering grimace in return. All I knew was that I had bruises on bruises. I had a fresh pair on my knees, and there was a pain at my left shin where the edge of a stone had caught it, but it was less that which made me pull a grimace of sheer dismay. It was my clothing. I looked as though I had been dragged all the way from Temple Bar to Tyburn, and had been deliberately trailed through every cow pat, every lump of horse manure, every dog's . . . you get my meaning. My appearance was a horrible mess.

Westmecott appeared to think so, too.

'You look like a man who has been treated as he deserves,' he said with a sneer.

'Why?' I demanded, with not a little irritation. 'I was only doing your bidding, and you chase me down like a felon!'

'Doing my bidding? You were following me! I ought to run you through for that,' he snarled, and it was the closest I have ever seen to a man imitating a mastiff.

'I was trying to find your wife, as you asked. And then, when I did, you decide to chase me with your companions, as if I was some kind of felon!' My tone was bitter, and I intended my words to sting, as I stood gazing down at my clothing, but they appeared to have no effect on him. Meanwhile, I was struck dumb with dismay for a moment at the sight of my jack and hosen.

'What is this?' a man asked. He was a slim, dark fellow with the look of an untrustworthy Cardinal about him. You know the sort, the type that holds his head down and looks at a fellow as if measuring him up for a good burning at the stake. I've known coffin makers like that, who, on meeting a man, get his full measure, if you understand my meaning. He had a suave voice which was unthreatening in a very definite manner – the sort of manner that makes a man think of the sound of his own bones breaking. When I looked at him, I was put in mind of a Spaniard I had known. He had the same slim features and swarthy appearance. But this one also had a look of tautness, like a wound-up spring.

'I'm taking this fellow back to my master,' Hal said. He edged round, so that he joined me at the side of the cart. I caught the whiff of stale wine on his breath.

'What has he done?' the man asked, turning a suspicious look at me.

'He's suspected of taking a boy and holding him to ransom.'

'What?' I squeaked. 'That is a terrible lie! I was looking—' I suddenly discovered the appeal of silence as his sword pressed against my jack.

'Evil bastard!' the man said, but he eyed Hal with suspicion. 'Where's your badge of office? Are you a bailiff?'

'No, he's a—' I began, but again was hushed by the soundless persuasion of a length of sharp steel.

'Here,' Hal said, 'this is my badge of office!' and flourished his sword near the man's face. The fellow barely flinched as the point almost caught his nose, and I got the impression that he was a mere breath away from drawing out his own sword. 'Hoi!' he cried, but he had no need of his own weapon.

Even as I watched the executioner waving his blade in that dangerous manner – feeling appalled at the sight, since if he was happy to threaten a stranger like this in the street, he would hardly be worried about introducing a number of unnecessary punctures in me – I noticed another man behind him. It was Geoffrey, who walked up behind Hal. With a calm insouciance, he glanced at me and then peered into the cart. Lifting a stave of timber from the cart's bed, he hefted it in his hand with a contemplative expression for a moment, while Hal muttered imprecations against fatherless fellows who interrupted others in their duties, and then brought it down smartly on Hal's pate. Hal's eyes widened briefly and then rolled upwards, and he fell to the ground, his head striking the cobbles with a sickening thud that I felt in my bowels. Geoffrey casually returned the piece of wood to the cart, smiled at me, touched the brim of his hat to the man who had so helpfully distracted Hal, and indicated the road to London. 'I think you should consider a change of clothing,' he said with a wince at the sight (and odour) of me. 'Come!'

'Hey!' the man called. 'You can't leave this man here!'

Geoffrey turned to him. I was in front of him and couldn't see his face, but the other blenched and stumbled away in the opposite direction.

'Come,' Geoffrey said.

At least the smell meant we had little difficulty finding our way through the crowds. With the stench preceding me, a passage opened before us, and we soon beat a passage to a tavern, where the host took one look at me and gave me to understand that I would be remaining outside on a bench.

'You look terrible,' Geoffrey said, casting a glance over my tainted clothing. His nose wrinkled. 'And smell worse.'

'He was chasing me,' I said irrationally. I was feeling peculiar. The run all the way from the Seymours' house, the little

matter of Moll refusing to be rescued, and the sudden appearance of Hal, while at the same time being smothered in all
the ordure from the road, had left me feeling oddly light-
headed. I have never felt the need of feminine comfort so
strongly. Visions of Peggy's slim figure rose in my mind, only
to be beaten aside by the memory of my neighbour's wife
opposite and the way that her chemise fell open so
enticingly.

'What have you discovered?'

'Hmm? Oh, I've found her. Moll, I mean, and she's with
the Seymours. But why is Hal with them? He said he wanted
to find his wife, but she was there, with him. I mean, why did
he come and ask me to find her, if he already knew where she
was? And he must have known what she felt about him . . .'

'Yes?'

'But that can't be right,' I said. My head felt as befogged
as a glass breathed on. You know how a glass will mist over
when you breathe on it? Yes, that was how my brain felt. I
tried to see past the dull greyness, but it remained opaque. All
I could think was that Hal must have lost his mind. I picked
up the jug of ale Geoffrey had placed at my side, and drank
thoughtfully.

'Well? What can't be right?'

'He came to me and said he wanted to find his wife. Then
he said that he wanted to have his son back. But the woman,
Peggy, told me that the boy wasn't his or hers, but she was
only a child-nurse to him, and it was for that that they kept
her on.'

'Who?'

'The Seymours. They employed her because she was
recently bereaved of a daughter. I suppose that girl was Hal's.'

'Yet now you learn that he was working for the Seymours
all the time?'

'Well, yes. Why would he come to me to find her, if he
knew where she was all along?'

'And the Seymours were the same men who took my brother
somewhere and then saw to his death.'

'Perhaps, yes.'

'Is there any doubt?'

I shrugged and downed more ale. It was more than my brain could cope with just then. I kept seeing Hal Westmecott's face in my mind's eye, and it was not a pleasant sight.

'I think you need to go home and get yourself changed,' Geoffrey said, eyeing my jack with increasing distaste.

I could understand that. The material was encrusted, and stains were spreading. It was, in short, utterly befouled. However, as I stood, I swayed. The bruises on knees, shin, jaw and elbow (when I had fallen) mingled with the sharp, stabbing pain at my shoulder. It was not a happy Jack who stood gazing up the road.

'You look as if you can hardly walk a step,' he said.

'I am fine,' I said, and set off.

There are times when I have wandered in London and have felt entirely at ease. Many times I have been so careless that I could have fallen prey to one of the many footpads of the streets, but by some miracle I have always remained secure.

Today I walked with a deal more caution. The haziness of my mind remained, and the only thing that kept me moving onwards was the pain. It was as though I was grown into an ancient, arthritic man. My legs and arms and shoulders were all throbbing, and they kept my mind working. Every time I thought I might stop and take my ease, another stab would jab at my injuries and I would sharply waken to the reality of my position.

What was my position? Well, just now I had no idea who was a friend or who was an enemy. I had thought Hal was an ally, but just now he had tried to take me to the Seymours' house, where I would hardly be viewed with warm bonhomie by Edward or his father, since I had killed Anthony. But why had Hal suddenly attached himself to the Seymours? He had wanted to find Moll. Perhaps that was it!

I stopped in the street, struck by this revelation.

Hal wanted his woman back. She was with the Seymours. Logically, he had decided to make himself useful to the family, and would do all in his power to win her. Did he think they would agree to his wooing her? It was hardly likely, but if they said he could take her, poor Moll would find it difficult to refuse them, surely. Where else might she go, if she decided to ignore her husband and new friends? Yes, so Hal had allied himself to the Seymours.

I walked on with a frown of concentration. Gradually, the fog was leaving my mind, and although I glanced at various hostelries along my way, I set my mind on a good pot of wine when I reached my house again. I had an urge to sit before my own fire and enjoy the comfort of my home.

Besides, none of the taverns would let me in, the way I looked and smelled.

Back at my house, once I had divested myself of the stinking garments, and taken a few moments to bathe my face and arms in warm water, I donned my second-best suit of clothing, dropping the filthy clothing on to the floor for Raphe to collect and take to be cleaned. I didn't want to touch them again. In fact, I was seriously thinking about buying a new suit of clothing. There was a particular green fabric that I thought would look well with a yellow lining, and a hatter along the way had a broad-brimmed black hat with a feather of blue that I thought would go well with a suit of such material. It was something to consider, certainly.

When I looked up, the buxom beauty at the house over the lane was in her bedchamber. She was wearing little more than when I had seen her in bed with her husband, and she made no attempt to hide herself from my gaze. I smiled lasciviously, and she raised an eyebrow, before drawing her drapery. I gazed longingly at the blank window and left her to it, walking down to my parlour. The fire was roaring merrily, a very welcome sight, and I sat, uninterested in food or drink, trying to make sense of the whole affair. Westmecott's appearance at the Seymours' house was confusing; Moll at their father's house was more so, especially considering her apparent conviction that they were looking after her, and her comment that she was waiting till the priest returned was also confusing. No one had told her of his death, apparently. Then again, Westmecott had tried to chase after me. I was relieved that he had been taken care of. If he had caught me, I suspected that my life would have been shortened considerably.

It was a remarkable coincidence that Geoffrey was there. The man had a habit of appearing when he was least expected, but that was all to my benefit, and I was glad to have seen him today. If he had not nonchalantly picked up the lump of wood and knocked Westmecott down, I shuddered to think what might have happened.

There was a sensible explanation for it all, I was sure. But, as I said, my mind was befogged. Meanwhile, I had the problem of the instruction to execute the child and, if possible, Moll as well. That was an issue that was made considerably worse by the sudden news that the boy Ben was the son of Elizabeth herself. Who could have ordered his death, if they knew he was her son? I am not squeamish generally, apart from when it comes to people trying to injure me, but the idea that some men could decide to kill a boy so young for no reason other than to get at his mother, that I found really distasteful. It made my stomach roil with unaccustomed vigour. Perhaps because I had been an unwanted boy, too – or more because of the vengeance that a Tudor princess would be likely to take on someone who had been so bold as to injure or murder her son.

There was more than just revulsion at the thought of such callous treatment of a youngster and trepidation at the thought of what might happen to me; I was also aware of a growing anger at the men who had decided on such a course. What right did they have to decide on the death of a boy like him? People who went around killing people for no reason should answer to the law and expect to be pushed off a ladder with a rope round their neck.

I didn't dwell on that. There was still a damp spot beside my chair where Anthony's corpse had lain. Instead, I began to think deeply about the men involved. The Seymours, who appeared to be preparing to sell Moll and Ben to the Queen's men, so that the Queen could have evidence to hold over her half-sister and perceived rival. But Moll herself seemed more than content with them. Had they so deceived her that she felt safe? Then there was the slaughter of the priest. Was that because the Seymours had already given him away to the Queen's men as Geoffrey had suggested? Was James arrested and burned not because of a slightly deranged sermon, but because he had knowingly baptized the boy in the English Church, rather than following Queen Mary's own Catholic instructions? Was he burned more because he had learned of the boy's parentage, and Mary had stored up that information, ready to make a case against Elizabeth? Had he been tortured to give away the boy, and then slain because he would not speak of the child?

The more I thought of this, the more I was convinced that the only people I could trust were those who were on the side of the boy himself. That meant Peggy, and probably Geoffrey, since he would want to avenge his brother. I didn't think Moll was sensible or trustworthy, not from the way she had indicated that she was happy with the Seymours. They did not strike me as honourable men. And now I had, albeit accidentally, killed Anthony, I didn't think that Edward would be a reliable ally, even if he had been so inclined originally.

Westmecott had appeared to be dependable at first, when sober, but I had reservations about him since he had tried to catch me.

I did have others I could trust, though. I could rely on Piers, so long as he was still sober. And there was Raphe, and Humfrie, of course.

But at present I was not sure about my safety. Piers was the other side of the river; Humfrie, too. And Raphe . . . well, he was good with a heavy pan, but I wasn't convinced of his ability with a sword.

There was only one man who could possibly help.

'Raphe? I need you to go out,' I shouted.

He appeared as if by magic in my doorway. 'Master?'

'I want you to go to Master John Blount. I must speak with him.'

FIVE

I t was a relief to see him go. With my conviction that Raphe would inform about all of my activities as soon as he met his uncle, Blount must be impressed to hear how I dealt with Seymour. I only hoped Seymour was not somehow a friend to Blount.

I sat back, musing over the affair once more. So much had happened: it was baffling. But I am always a careful fellow. Not for me the panic and tantrums of the feeble-minded. Not for me the sudden burst of terror. I am made of sterner stuff. Instead, I started to think about the people involved in the affair. Geoffrey was only interested in his brother's death, of course. He wanted to know who had tampered with my powder. Hal Westmecott was responsible for the condition of the powder since he had possessed the bag that evening. I had thought that the fool might have got the powder damp by accident, leaving it on a wet table in a tavern, but what if he had *meant* to disable it? Could he not have made the powder wet on purpose, so that he had an excuse to blackmail me into helping him find his wife? He could have so dampened the powder as to make it unusable. After all, I had wondered whether someone could have met Westmecott in a tavern somewhere and made the powder damp. But who could have known where he would be, and that he would have a bag of black powder on his person? No, it was ridiculous.

What if he didn't want Moll because she was his wife? What if he was only ever in the pay of the Seymours? Perhaps he wanted Moll because they told him to find her? But no, that was lunacy. The Seymours were happy with the service Geoffrey's brother had provided in baptizing the boy. Why would they willingly let Hal kill the priest? Unless, of course, he had not mentioned to them that he was going to do that. They might have had no idea that he contemplated giving

Geoffrey's brother a slow, lingering death just so that he could blackmail me into finding Moll.

In any case, I began to feel more comfortable. I allowed myself to think that, with a little good fortune, the whole affair would soon be over for me. The boy had disappeared courtesy of Humfrie, the woman Moll was in the care of the Seymours, and Hal Westmecott knew where she was. My tasks seemed to be coming to an end.

After all, if my master demanded to know why he had not heard of the child's death, I could happily tell him that the child had been 'removed', and the mother was even now at the house of Edward Seymour. Master Blount need never hear of them again, once we had liberated Moll. She had to be removed, else her evidence ended up in Queen Mary's hands.

If Blount chose to question my integrity, or demand to see the body of Seymour, I would reply coolly that he only need question my servant, his spy, about whether I was responsible for executing those who displeased me, and learn that Anthony Seymour's body had been thrown into the Thames. If he wished to go hunting from London's wharves all the way to the coast in search of a body, he was welcome to do so, but he could not expect me to go with him. I had better things to do with my time.

For now, I was left with the delightful prospect of meeting Humfrie and letting him know what was planned. In fact, I was surprised that he had not been back yet. I had expected him to return before now. No doubt Blount was interrogating Raphe with enthusiasm about the last days.

Now, admittedly, my next action was perhaps not the wisest, but my mind was running on two parallel roads. One was all about Humfrie and my protection, while the second was fixed rather more firmly on the woman in the house opposite. I was wondering whether her husband was at home, and whether she would welcome an invitation to sup wine or a little strong ale. Not that I was going to knock on her door. After all, her husband *might* be at home. Besides, I have always tried to have a golden rule in my philandering: never to enjoy the affections of those living nearest to me. If I were to go and introduce myself, and anything were to happen, and we

engaged in a happy coupling, her husband knew where I lived.
But even golden rules are made to be broken occasionally.

I moved my foot nervously at the thought of an enraged
cuckold banging on the door. My boot's sole caught, and I
glanced down at the dampness where Anthony Seymour's
blood had been washed away by Raphe. The moisture had
dissipated somewhat, and that was a relief. If Edward were to
come here, it would be hard to see that a man had died in my
house. And then I realized. Suddenly, I felt my spirit quail.

He knew where I lived!

'Oh, dear heavens! God's wounds!'

I dare wager you have already spotted this, but I assure you
that it had not occurred to me until that moment: Westmecott
had taken the body away from here. He knew that I had slain
Anthony, and he had taken the body away. And then he had
gone straight to the Seymours' house at Whitehall. *He must
have told them!* They must know that I had killed Anthony! I
looked about me at the floor.

Edward must be on his way here to see me!

Westmecott and Seymour both knew perfectly well where
I lived.

Yes, that was when I began to panic.

There was only one thing to do. I hurried upstairs, but the
woman opposite (what was her name?) was no longer in her
bedchamber. The drapery had been withdrawn, but she was
nowhere to be seen. I stared over the gap wistfully. It would
have been good to see her, to discover if she would do more
than raise an eyebrow. And then I heard steps in the street. I
craned my neck close to the glass to peer down, but it was
only a man with a great bale of goods on his back. When I
looked back over the way, she was there.

She wore a tunic with an apron bound about her waist. Her
bosoms strained against the thin material, and her hair was
demurely locked away under her coif. She looked the perfect
embodiment of serenity and femininity, I thought, gazing at
her. There were more steps below, but I could see no one
under the overhang of my jetty. I held my breath. They were
right under me now. When I listened, the steps continued along

the way, and I could breathe again. Looking over, I gestured to indicate I could go over to join her. Her face stiffened, and she glanced behind her. I guessed she was thinking about her servants, but then she looked back at me and nodded.

I cast a glance down into the street again. No sign of Westmecott or Seymour to left or right up the lane, and soon I was hurtling down the stairs, rushing to the door and drawing the bolts. There was only the lock remaining, and I turned the key and opened the door, and as I did so, I stopped.

The woman who had knocked me down and scarred my jaw was in the doorway, her knife at my face, and she stepped into the house, pushing me back while I whimpered, staring at the horribly shiny blade.

I do not think it was unreasonable for me to be alarmed. This maddened harpy had appeared several times, and never had she heralded anything to my benefit. My jaw still stung where that damned knife had marked me, and my head was still feeling battered from her blow when she had stunned me, and now the knife was back in her hand and threatening me.

No, it was perfectly reasonable to be anxious at the sight of her crazed features.

There are men, such as Blount or Humfrie, who would take this kind of event in their stride. They would dart back, perhaps slam the door in her face, knock her knife hand aside, deliver a blow to the side of her head, or something similar, and wrestle the knife from her feeble, womanly grasp.

I confess, I am not cast from that mould. Instead, I gave a sharp cry and tripped over Hector, who had chosen that moment to come and see what I was doing. He yelped, I gave a loud cry of '*Ballocks!*' and the woman slid in and closed the door quietly behind her. I heard the key turn in the lock.

At that moment I had other matters to occupy me. One was the benighted mongrel. I was on the ground again, and my arse had hit it heavily; I was forced to sit there rubbing my backside while glaring at the bitch with baleful anger and fear. All I could think right then was, if I'd left a minute or two earlier, I could even now be resting my head between the bounteous bubbies of the woman over the road, but no, as usual Fate had stepped in with a mallet and bludgeoned my potentially beautiful future.

'What in God's name are you doing? Who on earth *are you*?' I demanded.

Now I could see her more distinctly, I was much less alarmed than the last time she had me at her mercy.

'As if you don't know,' she sneered.

'No. I don't.'

'I am the wife of Hal Westmecott.'

It was obvious to me that she must be mad. After all, I knew what Moll looked like, and the last time I saw this woman, she had told me to leave Alice alone. I goggled at her on hearing that. 'What is your name?'

'I am Alice.'

Now I could smile. 'Then you aren't the wife of Hal Westmecott. His wife is called Moll. He told me so.'

'Are you really so stupid?'

'What?'

'You thought you could take poor Molly and her charge and sell their lives! I ought to kill you right now!'

She took a step forward as if persuaded, and I scrabbled my way back. Hector thought this enormous fun and started to leap up at me. I had to batter the foolish creature away while trying to keep an eye on the mad tramp before me. 'No! Wait! Look! Westmecott came to me and asked me to find his wife and son for him. It was only later I heard that he wasn't married, and that she had been a wet-nurse. I had no idea. I thought I was bringing a family back together, that was all.'

'You think me as stupid as you?' she demanded, the knife giving off nasty blue/grey flashes as she swept it from side to side, approaching me.

'No!' I squeaked as the knife came closer. 'I was hired by Westmecott to find his wife, or so he said. When I learned the boy wasn't his, I wasn't going to take the lad to him.'

'You were at Whitehall today with the Seymours.'

'Yes, and they chased me all the way to Temple Bar, almost. I was trying to persuade Moll to come with me, so I could release her. The boy isn't there – I sent him away for safekeeping.'

'And Westmecott told you to find them for him?'

'Yes.'

'Why would he do that?'

'He's your man! Why do you ask me?' I demanded, not unreasonably, I think.

She looked at me coolly. There was that calm serenity in her eyes that spoke of either large quantities of alcohol, or a religious conviction that was set several levels above mine. Don't get me wrong, I am not a heretic, but there are some people whom you meet who can plainly see heaven before them. All too often they are keen to help others to see their vision, aiding them on their way with a rope or a knife or a fire. Thankfully, I have never had that vision. My life has always been too chaotic.

'So this woman is called Moll, yet your man asked me to find her, saying she was you?'

She nodded.

I absorbed this with a puzzled frown. 'Why did he ask me to find Moll, then, and not you?'

She rolled her eyes. Speaking with the patience of a woman answering a child's repeated questions, she said, 'Because he knew Moll had the boy with her. He didn't want me! He got you to search for Moll, pretending she was me. He wanted the boy. It worked, didn't it? Anyway, did Moll say where her son is? Is he safe?'

'Yes, he's safe enough. As I said, I have placed him with a friend,' I said warily. 'It's me who is in danger. Westmecott will likely be here at any time, and when he arrives—'

'He knows you live here?'

'Well, yes. He came here to buy powder for the execution of the priest, and then—'

She interrupted again. I have no objection to people having their say, but this constant interjection was annoying.

'When did you last see him?'

'I don't know – in the time it took for me to get here from Whitehall and change my clothes.'

She turned and went to the door, slamming the bolts into place. 'Can we escape from the rear?'

'I suppose so,' I said. 'There is a gate to the alley. But wait! Why are you concerned? Surely he would be glad to find you?'

'Why?'

'He was looking for his wife, and you are his wife.'

'No. He was looking for Moll, pretending she was his wife, so that he can sell her and the boy to whoever will pay him the most money for them.'

I rubbed my temples. 'Say that again?'

'We don't have time!' she snapped. 'Come, show me this gate!'

I took her through the kitchen and out to the little yard behind. There was a gate in the wall which had three bolts. A man cannot be too aware of security. I drew them all, and she opened the gate and peered up and down the alley, quietly stepping out and walking on to the alley's entrance.

I left Hector behind. The stupid animal would only have been a distraction on our way, and, besides, Raphe would have been distraught if the creature had disappeared. He could easily bear my absence, but not that of his beast.

We made our way along the narrow way, her in front and me sheltering behind her. It was when we were almost at the south-western entrance that I heard the tramp of heavy boots. When I snatched a glance from behind her, I saw that there were four men, with Westmecott and Seymour in the lead. Two large, rough brutes followed on behind. They passed by the entrance to the alleyway, and thankfully did not so much as glance in our direction.

'They'll be on the way to my house,' I said sadly. I could all too easily imagine the damage the four could do to my home.

'Those men?' she said.

And suddenly I realized she didn't know any of them.

'Wait!' I cried, and took her by the shoulder, thrusting her against the nearest wall. When I think back to my action now, a cold stream of water runs down my back and makes me shiver. I wasn't thinking at the time, but her knife was at my belly. 'Do you mean you didn't recognize them?'

'I know Edward Seymour,' she said. 'The others were surely his henchmen?'

'The man in front on the left – didn't you recognize him?'

'No. Should I?'

'That is the man who called himself Westmecott,' I said.

She chuckled briefly, but then she saw my seriousness. 'You mean this? That was not my man.'

'It was he who told me to find you!'

She gave me an entirely puzzled look. 'But I've never seen that man before.'

'He isn't Westmecott?'

She made no reply to that, but gave me a look of such contempt that I guessed the answer.

'You were living with Westmecott?' I said doubtfully. 'You couldn't have mistaken him?'

'Yes, but that was not him.'

'What did your man look like?'

'About your height, but broader of shoulder. He wasn't a bad-looking fellow. He had a scar, here,' she added, touching her left cheek.

I frowned. A man with no scar was a rarity, of course, but this sounded familiar. 'What hair?'

She shrugged. 'Fair – sort of dirty fair. Not yellow like some. He wasn't a bad man. He was good enough by his own lights, but I could not bear to have him pawing at me, knowing what his hands had done that day.' She pulled a face. 'It was horrible. So I decided I had to leave him.'

'Where did you go?'

'I was able to find a job at the Cardinal's Hat.'

'So you knew Peggy?'

'Yes.'

Her tone indicated that there was little love between them.

'How did you meet Moll and Ben?'

'They were often down that way. Moll had been at the Hat before she was hired as a wet-nurse. As soon as that happened, she was taken away, but she returned to London some months ago, with the child in tow. I saw her in the street with the boy.'

'Did she tell you what had happened to her?'

'Who, Moll? Of course. She was . . . well, she needed help when she started out. I took her under my wing, as you might say.' She gave me a quizzical look. 'Do you want to stand here for long? If those men are looking for you . . .'

'Yes, yes,' I said. I had no wish to be discovered by Westmecott or the others. We set off at a fast pace.

'Moll told me that they took her to a big hall in Hertfordshire, and from all she said, she was treated like a princess there. She'd lost her own child, which was why she was needed there as wet-nurse, but she enjoyed it so much that when they offered the post of nursemaid to the boy, she took it like a shot.'

'Why is she back here now?'

We had reached the end of the alley. I motioned to her, and Alice peered round the opening. She gasped and snatched her head back, panting, leaning against the wall, her eyes wide with terror – and then began to laugh. 'Your face!' she managed between gurgles. 'You should see yourself!'

'What, is there . . .' I took a peep myself. There was no sign of anyone in the street. 'You stupid—'

'Oh, don't be so pathetic,' she said, and took my hand before leading us up the road away from my house.

As she went, she said, 'The Seymours wanted to come here, and they brought her with them.'

'Why?'

'I don't know.'

I nodded, frowning. 'So why did you attack me?'

'Moll was trying to keep away from her old life. I thought you were working for a pimp and trying to get her back on the game. I wasn't going to let you do that to her.'

I felt the scab at my jaw. The wound was still sore, and I disliked the idea that I might in any way look like a pimp. 'Next time, perhaps you could ask questions first, before attacking a fellow,' I said. I almost pointed out that I had a much more honourable profession – but that could have led to difficult explanations.

'Moll is with the Seymours now, you say?'

I nodded again. 'They seem to be treating her well.'

She frowned. 'The last time we spoke, she said she was

terrified of the man Seymour. He was violent, she said, and she didn't think he had the boy's best interests at heart.'

'If that was Anthony Seymour, I can only agree with her,' I said. 'He was a horrible man.'

'*Was?* Has something happened to him?'

I smiled with some bemusement. I didn't know how to answer. 'I only met him a couple of times,' I said at last.

'I felt sure that he was trying to use Moll to get at the boy.'

'I see,' I said. I didn't want to mention the Seymours selling Moll and Ben to the Queen.

'After all, the lad was worth a lot of money.'

'Really?' I said suavely, and was about to question her about this aspect of the matter when we reached the house of Master Blount. I knocked, only to be told that the master was not at home. It was enough to make me swear, but I informed his servant that we would be found in the Golden Cockerel, a tavern only a short distance away, and to send his master to me as soon as he appeared.

At the tavern, after buying us drinks, I took her to a table in the front room where I had a good view of the entranceway. I wanted to see as soon as John Blount – or Westmecott – appeared.

We had been there long enough for a quart and a half of ale by the time I saw Master John Blount in the doorway. He pulled off his gloves as he marched to our table. 'That was a merry dance you led me,' he said. 'Who did that to your house?'

'My house?'

'All the doors broken, chairs slashed and damaged, and a woman crying that they were fiends.'

I swear to you, the first thought in my mind was Hector. 'What of the dog?'

He shrugged.

For once I had a feeling of sadness at the thought of the scruffy mutt. It was the idea that I might not see him again. The tatty little fleatrap had grown on me, I suppose.

He must be dead.

'Who was crying?' I said with confusion. All I could think about was my lovely house, and especially my little strongroom with the bolt-studded, iron-lined door, which held my chest of money. My heart felt as if it had been gripped by a steel fist, and was being squeezed as the fist clenched. All that money . . .

Blount was looking at Alice. 'Who is this?'

'This lady is Alice. She was Westmecott's – er – wife. She knows Moll and the boy.'

'Oh. You can go now,' he said to her, and faced me.

Alice leaned back. 'And you can go swive a goat, Master,' she said equably. 'I'm enjoying my ale.'

I don't think any woman had spoken to Blount in so forthright a manner before. He had given her an instruction. Her refusal to pay him any heed was not expected. In his world, women were dainty things who obeyed. He blinked and stared at her, and clearly decided that she was determined to remain, so he dropped his voice and leaned towards me. 'This wench, she's a whore?'

'I can hear you, you know,' she said.

'Damn your eyes, woman, will you let us speak?' he blurted.

It was entertaining, I confess. I had never seen my master in quite such confusion of spirit. He glared at Alice, who nonchalantly ignored him. It became rapidly apparent to me that Blount had no idea how to deal with this woman. A man he could simply have bullied into submission, threatening him until he left us to our conversation, but this woman was a different matter. He had the sense not to try to manhandle her from the room, because, for all her tatty appearance, there was a confidence that oozed from her. Whores often have it, I've noticed. Since they have little shame, it's hard to embarrass them, and often a man will discover that any attempt to do so will leave *him* looking the fool.

Blount turned so that his back was half turned to her. Glowering at me, he said, 'So? Who did that to your house?'

I glanced at Alice, but there seemed little point ignoring her or trying to conceal matters from her. I began my story, telling him about the Seymours. 'You know that Thomas Seymour, the Lord Sudeley, married Lady Catherine? He was accused of treason and arrested, and had to be executed.'

'I know all this,' Blount growled.

'And you will know that Lord Sudeley had responsibility towards a young lady living with Lady Catherine and under her protection?'

'Yes, yes.'

'And that there were rumours of . . . impropriety between the Lord and his young ward?'

'Yes, and he was forced to confess, and was executed, as you say. So what?'

'A woman was working in the stews at that time. She was pregnant, but her child did not survive. However, she was invited to go and live in a great hall as wet-nurse to a child.'

'This woman?' Blount asked with frank distaste.

'No, another – a woman called Moll. She was engaged, and when the child was finally weaned, she was retained as maid and dry-nurse. It was a job that she found accommodating.'

'And?'

'Do you not see this? Moll, the boy – a lad who happens to have been born at about the time Thomas Seymour was arrested, and now many men expressing great interest in the lad and his mother?'

'There can be no connection.'

'Then consider this,' I said, fixing him with a serious eye. 'Whether the boy is or is not the son of a nobleman and his leman, could it be argued that he was? If so, others who worked for someone with a desire to earn favours at court might well decide to allege that the boy was indeed the result of an illicit union between Thomas Seymour and his . . . his . . .'

'Be very careful,' Blount grated.

'His companion.'

'Well and good,' Blount said. He eyed me consideringly, then shot a look at Alice. 'What of her?'

I frowned. 'Alice here was the companion of Hal Westmecott, the executioner. She left him. But when he asked me to find his wife and son, he told me her name was Moll. So he did not seek Alice here, but the woman who was Ben's nursemaid. That means, I think, he must know of the story, and he is trying to find Moll and her son to take them to the Queen and denounce the mother.'

'Which, true or not, would be embarrassing,' Blount nodded slowly.

There was no doubting that it would be easy to persuade a justice that Lady Elizabeth had indulged in adultery with Thomas Seymour, and that Ben was the fruit of that illegal relationship. And if that was the case, Lady Elizabeth could be in very great trouble. I didn't need to point it out to Blount.

'There is one other thing, however. As I said, Alice was the companion of Hal Westmecott. A man came to me to buy powder and said he was Westmecott, but according to Alice here, it was not him.'

Blount shook his head as though to clear it. 'What? You mean the man you were dealing with claimed to be Westmecott, but wasn't?'

I merely nodded, and Blount leaned back, his hands on the table, staring into the middle distance. 'So this man Westmecott is an imposter. Where is the real Westmecott?' He looked at Alice. 'What does he look like?'

'Not tall, but broad, fair-haired, with a scar on his face, and he's lost the top of his finger,' she said succinctly, holding up her finger to demonstrate.

I gaped, aghast. 'That was the man I saw dead on the floor in Westmecott's chamber!'

'Are you sure?' Blount said.

'Yes! I went there to talk to him, but when I walked in, he was dead on the floor. I didn't know who it was, because I'd already met Westmecott, or the man who called himself that, and he appeared a little later with a rug, and seemed to suspect me of the murder.'

'He was carrying a rug?'

'Yes.'

'So he had murdered the man and was bringing a means of removing him.'

'Oh!'

There seemed little else for me to say, really.

'You didn't suspect him?' Blount said.

'No. Why should I?'

'The fact that he was there, that he had brought a rug. How did you dispose of the body?'

'He said he could do that. He had ways, he said. So we rolled the body into the rug to conceal it, and he took it away.'

'So you had seen him arrive with the article and didn't suspect him?'

'Of course not! I am not a murderer. I don't think like that!'

He looked at me with a keen sharpness. It was like being stabbed with a dagger that had been hidden behind a fine veil. Since he had hired me and paid me to be his assassin, I suppose I deserved it. He was not to know that I had never killed on his orders.

'Raphe mentioned that you had some other difficulty,' he said pointedly.

'Um.' I had no desire to discuss Anthony in front of Alice.

'What did you do then? Did Westmecott come around again?'

'Yes.'

'Where did he go?'

'I don't know. But a little later I saw him at the Seymours' house.'

He winced. 'And a little later I found your house sorely battered. I think you can assume that Edward Seymour has learned of his brother's death.'

'The man calling himself Westmecott was with him when he marched to my house,' I said.

'You saw him?'

'We saw the party, yes.'

Master Blount nodded to himself. 'So it would seem that the Seymours have you marked as a person they would like to speak with.'

'What can I do?'

He rose. 'I would run and hide. I see little else you can do.'

'Can we stay at your house for a little? Just until . . .'

'No. You can return to me when this affair is sorted one way or another,' he said shortly. 'Until then, you are an embarrassment – and dangerous, both for me and for our principal. You can seek me out when Seymour is no longer a danger, or . . .'

That was the point. The '*or*'. Because either Seymour must be removed, or I would die. Blount's eyebrow lifted just a fraction, and we both knew which was the more likely outcome.

Blount stalked from the room, and I was left staring at a crack in the wall's plaster. I had no very happy thoughts.

'What are you going to do?'

'I don't know what I can do. I should leave London, I suppose. What of you?'

She shook her head. 'I can't go back to my house, and I can't go to work again. I'd be too easy to pick up on the streets. If they were to find me . . .'

'Why should they want to hurt you? I'm the one they'll want to kill,' I expostulated.

She shrugged. 'The man who killed my Hal won't want me to be here, in case I tell stories about him and people realize he isn't the real Hal. I am as much at risk as you. If he was happy to kill my husband, he'd hardly worry about removing me, an old whore.'

Her tone was matter-of-fact, laced with a little stoicism, but while there was not a trace of self-pity, she looked distinctly mournful. And with her face like that, she was a different woman. With her features softened, the harsh lines of rancour were smoothed over, the trials of her hard life were swept away like old rushes, and in their place I saw a woman who had once been a young, attractive wench, with large eyes that would melt the heart of the most pitiless outlaw and have him begging her to take a sup with him.

'What are you staring at?' she demanded, catching my eye, and normal life was resumed.

It was clear that I could not return to my home. Even if the housebreakers had left me a seat or table undamaged, the danger was that they could return at any moment. What I needed was a place where I could rest and think what I should do. Master Blount was clear enough that I was not welcome at his home, and I didn't think it would be a good idea in any case. The fact was, many people knew I worked for him, and it would take little to realize that I might go to his house.

Where else might I go? The Cardinal's Hat? That was safer,

no doubt, but I didn't think that the bawd who ran the house of relaxation would welcome me. She had a soft spot for me, as so many of these tarts do, but the fact that I was a refugee and could bring danger to her own place meant she would be unlikely to want me there. I needed somewhere else.

One man occurred to me.

'I know where we can go. We should be safe there,' I said.

I knocked loudly on the door. There was an interval in which not a sound could be heard, and then the sound of slowly approaching footsteps.

Jonah, Mark's servant, opened the door, and subjected us to his most morose scrutiny. He glowered all the while with suspicion. He was a wizened, ill-kempt fellow, who looked as though he should have had a dewdrop fixed to the end of his nose permanently. He would not have looked out of place in a dungeon, serving the torturers with ale and cheese between the clicks of the rack's ratchets.

'Jonah, it is me. Is your master in?'

'I'll have to go and check.'

'Be quick, then!'

'I'll take as long as I need to,' he said. He slowly withdrew and closed the door again. I heard the bolt lock.

I had a sudden thought. 'Do you like hounds?' I asked.

Her look could not have been more confused if I had grown a second head. 'What?'

'I suppose I'll soon find out,' I said.

It is fair, I think, to say that while Alice might have liked the companionship of a small lapdog, Peterkin was not built on those lines. When Jonah opened the door again, grudgingly admitting us to the hallway, there was a sudden plodding of paws. While Jonah slammed the door and thrust the bolts home, Alice suddenly caught her breath. If she had been confronted by a demon, she could not have looked more appalled.

I have noticed that some people are more keen on keeping cats. They are less trouble, they say, and affectionate, without fawning. And they keep rats down. Except in my experience, they do nothing to control rats which are almost their own size. Rather, they assault the prettiest songbirds, any shrews or mice, and occasionally me, as the scars on one wrist can attest (the cat was lying on its back, and I thought it wanted its tummy rubbed).

On the other hand, dogs will protect a house, see to the defence of their master, obey commands and, in short, be reliable members of the family.

However, not all people feel as comfortable with a dog like Peterkin. This hound of Mark's was as tall as Alice, if he stood on his hind legs – no, taller. As she took in his size, I had the impression that he was measuring her up for future amusement. Perhaps he considered her a dainty little treat to be consumed later. I could not be certain, but felt that there was a flaring of interest in his eyes as he took her in – a little spark, such as one might see in the eye of a demon welcoming a new victim to his pit. He padded towards us on paws the size of my fist.

Alice was unimpressed by the sight of him, and as I remembered my scarred jaw and the lump on my head, it gave me no little pleasure to see how she recoiled at the sight. She retreated before him, until her back was at the door, and then, as he shoved his nose into her groin, she whimpered.

I patted the brute's back with a sense of comradeship before strolling off after Jonah. After some moments, Peterkin followed after us, and then there came the slightly frantic pattering of Alice's feet. Reaching me, she took my arm in her hands and clung to me all the way to Mark's chamber. It was not an unpleasant sensation.

The room was, as usual, a precise duplicate of a room that has been struck by a cannonball – no, an artillery barrage. Papers had been flung on every surface. Where there had been space, more armour and weaponry appeared to have materialized for little reason. The great hound sauntered in and shook his entire body, and slobber flew through the air to land on a sheaf of papers on Mark's lap. He glanced at his pet affectionately and looked up at me.

'What do you want now?'

Hardly an encouraging welcome, but I indicated my human limpet. 'This lady is Alice. She was involved in the matter I spoke of with you . . .'

'Come in, my dear, please,' Mark said immediately. His attention, once distracted from the papers, was wholeheartedly in favour of the wench. He all but threw the papers aside and tried to spring to his feet. His age and infirmity were against him, but he yet cast a languishing glance at her. The man was already undressing her, I saw, but that was the sort of man Mark was. He could never pass through a room without doting on every female form within it.

I interrupted his gaze quickly, saying, 'Mark, the lady is under threat of her life.'

'Are you the lady he told me of?' Mark said, seemingly deaf to all but Alice's voice. 'Please, you must be chill. Sit yourself by my fire, my dear. It must have been a terrible shock to you, you so young and . . . Please, you will partake of some wine, and a little cheese and beef?'

'I—'

'Quite. Jonah, would you . . . God's teeth, where is the useless . . . *Jonah!*'

'What?'

At the response behind him, Mark gave an instructive impression of a startled faun. 'Well, I . . . wine and—'

'I did hear you.'

He wandered off, his head bowed, and Mark continued to survey Alice with much the same gleam in his eye that his hound had borne. 'So, are you the lady my friend here was looking for?'

'Yes – and then again, no,' I said, not that my presence was required. I felt rather superfluous, if you know what I mean.

'How intriguing,' Mark said, without for an instant taking his eyes from Alice.

I told him briefly of the matter, how Alice and I had met and the situation in which we found ourselves. 'And so I was hoping that you could help us,' I finished.

Mark said, 'Oh, yes. Of course. I see. Here? Oh, I don't think we have space for both of you. It would be . . .'

Alice had been fully aware of his attention. While he had been studying her figure in the way of a paederast artist studying a possible subject, she had been keenly giving the room her own minute examination. Clearly, what she saw was pleasing. I could almost hear the chink of coins being counted in her brain. 'I think it would be very kind of you to put us up. Obviously, I need Jack for my protection.'

'Oh, don't have any fears on that score. Our Peterkin will drive away any foe foolish enough to try to break in or harm you,' Mark said.

We all turned to view the hound, who was currently sitting before the fire and assiduously scratching at his ear with an expression of acute gratification. On noticing our stares, his paw gradually slowed in its whirling motion, and he clearly grew uncomfortable, until his paw came to rest some six inches from his head, while he looked from one to another of us with an air of questioning innocence, as though he knew his own behaviour was irreproachable, so why were we viewing him in such an accusing manner?

'Yes,' Alice said. 'I think I would like Jack here, too.'

SIX

I woke and stared about me in alarm for some moments before my brain caught up with my eyes and reminded me that I was safe. So often I have awoken to a strange room, and shortly thereafter been reminded of my activities by the size of the bruise on my head or the aching from within. This time, I recalled no reason for a headache, other than the foul wine that Mark foisted upon us. He was fondly convinced that it was as good as the finest Bordeaux, but I could tell from the first sip that either he had been sold foul dregs from the last of an ancient barrel or he was so foolish as to think that he could buy the best for the price of the worst vinegar in London.

My head was a little fragile, it is fair to say. However, as soon as I recalled where I was, I felt considerably happier, and lay back on the bedding with a contented feeling. After all, it was a warm chamber, this. And the bedding might have smelled a little, but it was soft enough. The pillow, however, was . . . well, it was odd. Warm, soft, but . . . when I prodded it, there was a low rumble that I could feel through it.

I sprang from the bed. 'What are you doing here?' I shouted.

Peterkin blinked at me with apparent surprise. It was not, in his opinion, my place as a guest to complain about my bed companion. Which, when I glanced about me at the room, was fair enough. This was clearly a chamber that had been allocated to guests, but which had been commandeered some little while ago by the hound. His fur lay thickly all about. It made me begin to itch at the very sight.

I left the chamber, which was a room at the side of the kitchen, and went through into the main hall once more. There was no sign of Alice or Mark, and I felt sure that there would not be for some time. Mark, I knew, was a late riser by nature, and the idea of getting up early was anathema to him. Alice, I guessed would be content to stay abed with him. Her past

career at the Cardinal's Hat would have persuaded her to shun
the daylight, and since she looked so haggard now, I felt it
likely that she might be keen to keep to the shadows. They
are much kinder to an older whore's wrinkles, after all.

Not that Mark would mind. He had the discrimination of a
feral cat when it came to women. Availability counted for
much more than any other attribute, in his mind.

However, I had a need to be up and about. There were
matters that needed my attention, and soon. Some thoughts
had been raggedly meandering through my mind as I slept.
For instance, why had the man calling himself Westmecott
decided to come to me for his powder? If he was, as I suspected,
an agent of the Queen, who was bent on capturing both Ben
and his nursemaid with a view to proving that Ben was the
illegitimate son of Lady Elizabeth, why had he decided to use
me to supply powder? Was it only to make sure that I would
help him to find his 'wife' and 'son', or was there some other
reason? Perhaps he wanted me out of the way for some reason?
If that was the case, I must be careful, because he had the
easiest means of removing me, knowing that I had killed
Anthony Seymour.

What reason could he have for wanting me to be the target
of the Seymours' ire? Could it be that the brothers suspected
him of some offence, and he was deflecting their attention
towards me as a shield for himself? Or had he some idea that
I was a threat to him? And either way, what a convoluted
approach to take, soaking my powder in water or ale to make
it ineffective. How could he know how poorly it would respond
to the moisture? And how did he get it wet? Was he, as I
suspected, a drunken oaf who set his powder on a wet surface
in a tavern, and who let the damp seep into the leather, or
was it possible that someone else saw the bag and sought to
soak it to prevent it functioning when it dangled about the
neck of his victim?

Then there was the matter of the visit to the Seymours. Why
would he go there, unless to inform them that I had killed
Anthony? Afterwards, naturally, the family had sent their party
to my house and conducted their savagery on my belongings.
But, I hoped, had not stolen all my money. Was it safe there,

if the house was left broken and open to any drawlatch with a hankering for a quick profit?

I rubbed a hand over my face. This was pointless. I needed time to think. Ideally, I needed Master Blount to help me. His mind was like a steel trap. When he was not discontented by a strange woman, he was rational and logical, whether I liked his thinking or not. But he had made it clear he wanted nothing to do with me.

Alice should be safe here with Mark, I thought. She would be forced to entertain him until she was exhausted, but apart from the risk of being worn out, she was secure. Jonah, for all his moaning and complaining, was a loyal man and devoted to Mark. If Mark indicated that he wanted Alice protected, Jonah and even the drooling mutt would lay down their lives for her.

The house was quiet. I returned to the kitchen and cut a crust of bread. There was ham and some beef remaining from the previous evening, as well as a jug of the vicious wine. I ignored that, and sought a flask, which I filled with ale from a barrel in the buttery. Armed with food and drink, I settled my baldric about my shoulder, checked my pistol and thrust it into my belt, and set the flask of powder and pouch of balls to rest with the baldric.

Taking a deep breath, I slid the bolts and stepped out into the thick air of a cool London morning.

I needed answers, and I thought I knew where to find them.

A priest was holding a crowd spellbound at the great cross in the road just up from the cathedral as I passed, and I paused to listen to his depiction of hellfire and the dreadful punishments that awaited sinners as they descended into Hell.

This was quite a good fellow. He had a strong, clear voice, and the sort of youthful, dark appearance that appealed to a certain sort of woman. There were several in the crowd who hung on his every word and shuddered deliciously at his depiction of the worse levels of Hell. I wouldn't have minded soothing a few of those troubled breasts, had I been given the chance. As it was, it was hard enough to keep my eyes from their bounties. Many of the women and men had well-filled purses which caught my attention. Well, I was a cut-purse for many months – and a good one, if I say so myself. I could dip into many a man's pocket in a crowd and empty it of all his money in an instant without him ever knowing. It is a skill, and I was proficient, I have to confess.

There was one wayward beauty with a heaving bosom who had a most appealing sideways glance at me a couple of times, and I was tempted to go to her and try an exploratory introduction, but today I was more keen on finding Humfrie, and so I pushed through the crowds and would have hurried on, but for a sudden roar.

After the sermon, and the priest's blessing, another man stepped forward. This was a crier for the city, and he now made a great bellow, with the important announcements for the day. And there were several, but only the one caught the attention of the crowd: a conspiracy had been uncovered against the Queen herself. A number of people had been arrested, and others were sought. Men from the household of Lady Elizabeth had been taken and were now on their way to the Tower (at this, my own heart began to beat faster, and I wondered if the woman I had been eyeing would be thinking of offering me some medicinal comfort), and among them were some fellow called Verney, Kat Ashley and Sir Thomas Parry. Apparently, there was proof that the French were involved, and their ambassador had already fled the country.

I was flabbergasted. This was terrible news! There was no mention of Blount as yet, but if his master, Parry, was arrested, it could only be a short while before Blount was also taken. I could have sunk to the ground in despair; it already felt as if the roadway was tottering beneath me, and I felt as if my reason was failing me.

Parry was Lady Elizabeth's Comptroller, and Kat Ashley was her chief lady-in-waiting. If people of *their* standing were being arrested, there was little to be done. No doubt evidence of their complicity in this conspiracy would soon be discovered. After all, when they have been held in the Tower and exposed to the clever techniques of interrogation that the equipment inside provided, few men or women could withstand the persuasion. Anyone would confess just to stop the pain.

I hurried to the nearest tavern, wishing I might find Humfrie, but as I expected, he was not about. He must still be with Peggy and Ben at his sister's house. Instead, I made good use of my time by drinking a quart of sack and bemoaning my fate.

There was little doubt that my position was terrible. My life was bound up with that of Lady Elizabeth – if she was lost, so was I. There was the other matter, too, which was that if Parry and, possibly, Blount were captured as had been said, then they would both likely be keen to use any information they could to provide themselves with a level of safety. They would use any intelligence they could think of to protect themselves. If that meant telling of an employee who was used as a professional assassin, they would sell me in the blink of an eye, and deny that they themselves had anything to do with me. I could imagine Parry now, in his lilting Welsh accent, speaking of a dangerous man that Blount had engaged to go out and perform unspeakable acts against the innocent.

And then another thought struck.

I had been ordered to kill Ben. Yes, Humfrie had been most reluctant, and had said he was taking the boy to safety, but if someone else had followed Humfrie, or worked out where he had gone, and chose to remove the embarrassment of Ben, my position would be undermined. If Ben were to be discovered dead, after all, it was very likely that it would be my name announced at the cross here at St Paul's. And there were many who would enjoy seeing me arrested and forced to a cell.

Quickly, I demanded another pint of sack.

'Why, good day, Master Blackjack,' came a voice, and I turned sharply, fearing the worst, but it was only Geoffrey. 'What are you doing in here?'

'I wanted a drink,' I said, trying not to hiccup. The last gulp had seemed to go down unsteadily, and I was assailed by a wave of the irritating spasms. 'What brings you here?'

'I was passing St Paul's cross, and heard a most interminable sermon,' he said, and then took his seat at my side. He carried a metal tankard and leather jug, and set them on the table before sitting, leaning towards me conspiratorially and hissing,

'So, have you heard what the criers are saying? Apparently, there has been a conspiracy, and Lady Elizabeth's lady-in-waiting and Comptroller are arrested. It's said they're being held in the Tower before they are condemned.'

'Before they are tried, you mean, and, if found guilty, then possibly condemned,' I said. When one has been a pickpocket, one develops a regard for the integrity of the law and legal processes.

'Quite,' he said with a grin. But then he lowered his head again, glancing about at the others in the tavern as if expecting to see a spy listening intently. But there was only the usual crowd of tradesmen and merchants growing redder of face with every passing moment and every extra pint consumed. Geoffrey continued more quietly, 'But this time the Queen will hardly allow traitors to escape. She has the ringleaders already. Next, she must remove their figurehead, don't you think?'

'I don't know what you mean,' I said stoutly, and buried my face in my tankard again. This was terrible news!

'There is one thing, of course,' he said thoughtfully. 'Her child must never be found. Can you imagine what would happen, were the son of Thomas Seymour and the Lady Elizabeth to be discovered? Instant condemnation for her adultery, and an instant belief in her guilt. No one would believe her word if it were known that she was guilty of treason to her guardian and had seduced her guardian's husband.'

I swallowed. 'I'm sure no one would find the boy.'

'I am glad you are so sure. It would be terrible if he were to be found. I mean, the lad would suffer torture to force him to confess all he knew, and Lady Elizabeth would be tormented to think of her own son treated in such a foul manner – and then, just think of her feelings as she saw all her servants punished for what they might have known. It would be so terrible a situation.'

'What is your interest in all this?' I said. I think it came out rather sharper than I meant, because he sat back and held up both palms as though pushing away any allegations.

'Me? You know my interest from my brother's religion, I think. Obviously, I am a loyal man to those of my religion. Lady Elizabeth is of a similar mind.'

'You should be careful. The Queen may be interested in hearing your views,' I said sourly.

That registered. His face paled a little. 'Don't think me a traitor, Blackjack,' he said tersely. 'But, like you, I work for those who serve the true religion.'

It was a strange argument, that. Truth be told, I had no great interest in religion. I was more keen on ensuring that I kept well away from such arguments. The Lady Elizabeth had enough trouble on her plate, and I didn't want to be yet another small issue. In fact, I would prefer to remain invisible to both half-sisters: the Queen and Elizabeth. It was never a good idea to get involved in the lives of royalty. All too often it led only to tears and anguish. I had enough on my plate already worrying about Seymour.

'You are sure the boy is safe, anyway?'

I glanced across at him. 'Yes. He's fine where he is.'

'That is good to know. If you need help in defending him, you can always call on my help.'

'Thank you.'

'Do you know where to find me?'

'It seems as though I only have to turn around and there you are,' I said, and lifted my ale again.

'We do keep bumping into each other, don't we?' he said easily.

'Yes,' I muttered. I stood.

'Where are you going?' he asked.

'I have some errands to run,' I said.

'I'll join you.'

'No need.'

'I would like to. The streets are dangerous, especially now with the conspiracy uncovered,' he said.

'No. I will be going alone.'

'Very well. But don't forget I offered to help. Good luck. I hope you don't see him.'

'Who?'

'Why, Westmecott. He's the one who is likely to try to harm you, isn't he? Master Blackjack, do you think a little food would be a good idea? They sell good pies here.'

* * *

He ordered from a young serving wench, and when two pies
arrived, he made me sit and eat with him. I had no appetite,
but it was not bad for a London pie, with some meat inside
that could indeed have come from some form of bovine. After
a bite or two I found myself ravenous and scoffed the rest,
washing it down with the last of my ale. He sat back, and I
leaned against the wall.

Geoffrey was a good man, I considered. He was one of the
few people I knew I could trust, a man with no reason to want
to hurt me or make things more difficult. All he wanted was to
know who was responsible for delaying his brother's death.

'The Seymours – do you think they were the ones to make
James suffer?'

'I know it was not me,' I said, burping softly. The food had
helped, but every so often it felt as though the room would
begin to revolve about me. It was very disconcerting. 'If not
them, then who?'

'It does seem strange that they should ingratiate themselves
with the Queen by denouncing James when he is the same
religion as them.'

'But religion counts for little compared with the other things
that motivate men,' I said. The serving wench was buxom and
had a pleasingly wanton look about her. She caught my eye
and smiled broadly. I thought that matters could be looking
up, if her grin was anything to go by.

'What other things?'

'Hmm? Oh, money, women, power. Mostly money, though,'
I said, trying to wink at her. She laughed and turned away. I
had a horrible suspicion she was laughing at me. It was very
hurtful, if so.

'James had no money, no woman and no power at all,'
Geoffrey said.

'Could he have had influence over someone else?'

'Who?'

I racked my brains. 'Someone in his congregation? Was there
a very rich person there whom he could have influenced?'

'I don't know.'

'Because if not, then he died to keep him silent.'

'They killed him to still his tongue?'

'Yes.'

'That would be a terrible deed. He would never have betrayed a secret; he was very discreet. And besides, what secret could he have betrayed? We thought he had baptized the child. What harm could there be in that?'

'He could have baptized the lad in the wrong faith?' It was weak, I knew. Many children were baptized into different faiths daily, but their priests were not executed immediately afterwards.

'Perhaps. But I keep coming back to the idea that if they wanted to keep him silent, they would have killed him more quickly,' Geoffrey said.

'Eh?'

'If they wanted him quiet, they would have killed him more speedily. Why have him arrested and run the risk that he might not be convicted, if they wanted him silenced forever? Surely they'd have just stuck a knife in him and dumped his body in a ditch?'

That was a thought, certainly. Not that it was cast-iron. When a priest was accused of heresy, his fate was almost sealed.

'You were over at Whitehall, I think you said?' He took a pull of his ale. 'What were you doing there?'

I shook my head. 'I hoped to see Moll and get her away from the Seymours, but I couldn't persuade her.'

'So you know where they live?'

'Yes, at Whitehall itself. They have a place on a path that leads to the river.'

'I see.'

'They nearly caught me, too, you will recall.'

'You were fortunate.'

I gave an emphatic nod. It had been fortunate for me that Geoffrey had been there. 'Yes, I was! I could have been hauled back to the Seymours' house like a snared badger, and murdered, and no one would ever have known. I'll bet they would have killed me and thrown me into the Thames. That's the easiest way to get rid of a man down there.'

'I see. And she has her son with her?'

I gave a non-committal grunt that could have meant anything.

It was not until later that I wondered about him. That he had been there when Westmecott had hunted me down, that he had happened to enter the same tavern and bumped into me. It seemed a great coincidence.

But as I say, that was later. Just now I had plenty of other things to occupy my mind.

I left him in there and went out into the street. It was mayhem, with people running about, children screaming and darting in and out between cars, carts and sumpter horses. More than one oath was flung at the little brutes as they played in the streets with balls, hoops or sticks, pretending to be bold knights.

At one corner, I saw a man watching me. I confess, I do not have a good memory for faces on occasion, but he looked familiar. He was lounging against the wall as though he had not a care in the world, but I was sure he was watching me. A second fellow was at the other end of the road, as if they were waiting for something, or someone. Like a thief-taker, or like a man sent by the Queen to capture me.

There was a loud noise in my ears, like the sea at Whitstable when I was a child. With it there came a bubbling sensation in my bowels that I recognized: it was the horrible beginning of a sick panic. Once, when I was young, I saw our neighbour put his pig to the slaughter. He had a friend come, and the two set the pig in a pen and bound its legs, and then they hauled it upright on a small frame like the cranes stevedores use to lift heavy loads from ships' holds. As soon as the animal was hanging upside down, it began to scream, a horrible noise. The men laughed and chattered as they held a bucket to the throat while it died.

Just now, I knew what that pig had felt. Seeing instant death no matter which way I turned made my bowels turn to water. It was enough to make me lurch back into the tavern, breathing deeply while I attempted to lose the feeling of shivering terror.

I was only partly successful. My hand was shaking like a willow in the wind. Still, I had my knife and sword and pistol. I was no mere simpleton to be captured, I told myself.

Squaring my shoulders, I lifted my chin and walked to the

doorway again. The man to the left was still there, but the
other had disappeared, and I searched for him without success.

Wherever I looked, I felt that people were staring at me,
that all around were hundreds of soldiers, all waiting for a
command to come and arrest me, to take me to the Tower and
torture me, or simply to murder me on the streets. And it was
so unfair! I had done nothing, really – or at least, very little.
Yes, I did kill Anthony Seymour, but it wasn't on purpose;
accidents happen, you know. All the other people I had been
told to kill, I had subcontracted to Humfrie. They weren't my
fault – well, they weren't my doing, anyway. But with Parry
arrested, surely Blount would be too, and they would be bound
to give me away. I was certain to be accused. And I could do
nothing about it. Oh, it was all very well thinking I could
instantly tell people that it was Humfrie, but he had already
let me know that if I were ever to think of giving away his
part in my career, he would see to it that I would die slowly
and very painfully. And while I knew that his own attitude
was more to kill quickly, and not make his victims suffer, I
equally knew that he could be induced to change the habits
of a lifetime, if someone were to give him away. And I
was certain that he would be even more inventive than the
Queen's interrogators in the Tower.

But in reality, life seemed to be going on.

The odd passer-by glanced at me, but only with the contemp-
tuous curl of the lip that people held for those who were clearly
quite drunk. And I was, I suppose – but I didn't feel it any
more. As I stared about me, I realized that I was being foolish.
There was no threat to me here. The queasiness had left me,
and instead I felt as though my body was perfectly balanced,
that I was alert, attentive, keen and ready for anything.

With a saunter, I went to cross over the road, but my boot
caught on a loose stone and I was nearly pitched into the path
of a cart. The carter swore at me at some length, and I tried
to ignore the ribald comments and laughter at my expense,
turning up the road away from the lounging man, but it was
hard to make any headway with so many people in the way.
I pushed and shoved with the best of them, earning a smack
on the cheek from one shameless harlot, and a threat from a

man carrying a cudgel, and suddenly I was confused, unaware of my direction. I wanted to return to Mark's house, but with the disconcerting dizziness assailing me, I was unsure of my direction. I stopped and gazed about me, and it was then that I saw the lounging man had gone. That was at least some comfort.

I made sure of the road, and soon remembered where I was – only a short distance from St Paul's, close by the Fleet, so only a short walk from Mark's. Thereto I bent my steps, but as I peered ahead through the crush, I suddenly saw a face. It was the lounging man!

Turning, I was about to make my way back up the road when I saw the second man striding towards me. Both routes were blocked. I panicked and turned to flee across the roadway to safety on the other side, but even as I began to move, a pair of horses blocked my path.

'Going somewhere?' a voice said in my ear, but it wasn't so much that which took my interest at the time. Rather, it was the sharp pain that told me I had a fresh wound in my second-best jack. He was holding a knife to my kidney.

That was when I remembered where I recognized him from. He was the man who had held a sword to my guts while I lay sprawled on the floor in the house where Peggy had taken me. He appeared to be making a habit of threatening me with being punctured.

'Hello?' I said and tried to smile winningly.

It was some relief that they did not have to take me very far. Whitehall was quite close, and the two held my arms as they marched me down the road, out through Ludgate and along the street to the palace. This we entered by the Scotland's Yard gate, and the two took me all the way to the Seymours' house.

I know it takes little time to write this; however, in setting out the scene, I should not like to mislead you as to the facts.

Was it a silent walk? Not on my part.

Were the two responsive? As church gargoyles.

Could they be bribed? No. I tried. In fact, I kept up a constant jabber all the way, promising them wealth, women and long life, if they would only let me free. I might as well have been shouting at the moon for all the notice the two took. They were grim-faced and uninterested. I mentioned money, bags of money, but they heard nothing. I did wonder whether they were deaf at one point, but then someone shouted, and both turned their heads sharply. I was quick to jerk my arms in an attempt to free myself, but that only earned me a clout about the ear, on the bruise caused by Alice's stone, that made my eyes spin and my brains rattle. The two didn't even break step, but I did. Both feet missed their place, and I was borne along by their grip on my arms, my boot-toes dragging in the dirt. It took a while to recover myself and begin walking with them.

I didn't try that again.

We turned down the lane towards the Seymours' house, and I was aware of a growing trepidation. These men were not the kindly sort who would break an uncomfortable silence with chatter about the weather, the latest play at the theatre or the threat of war with the French. No, the words I last heard from the man on my left indicated that he wanted to destroy me. That leaves a fellow feeling a certain dismay, and leaves him with the conviction that his companion has little interest in his well-being. It means conversation withers. A lack of empathy is what I mean. I didn't feel that he truly cared about me. As to his friend – he said nothing as well.

They knocked on the door, and it opened. With a squeak of protest from the hinges, it was drawn wide; with a squeak of protest and alarm, I was flung in through the door, to land in a heap before a pair of boots. I stared at them. They looked like hard-wearing boots, the sort that could all too easily be imagined kicking out at a fellow's head or belly. They had the appearance of boots that had seen a lot of life – and, quite possibly, death.

They were not attractive boots.

There is no easy way to begin a conversation with a fellow when you are looking up at him from a recumbent position. Many topics for a chat may occur, but when you are in the position of staring up into his nostrils, it is rather difficult to remember them all. When you add into the mix the fact that

I had just been thrown to his feet by a pair of his henchmen, you will understand that it was a more tricky situation than I could have wished for. That wasn't really helped by the fact that I had killed his brother, of course.

You will understand that I felt a certain trepidation lying there, waiting for him to make some form of pronouncement.

For his part, there was a terrible, cold blankness in his eyes as he stared down at me. I had the impression of great emotion only barely held in check. His eyes fixed on me and I felt like a mouse seeing a falcon. There was no feeling in his eyes. Only a terrible detestation and contempt. Well, I'm perfectly used to the latter, but the former was hard to accept.

'Oh, er—' I began.

'What did you do with him?'

Now, you will understand that this was a difficult one to answer. I looked about me quickly and was relieved to see that there was no sign of Hal Westmecott, or whoever he was. Still, it's hard to admit to a man that you tested the sharpness of your knife on his brother. It doesn't inspire the spirit of camaraderie that a man would wish, when you think about it.

I could have said, perfectly honestly, *Nothing. I just left him there, and it was Hal who took him away*, but that probably wouldn't have won him over. *Ask Hal* would have a similar result. I lay there, trying to work out the best response, while the room remained silent. Then there was a horrible, slow sound. My silent escort, the one I hadn't met before, had taken his knife from its sheath, and now he had wrapped a strap of leather about his fist, and was stropping his blade over and over. It was a sight – and sound – to chill the blood, and I felt suitably intimidated.

I swallowed. 'Well, I—'

'Let me start on him,' the man with the strop said. 'I'll soon loosen his tongue.'

He had a sort of quiet, reflective, soothing tone which appalled me. It made him sound utterly unfeeling, like a man talking about pulling the legs off a spider. I didn't like to think that I was no more than a spider to him.

'Well? Should I let Finch test his knife on you?' Seymour said coldly.

I swallowed. 'It wasn't me!'

'What wasn't?'

And here I had that quandary again. I did not want to admit to having killed his brother. I opened my mouth, but nothing came, and at that moment I was saved by Moll.

The sweet-natured besom took in the atmosphere and my position on the floor and gave a little moan of horror. 'Oh, Edward, no! You mustn't do that!'

'What else can I do? I want to know where he is!'

'Then come, just ask him politely! I am sure this fellow wouldn't want to hurt little Ben, would you?' she said, crossing the floor to join Edward and gazing down at me in a most appealing manner.

I thought quite seriously, for a moment, of giving her my best lecherous grin, but quashed the idea immediately. Seymour and his men were not the sort to understand mere friendliness of that sort. They would look on any overtures by me with extreme suspicion, I thought. Not for the last time, I found myself thinking of the neighbour's wife opposite. She had a much more accommodating attitude, I felt sure. Just now I wished myself in her bedchamber, unfastening the laces of her chemise . . .

I was rudely called back to the present by a boot in my flank.

'Where is he?' Seymour rasped.

'We want little Ben back,' Moll said, dropping to a crouch by my side.

It was now that they had driven thoughts of my neighbour's wife from my mind that I latched on to Moll's words. She had said I wouldn't want to hurt 'Ben'. This was not to do with Seymour's brother: it was the boy!

'I have him safe,' I said, glaring at Seymour and rubbing the spot where he had kicked me.

'Where is he, I said. I want my son back here, you ruffian!'

'I . . . *your* son?'

'Yes, my son! He was born out of wedlock, it's true, but he is yet my boy. And now I have a wife to help bring him up, I can acknowledge him fully.'

My eyes slid down to Moll's finger. There, on her wedding finger was a large ring. 'Oh!'

And yes, that was a big '*Oh*'!

I suppose my face registered my surprise. Moll allowed a slight frown to pucker her perfect brow. 'What?'

'You have married?'

'You asked me about it.'

'Eh?'

'The priest. I said he conducted our ceremony.'

'And why should we not be married?' Seymour said.

'Because of your father,' Moll said, somewhat tartly.

'And my brother. But they are too late now. We are married, whether they like the fact or not.'

'So you want the boy back because he is your son?' I said.

'Every village has an idiot, but there they are based on a small population. You must be the idiot of the city,' Seymour said with disgust.

I ignored his rudeness. 'That was why you had the priest taken from his church. You sent for him to marry you,' I said.

Seymour stared at me uncomprehendingly for a moment, then motioned to the man with the strop. 'Enough of this!'

The man stepped forward, his knife held lightly in his hand, like a man who was wielding a paint brush.

'I will fetch him,' I said.

As we left the house, I was aware of a sense of befuddlement.

I had thought that Hal Westmecott was keen to find his wife and son. Then it transpired that the boy was not his, and the woman was not his wife either. Before, of course, learning that Hal Westmecott was not Hal Westmecott. Who was he?

All through the last days I had been convinced that the priest killed with my powder had been killed because of his sermon, and then I believed that he had been taken to perform a service on the boy – to be baptized or confirmed in his religion – but now I learned that the woman and his father were instead making use of the priest to marry them. And now they intended living in wedded bliss with Ben as their son.

It would not have surprised me to learn that Geoffrey was

not Geoffrey, that Peggy was not Peggy, and that Alice was in fact the Queen's mother!

'Hurry up!'

I had been granted the support and companionship of Master Knife-Stropper and his friend, but also Moll herself. She had declared herself determined to find the boy at the earliest opportunity, and now she trotted lightly at my side, her skirts held high over the filth of the street. Our companions strode on either side of me, their hands on my upper arms. If they had allowed me to keep my sword, dagger and pistol, I could have attempted to grab them, threaten the pair and free myself, yet, looking at them, I had the distinct impression that I would have ended up with two broken arms. Knife-Stropper had that sort of imperturbable confidence that gave me to understand that, were I to try any sort of foolishness, I would be crumpled like a parchment under the first blow of his fist. Even if I attempted to shoot him, it was plain to me that my bullet would almost certainly bounce off him. His confidence formed a carapace as strong as a steel shield. As to the other man, well, he was tougher.

'Where did you take him?' Moll asked me.

'It is a small village called Clapham, some miles to the south of the city,' I said. 'We thought he was in danger here.'

I felt my upper arms being gripped more tightly, as though the men wanted to warn me to be silent, but when I cast glances at them, their expressions were entirely blank.

'What are they doing?' Moll asked.

There was a group of soldiers with polearms surrounding a man striding along the road eastwards. A crowd had gathered and was hurling insults with gay abandon, and the troopers were glaring back, eager to throw themselves at the throng.

'Another man who wanted to kick the Queen from her throne,' an old woman said.

'Who would want to do that?' Moll said, and I glanced at her to make sure she was not being sarcastic. She wasn't. That time when I saw her in her . . . well, her father-in-law's garden, I suppose, she had struck me as two bales short of a cartload. At the time I had thought it was the wine she had been drinking, but now I wondered whether it was her usual frame of mind.

'You do know what happened to the priest who married you?' I said.

'Yes, he was paid well,' she said happily.

'No, he was burned at the stake,' I said.

She stopped in the road, her mouth forming a perfect 'O' of surprise. 'No!'

I shrugged, although my shoulders didn't want to move very high with my companions gripping my biceps so tightly. 'It was days ago.'

'He was a nice man,' she said, and her whole demeanour changed. She looked like a dog that had been kicked once too often. 'Why would they burn him?'

'Perhaps he didn't comply with the orders about the new religion,' I said.

She opened her mouth, but said nothing. Instead, she hung her head as we walked on. 'He was a kind man,' she said again.

At the south side of the bridge, I was taken to an inn, one of the many down there, and we procured horses to make the journey to Clapham. It was only a league and a bit, the groom told us, so should not take above a half day to ride there and back. Moll was reluctantly helped to an elderly mare, and I was given a young brute who, the groom informed me, needed a firm hand, and so we set off, a spare mount in tow to bring back Ben.

I have never liked horses. When I sit on one, all I am aware of is the distance to the ground far below. Today my mount appeared to be one of those frisky types which is always likely to remove an unwanted encumbrance such as a rider at the earliest opportunity. He jerked his head alarmingly as though to test my resolve, and then began to nudge closer to Moll and her steed. Soon the reason became obvious to all but me, as urchins pointed and laughed. My own companions allowed themselves to unbend so far as to grin at the sight, for apparently my fellow had become utterly enamoured of Moll's, and his pizzle was most prominent. It led to some ribald comments from those in the streets, and soon we had quite a following of youngsters whooping and cheering us on our way. It was a relief to leave behind the ragamuffins and enter the fields and woods of the countryside.

The sight of fields and trees are calming to many a man, so I'm told. They praise the sound of birdsong, the peace, calmness, clean air, lack of stench of kennels full of shit and piss. I suppose it makes sense. However, highest in my mind just now was that any one of a thousand little bushes or hedges could conceal a man with a bow or gun. And that led me to the next thought, which was, once I found Humfrie and his sister and little Ben, these fellows would have little use for me. I've heard it said that life is cheap in London – although my profits tend to dispute that – but I had the distinct impression that, once I had delivered Ben, my life would be exceedingly cheap. I had the feeling that Knife-Strop would happily blunt his dagger's edge on my throat without compensation. And here, in the midst of all the greenery, I could see nowhere to run to where I would be safe. There were no peasants, only occasional riders or carters bringing produce or business to London. It would be ridiculously easy to murder me and leave me at the roadside.

That was a thought to make my heart thunder. I could feel a sweat breaking out on my forehead at the idea of it. In my mind, it was easy to imagine the blade being drawn across my throat, and if I really thought about it, I could imagine the blade raking across my spine after severing my veins and windpipe and all the other stuff that shows up as gristle in a beheading. I almost disgorged at the thought.

'Hoi, keep that brute under control!' Knife-Strop said, and I realized my beast had wandered back towards Moll and was nuzzling at her mare's tail. I wrenched the reins around as best I could, and the damn thing jerked his head, almost pulling the leather from my hands. Meanwhile, the two guards were laughing, one pointing at my mount's obvious excitement, and then my monster pranced, reared, jerked himself from side to side, and did everything to dislodge me other than buck. I found myself clinging on for dear life, while the cursed animal did all in his power to evict me, until he tired of the game. By then I was facing back the way we had come. There, far in the distance, was a rider, I saw. He was approaching at speed, and I thought I could perhaps kick this recalcitrant nag into a momentary obedience, and escape quickly in the direction of the man following, but before I could do more than let the idea slip across my mind, Knife-Strop appeared before me. He wore a broad grin, but there was no mistaking the cold menace in his eyes as he nodded his head back the way we had been heading. I managed, on the third attempt, to have the horse turn and begin to walk joltingly again towards Clapham.

We reached the village in the middle of the afternoon. The rider behind us had not been in a hurry, because he had not caught up with us. I was weary, irritable and, most of all, sore. It had been a warm ride, and the dust of the road was choking me. I wanted nothing more than a simple drink to wash away the miles I seemed to have swallowed on the journey.

'Where is he?' Moll asked eagerly.

There was a single street running through the centre, and a sprawl of buildings spread out from it, with a decent pasturage and fields visible, bounded by a series of small woods. Near the church ahead of us, I could see some idlers at the front of an old building with the appearance of a happy inn. I guided my horse as best I could and dropped thankfully from the saddle.

'Wait!' Knife-Strop said sharply.

'I don't care if you throw your knife into me,' I said. 'I am tired, hungry and thirsty, and I'm going in here.'

The two may have thought of sending a knife into my back, but the idea just then was less alarming than the thought of riding past this alehouse.

There were three fellows outside, one standing, the other two sitting on a bench with their feet to the road. All had the appearance of peasants at the end of the working day: weary, suspicious, acquisitive, as though they could believe anything evil of us, and probably did. They had that look of men who would happily knock me on the head to see what was in my purse. Yes, I know, I was in a bad mood already, and feared that I might not last the day, but even so, these three were not the sort to send a warm feeling of bonhomie to my heart. One had a terrible squint, and his neighbour only had a thumb and forefinger on his left hand. It looked as though someone had taken off the rest of it with an axe. Well, accidents will happen in the countryside, I've heard. Especially when a fight breaks out in a tavern, or when a man discovers his neighbour in bed with his wife.

I put them from my mind. Just now, being knocked on the pate would make for a welcome respite from riding with the two gorillas.

The innkeeper was a big, bluff fellow with an accent I could barely comprehend. In the end, I took the simple approach of pointing to his barrel and demanding a quart. Soon I had a large, foaming jug of ale, and had just lifted it to my lips when a quiet voice behind me all but made me burst the liquid forth like a dragon spurting fire.

'Humfrie!' I managed at last.

'What is this?' he asked. 'I thought we said I would stay here and protect the boy, and . . .'

'No time for that now. The woman outside is his mother now. She was his wet-nurse, but now she has married his father. The dead priest? He married them.'

'What of the other two?'

'They are Seymour's men, set to guard her, and to keep me with them.'

'Both have the look of fighting men,' he said thoughtfully.

'Yes, and I think they were intending to kill me as soon as they have the boy.'

'We'd best keep you from them, then.'

'I just want to be rid of them, and the boy. Is Peg here?'

'No. I sent her away yestermorn. She was little use here, and I didn't want her setting up trade in my sister's house.'

'Oh. No, of course. I see.' I drank deeply of the ale. Humfrie took the jug from me and swallowed, and I finished it off. 'Good! Let's get the brat, deliver him, and then I can get home and back to real life,' I said. Momentarily, a vision of the mess of my house sprang into my mind. Blount had described a broken door, belongings all hurled higgledy-piggledy, everything broken or destroyed. I had a sad vision of Hector lying in the midst of the destruction, and it made me steel myself angrily. If I had been armed, and if the two outside had not been quite so large, I might have gone out and attacked them. As long as Humfrie joined me, of course. 'Let us go and fetch the boy. The sooner they have him, the sooner I'll be rid of them.'

Humfrie told me which house to go to. 'You can't miss it. I'll follow you and make sure that the two don't attack you on the way,' he said.

I walked out again. The two were standing. Knife-Strop, having passed his reins to the other, seemed in the process of coming to fetch me. 'You took a long time,' he growled. Moll was still in her saddle, and gave me a nervous smile as though she had been worried that I had fled and taken the boy with me.

Ignoring them, I walked to my own beast and eyed him. He rolled an evil eye to me and stood still, as though contemplating snatching his reins from my hand, but I was not bothered. I pulled him and strolled my way down the street. The others remounted.

Humfrie had told me to look for a cottage of cruck construction. It was the only one, he said, that had solid oak timbers at either end, all curved towards the thatch. I soon saw it, further along the roadway, and headed straight to it, binding the horse to a tree near a trough. He bent his head and began drinking.

It was a small cottage, just one room below, and a small apartment built into the roof space reached by a hazardous staircase. I doubted it had changed much in the last two hundred years. From the smell of the place, it had been around at least that long. But it was warm and cosy with a fire smouldering gently on the hearth, and a pottage bubbling gently above it. I called out, and a voice answered from the garden behind. There I found a woman with a severe face under her wimple scattering grain to a number of chickens. The boy was with her.

'Who are you?' she demanded.

'I am a friend of Humfrie. I asked him to bring Ben here for his protection.'

'So you say,' she snapped, and dropped her basket to pull out a long-bladed ballock dagger. It swept past my belly and I squeaked in alarm. She was clearly her brother's sister. Except she had fewer inhibitions about using violence – and he was a murderer!

'Ask Ben!' I said, and I don't deny that my voice was pitched rather higher than usual.

She said, 'Well?' over her shoulder, and the boy, thankfully, indicated that I was indeed his friend.

I was against the wall by now, with my hand placed on my belly in case there was any blood. I hadn't felt it cut into me, but a fellow never knows. It's better to be safe than collapse. 'Mistress, you could have killed me.'

'There's little point unsheathing if you aren't going to use it,' she said. I'll swear she was disappointed not to be laying me out in my own gore on the ground. She grimaced as she shoved her dagger into a sheath at her belly. I was relieved to see it go.

'Master Ben, come with me. Your nurse Moll is outside.'

'What, here?' he said, and for, I think, the first time without a dog to tickle, I saw him smile. It made me think of Hector, and how he would never be stroked again, never sit beside me and rest his drooling mouth on my best hosen, never steal my breakfast . . .

Ben ran outside, and I followed at a more leisurely pace, the woman uncomfortably close behind.

'Moll!' he cried happily, and threw himself at her. There was clearly no lack of affection between the two, and, I confess, it was heart-warming to see them. Moll pulled him up to her, as best she could, and seated him on the mare's withers, and then she gave me a broad smile. 'Thank you,' she said simply, and turned her horse around.

Humfrie was at my side when I turned.

The men were already passing around the tavern, and I watched as they disappeared from view, seeing that the little cloud of dust followed them. They were not returning.

I said a heartfelt, 'Phew!'

'What?'

'It's a relief to be rid of them. The boy and the woman. I had thought I would be caught for . . . well, for the accident with Anthony Seymour, but in the end it seems that I've been saved.'

'Aye.'

'You don't look convinced.'

'I'm not.'

I frowned at him. He had a habit of looking on the bleak side of life, and on occasion it was wearing. 'You look on things in that manner, if you wish. Personally, I intend riding home and seeing what has happened to my house. It was trashed by Seymour and his men, and I'll have to see what I can rescue. Are you coming back to London?'

He had a horse which he had hired from another inn south of the river, and it took little time for him to take his farewell with his sister. Soon we were jogging along on the road northeast again. Neither of us was comfortable, but at least there was satisfaction in knowing that each of us was growing as sore as the other.

There was a small village on the way, which I had noticed on our way down. Just beyond it was a small stand of trees. When I mentioned before the risks of ambush and being attacked, it was here that I was first thinking of such events, and as we approached, my horse grew skittish. He threw his head up and pranced in a very pronounced manner, as though something had scared him. Humfrie held up his hand when I began to berate the animal. He slipped silently from his saddle, throwing me the reins, and crouched low. Stepping forward, he felt the ground and rubbed some soil between his fingers, sniffing at it. Then he threw a look behind us before plunging into the undergrowth where there was a patch of lower shrubbery.

Soon he returned, and, taking back his reins, he mounted in a hurry. 'Come, we need to hurry.'

'Why?'

'His body isn't yet cold.'

I gaped at that. 'Whose body? What are you—'

'You remember the two guards with the woman and little Ben? One of them is back there with his throat cut. His blood's all over the roadway. We'll cut around here,' he said, leading the way. My mount had to be urged on, but at last he complied, and we were on our way.

I was trying to find the words to express my feelings. 'There was an ambush? There are outlaws about here?' I gazed about me with increasing panic. 'We could be murdered at any time, and—'

'Master Jack, be still! Don't you realize? Someone else killed one guard, but escaped with Ben and Moll. What does that tell you?' He had a long face at the best of times, but now it lengthened further as he became increasingly grim. He continued, 'Someone wants the boy and his mother to be taken to be questioned. It must be the enemies of Lady Elizabeth.'

'Have you heard of the arrests?'

He looked at me, and as I spoke of the matters that had sprung up, especially the arrest of Lady Elizabeth, his mouth dropped, giving his face the appearance of a depressed mule. 'Is there news of her?'

'Not that I have heard, but since they have taken almost all of her household, it can only be a short while before they arrest her too. She has been in the Tower before. I am sure she will survive that, but I am worried about her.'

'Aye, so her enemies have taken the boy to prove that she was incontinent and committed adultery with Thomas Seymour.'

'But the boy was not his. He was Edward Seymour's son.'

'You think that matters? They'll torture them both to get the answers they want, so that they can execute Lady Elizabeth.'

I could see this, now that he spoke. It made sense. Someone had paid the guard to betray his master, and take his mistress and the boy. Oh, and slaughter his companion. I must do what I could to prevent a disaster. If my strongroom was still secure, there was money in there for me to find a new life. I could leave London, perhaps take a boat to France, and live well enough with the money I had.

'We have to catch them,' Humfrie said.

'*What?*'

There are times when Humfrie can be as pig-headed as a . . . as a mule.

'What, do you mean go after them?' I asked.

'The man has the woman and the boy.'

'But they are in no danger, surely,' I said.

'Someone killed one of their guards,' he said.

'But maybe he was going to attack them? The other guard protected them?'

'The dead man didn't draw a weapon. He was slain unawares. That means his companion killed him.'

'Unless it was Moll? Your sister was quick to pull a knife on me, and perhaps Moll is formed from the same mould?'

He looked at me without commenting.

'Perhaps,' I babbled, 'he was killed by his companion, because his companion realized he was a threat to Moll and Ben? He stepped in to protect them, and even now they hurry back to London. He is taking them to Seymour to make sure they are safe.'

'Or he killed his companion, and Moll and the boy fled from him, knowing he was going to kill them next.'

'Why would he—'

'He might catch them at any time. Or *they* might.'

'They?'

'He likely had an accomplice. Someone not on horseback, but who was around here during the attack. Someone who could hang back and attack anyone else passing him.'

'Eh?' I glanced about me. 'Wait! Where are you going? Humfrie! Stop!'

I had not asked which of the men was lying dead, and it was some surprise to realize it was Knife-Strop. The other was clearly alive still and well, because I could see him.

Humfrie, convinced that we may not be far behind the man, was setting a furious pace, and it was only when the horses were close to expiring, unused to such harsh treatment and racing, that we saw them: two men, both large and strong-looking. The guard, of course, I recognized, but it took some galloped yards to realize who the other man was.

'That's the man claiming to be Hal Westmecott!' I shouted.

'Claiming?'

'The man who told me he was the executioner, the man

who got me involved in the mess from the beginning,' I said. 'He told me to find his wife and child, but that was a lie, just to persuade me to do his bidding, the bull's pizzle!'

'So what does he want with the woman?'

'I thought he was working for Seymour, but perhaps he's working for someone else? The Queen wants anything she can get to ruin Lady Elizabeth's reputation, after all,' I said. 'He must be working for her, and he's taking Moll and Ben to her to be questioned.'

Humfrie shot me a look. 'We have to stop them and save Moll and Ben.'

'How? I don't even have a dagger!' I said.

He pulled his ballock knife from his belt and held it out to me. I tried to grab it, but . . . Look, if you think I'm just incompetent, let me remind you that I was galloping on a horse, being bumped up and down with every pace he took, and that Humfrie was riding at the same pace. The knife was bouncing around like a pea on a drum, and our hands just didn't connect. I felt a quick pain and yelped as his razor-sharp blade cut my finger, and then the knife went whirling behind us.

Humfrie gave me a long stare of contempt. Then, 'Keep close to me!'

He lashed his beast's flanks with the flat of his hand, kicking to increase the mount's speed, and crouched. I tried to emulate him, bending low over my horse's neck, but that was more to avoid the risk of a bullet than to go faster.

Humfrie hurtled on, and we were gaining on the quartet. They were riding at a decent pace, but not stretching themselves, and then I saw Hal, or whatever his name was, suddenly turn in his saddle. He caught sight of us immediately, and I saw his jaw drop. In an instant, he had grabbed the sleeve of the man at his side and drew us to his attention. That man turned, and I saw him pull my pistol – yes, he was going to loose my own blasted pistol at me! – and take aim. He clearly snatched a shot, because I saw the pistol jerk in his hand, but he cannot have wound it, else he hadn't loaded it or checked the priming, because it did not fire. As if thinking he hadn't pulled the trigger hard enough, he tried it again, and then clearly cursed and flung it away, pulling out his sword and spurring towards Humfrie.

Nothing loath, Humfrie dragged his own sword free, and soon the two were at it hammer and tongs. Meanwhile, I stopped my mount, slid from the saddle and retrieved my pistol. I was right, I saw: the mechanism had not been wound. Quickly, I set the key to the cog and twisted, then remounted, thrusting the gun into my waistband. Hal was some distance away now, and I set off after him.

You may think this was brave. All I can say is, if the man Humfrie was fighting bested him, he was not a fellow I wanted to meet, and just now the ringing clashes of their swords was very clear to me. I was happier leaving them far behind.

We were entering the outskirts of Southwark's sprawl south of the river now, and ahead I could see the smoke that lay over the city like a blanket designed to conceal the behaviour of the inhabitants from God's appalled gaze. Hal turned and stared at me several times, and I could only hope that he wouldn't realize I was all but unarmed, for a pistol at any distance is a terrible, inaccurate weapon.

The wind was a devil shouting in my ears. I could feel every hoofbeat through my backside. I tried to stand up in the stirrups like a real horseman, but even then the brute managed to slam the saddle into my arse as he took a little leap over a stream in the road. My face was fixed into a rictus, my teeth clenched, eyes staring, as I realized that Hal was going to fight. He had whirled his horse around, and now he rode straight at me, his sword whirling in his fist like a windmill in a gale. It glinted evilly, and I felt my scalp crawl with fear at the thought of what that might do, were he to strike me.

I tried to crouch lower, as though I could climb into the horse's neck, but then terror made me cast aside foolish cowardice. This was a time for serious action. I hauled on the reins to make the brute turn around so I could ride away, but the hard-mouthed monster refused to pay me any attention. He appeared to have got it fixed in his head that I wanted to run at Hal, and the devil take any other command. I bleated, gazed at the ground whizzing past me so close, and gave up on the thought of dismounting at that speed.

There was nothing else I could do. I pulled the pistol from my midriff, checked the dog's jaws still gripped the piece of fool's gold, that it was resting on the wheel, and pulled the trigger.

It is a strange thing, but sometimes when you fire a pistol, you are convinced that you will hit the target. But you jerk the gun, or you don't hold it in a firm enough grip, and there's a roar and belch of smoke and flame, and when it is all clear, you look at the target and see it is entirely free of injury. Other times, you let it go off without care or thought and see a hole the size of a farthing appear just where it ought to, much to your amazement.

Today was a new experience for me. I had never released a bullet from the jerking, unstable back of a horse before. As the gun bellowed, I was instantly blinded and choked by the swirl of greasy, foul smoke laden with sparks of burning powder. I felt the scorching of embers on my cheeks and hurriedly closed my eyes, but having inhaled, I could do nothing but gag. At the same time, I was to discover, I had managed to capture the full and undivided attention of my mount.

He had been running happily, no doubt imagining that he was a free beast roaming the wilds of Surrey like a lion, when the gun went off somewhere near his right ear.

If you have experienced a gun's shot beside your ear, you will know that it can startle and alarm. There is the report, then a loud hissing and whistling, accompanied by a near total deafness. As I closed my eyes, he bolted. Now, it is one thing to cling to the back of a horse in a gallop, and quite another trying to hold fast to the brute when he is terrified out of whatever wits he might once have possessed. And, I discovered, although I was competent with the former, I was not with the latter.

There was a curious series of sensations, beginning with a series of jerks and culminating in a strange feeling of lightness. Suddenly, I wasn't being beaten about the arse. I was as free as a bird – with the disadvantage that I didn't know how to land. The horse had thrown me.

I was aware of a sudden, slamming shock that went through

my body, then someone took a maul to my shoulder and struck my back and buttocks repeatedly. When I could at last open my eyes again, there was a loud singing as of a thousand birds tweeting over me, and I could see little bursts of stars. When I wafted at them with a languorous hand, they appeared to dart aside, and I was left bemusedly staring after them.

'Are you all right?'

I looked up into Humfrie's concerned face. And then up into Moll's. My head was in her lap once more. I gave her my broadest smile.

'He's well enough,' she said.

I had no memory after loosing my gun at Hal. All I could recall was that greasy smoke cloud and the stinging of the grains of burning powder and quickly closing my eyes.

'Where is he?' I demanded now, sitting up and moaning as the movement made my head hurt. It felt as if Hal had been at it with a blunted axe.

'He made off. Your shot went wide, I suppose,' Humfrie said disappointedly, 'but it did scare his horse, and sent him flying off towards the Thames. His horse liked your pistol as much as your own mount.'

'Damned brute,' I said. I looked about, but there was no sign of the knock-kneed nag.

'He took off like you'd shoved a nettle up his arse,' Humfrie said, and then, 'Oh, sorry, Mistress. I meant no offence.'

Moll smiled at him and lifted my head from her lap. I tried to sit up. 'Ow!'

'You'll be a little bruised,' Humfrie said without sympathy.

'I noticed.'

'You were thrown quite a distance,' Moll said. Ben was behind her, and now he sat in her lap. She put her arms about him. I was jealous.

'We have another horse, though,' Humfrie said. 'You can ride that.'

'Ride? Now?'

'We have to get this lady safely to her husband, and the boy, too, of course,' Humfrie said. He glared at me meaningfully.

I assume he was trying to tell me without words that we should hurry to protect the woman and boy, but in my mind there was only the thought of Hal riding at me with that damned great sword whirling fit to take a man's head off. It was not a sight I wished to revisit. I opened my mouth, and he gave me a look that required no translation. There was a threat in it that involved a great deal of pain. It was pretty non-specific as to the form of pain that would be inflicted, but that was unimportant.

'Help me up, then. We should be on our way as quickly as we may,' I said, and drew an admiring little gasp from Moll as I made my way to the spare horse, trying unsuccessfully not to notice the splash of blood on the beast's back where my friend from Seymour's entourage had been severely punctured by Humfrie's sword.

The ride to London was only brief, and as soon as we had clattered over the bridge, we made our way along the road to Whitehall. There, we found a stable and left the horses with a groom before making our way along the busy lanes to the house where Seymour lived.

I knocked, while Humfrie stood in the roadway with Moll and Ben, and when the door opened, I demanded to see Edward Seymour at once. There was some annoyance at my high-handed manner, but I was in no mood to be delayed. I stood tapping my toe while trying to keep an eye on the lane in both directions and failing.

'So, you return,' Seymour said.

'No thanks to your guards,' I said. 'One was loyal enough, but he was slain instantly by the other and the man who calls himself Hal Westmecott.'

'Oh, really?'

'Here are your wife and son,' I said, and motioned them forward. As I did so, I saw a flash of something behind Seymour, and peered. As I did so, Ben pushed me to one side, and I was unbalanced. I had to take a step inside, and as I did, I realized what it was that I saw: the man calling himself Westmecott was there in the room.

'What is *he* doing here?' I shouted. As I did, Hal stepped

forward. His sword was already drawn, and he looked daggers at me.

'I told you he would come,' he said. 'He wants your money now for bringing her to you! Kill him and be done!'

'He is the man who tried to kill Moll,' I said. 'Ask her!'

'I was trying to defend her against him and his assassin,' he countered. 'Didn't I tell you how he murdered your brother? This man cannot be trusted.'

'That man claimed he was Hal Westmecott, and made me find Moll for you,' I said, and as I said it, a sudden doubt occurred to me. After all, she had already been in Seymour's house with him when I first met her.

'Is it true that you murdered my brother?'

'I . . . no!'

'My man says you did.'

'Did he tell you how he killed the executioner, Hal Westmecott? How he disposed of that body, how he disposed of your brother's? He was here to catch your wife and son and deliver them to the Queen's men!'

'He is my servant,' Seymour said with a curl of his lip.

'Did you know he was getting paid to find Moll and your son? When you first saw me, when you had me on the floor of your house near London Bridge, when Peg had brought me to you, I was searching for Moll and your boy because *he*' – I pointed a trembling finger at the fellow – '*he* had told me to find her! Was he your henchman then? Or did he come to you more recently?'

I thought I could see a small cloud pass over Seymour's face, but he was determined enough. 'You killed my brother, didn't you?'

'He attacked me in my own house,' I said.

'And you killed him.'

'We fought. He was in my house,' I repeated. I saw little reason to describe the bonds which had held the man when he died. That blasted knife should have been too blunt to injure him, I reminded myself, but I didn't think that this was the right time to mention it. 'He broke into my house after bribing my servant . . .'

I broke off. Suddenly, it had occurred to me that Anthony's

words had been curious in retrospect. 'He said that Hal Westmecott had visited me,' I said. 'He saw your man, and said to me that he was Hal Westmecott, the executioner. But it wasn't. It was this fellow. And why should he have told Anthony that he was Hal Westmecott? So surely he and Anthony had been working together? Anthony was planning with him! That's it, isn't it?' I said to the man who claimed to be Hal. 'Anthony was going to have you take Moll to him, so that he could curry favour with the Queen?'

'He's talking rubbish!' he said. He spat on the floor. 'Listen to him! He'd say anything to get himself safe! Why would I speak with your brother?'

'He was against our marrying,' Seymour said. 'He wanted me to throw her over, but I refused. I wouldn't give her up – or my boy.'

'The question is,' I said, 'how far your brother would go to achieve what he wanted. He wanted power, I've no doubt, and money . . .'

'He wanted to have the family name cleared. After our uncle had an affair with the Lady Elizabeth, our stock fell at court, and Anthony wanted to be back at the seat of power, always. Me, I was happy to make a life with my wife and boy. But Anthony would not have taken Moll and Ben to the Queen. He must have known what would have happened to them.'

'The man who was with Moll and Ben at Clapham, and when we rescued them, was one of your men from that chamber when Peg brought me to you. He was an accomplice of this fellow Hal, or whatever his real name is, when he came knocking at my door. Then your brother broke in and attacked me.'

'And you defeated him? My brother was a trained swordsman.'

'Even a swordsman can be bested in a small room by a determined man with a dagger,' I said, trying to look as ferocious as I knew how. 'Why did your brother bribe my servant? He was asking about the executioner visiting me. He knew that man was pretending to be Hal Westmecott,' I said, pointing at him again. 'And that same man persuaded one of your henchmen to join him. It's true, isn't it, that your henchman persuaded you to bring him into your household only recently? I thought so. Because this fellow, Hal, wanted to find Moll as quickly as possible. He set me to find her, but thought you must know where she was. Why? Did you keep her from your brother? Didn't you trust him?'

'Anthony had indicated he might not treat her kindly,' Seymour said. 'I thought it better to keep her away from him. It was only after you appeared that it seemed a good idea to bring her to the protection of my father. And Peggy guessed, I think, that Anthony wished Moll harm, and stole Ben away for his own protection.'

'But someone told Hal, or he guessed, and followed me and your man when we rode to fetch Ben. But don't trust me: ask Moll. She was there when the other guard was murdered, when Hal took her captive with Ben and was bringing them back here – but not here, was it, Hal? You were going to take them to the Queen and claim all the reward for yourself, weren't you?' I said.

Hal suddenly pushed Seymour aside. His dagger appeared in his hand, and he thrust at me in an instant, and I felt the point sink into my breast. I gazed down at the blade with silent horror, as Humfrie sprang forward swinging his leather cosh. I saw Hal collapse, and then, as I brought my eyes up to stare at Humfrie, I felt myself slipping into a hole that appeared to have opened at my feet, and I swooned.

There are times when a fellow just wants to wake up without wondering what has happened to him. I've woken with bruises on my pate often enough to treat such injuries as part of the normal rough and tumble of my life. But there are other times, such as when I woke up on the floor in Seymour's house and Moll treated me with such consideration, or when I woke up on the ground after Hal tried to kill me and the horse threw me, when I am aware of a degree of irritation that once more I've been wounded for no reason.

At least this time I could understand why Hal had tried to injure me. He was furious at my exposing him. No doubt he had been expecting to receive a small fortune from finding Moll and taking her to the Queen. That would have been a day of great rejoicing in his house . . . or in a tavern. He was obviously the sort of man who would have lost any money in a week of carousing with the whores of the lower alehouses of London, if I was any judge. And I was. I knew enough like him.

From experience, there is a sequence of thoughts that strikes a fellow when he returns to consciousness after an injury. First, there is the moment of wondering where he is; that is followed by a quick recapitulation of the last waking moments and a mental check of all extremities and organs in case any are now missing; finally, he tests the environment with the ears to see if there are any hints as to what his reception might be on waking.

'He's awake,' I heard. That was Humfrie's voice, I knew, and I knew as well that there was no point feigning further unconsciousness. Running through my list of essentials, I remembered entering Seymour's house and Hal's attack; I recalled him springing forward like a bolt from a crossbow, and my falling. I could not discern any missing limbs or digits, and the sound of Humfrie's voice led me to believe that I was not in danger of being attacked in the immediate future.

I opened my eyes and the first thing I saw made me whimper. My breast was enwrapped with a strip of linen, and a pad on the left of my breast was crimson with my precious blood. It was the sort of sight to make even a strong man feel weak, and after my troubles of the last few days, I was already weakened.

'It's only a scratch,' Humfrie said unsympathetically. 'He glanced off a rib. You were lucky.'

Lucky! He wasn't sitting on the floor like a man-sized pincushion! It was easy for him to be so blasé, I thought, and as I did, I realized that my head was cushioned on a soft pillow. When I looked up, I saw it was Moll's lap that was so softly accommodating. I smiled at her, and this time for once she did not seem to mind, but shook her head as though in amused exasperation at nursing me for a third time.

'Are you feeling well enough?' she asked.

'Of course! I have never felt better,' I said. I could not show myself to be weak and feeble in front of her. 'Where is Hal?'

Humfrie indicated a figure in the corner of the room. Peering, I was relieved to see that the figure was swaddled in rope. It looked as though he was unlikely to be leaping upon me with deadly intent in the immediate future.

Seymour was sitting at a table with a goblet in his hand, studying me with a quizzical expression, and I could not help but recall that I had told him I had killed his brother. I gave him an anxious grin, but it appeared to serve only to make him more pensive, and not necessarily in a good manner for me.

'You say you killed my brother?'

'In self-defence. My servant, he was there, and he could . . .'

'He would support you, his master, of course.' He rested his chin on his free hand, like the devil assessing a new demon. 'You say this fellow killed Hal Westmecott?'

'He appeared carrying a rug to hide the body while I was there, so I think—'

'Quite.'

My head was lifted and Moll rose. I rolled half over to climb to my feet, trying to avoid glancing at my fresh wound. My shirt was on the floor, and I picked it up and began to drag it over my head as Moll spoke.

'He saved Ben and me. If it wasn't for him, I'd have been brought here and taken straight to the Queen.'

'There is that,' Seymour said, but his expression gave me little comfort. There was not much of kindness or understanding in his eyes, or I'm a Welshman. 'Very well, Blackjack, I will ignore your killing my brother. You have saved my son and my wife, and I know that Anthony was keen to take them to the Queen, so I can only assume that you were justified in defending yourself. But I don't want to see you again.'

'What of him?' I said, pointing at the huddled figure in the corner.

'Him? You need not worry about him. My brother disappeared. He probably swims the Thames even now. This man will join him,' Seymour said with a kind of cold ferocity that made ice run down my spine.

*   *   *

My house, from the outside, looked undamaged. That was good news. I stood in the street for a few moments taking it all in. It felt as if I hadn't been back in weeks, but it was surely only yesterday that I had walked from my door. So much had happened in so little time, and yet I had managed to return without too much injury.

I pushed at the door. It opened, and I saw that the lock had been broken, the staple in the door frame broken all to pieces. I was studying this, with anger at Seymour's vandalism, when a furious barking erupted at ankle height. I gave an involuntary yap of my own and leapt, I judge, about a yard and a half into the air. When I landed, my legs were weak enough, after all my trials, to give way. I collapsed just as Hector was living up to his heroic name by launching himself at me. I had a vision of a red, gaping maw surrounded with perfectly white teeth, before Raphe appeared to rescue me. He flicked a wet cloth at the brute, and he receded, still snarling and grumbling as only a small dog with a vindictive nature can.

Rising to my feet, I looked about me. I had returned to a scene of horror.

The walls had been bashed and broken, the dried plaster and whitewash submitting a fine white powder like chalk that lay over everything, including my backside from sitting down. The bannister rail was chipped and rough where someone had taken a hatchet or sword to it. In the parlour, my chair was smashed to pieces, and my favourite table had been savaged as though with a maul.

'I couldn't stop them, Master,' Raphe said.

This was curious. In the past, I have grown accustomed to a sneering, sarcastic servant of the worst form. Today, he appeared quiet and submissive. Naturally, I was immediately suspicious. 'You don't appear to have been injured while trying to defend my property.'

'When I heard them at the front door, I took Hector and we fled, sir. They were using heavy mauls at the timbers. I knew the door couldn't hold them, and I knew that I couldn't keep them at bay on my own.'

I narrowed my eyes and he paled. 'Fetch me wine, if there is some left in the house, and if there isn't, go and get some!'

'Yes,' he said, and scampered away. A rat seeing a cat give chase couldn't have been more fleet of foot.

Well, that explained his manner. He was still petrified of me and what I could do to a man. That gave rise to a fresh thought. When he had returned after only a few moments, my favourite goblet in his hand, I took it from him and then fixed him with a stern look. 'How is the rest of the house?'

'No better than this, Master.'

I glanced about me. 'How about my strongroom?'

'That's secure. They couldn't break down the door.'

I breathed a sigh of relief. Only recently I had been taken in by a pretty, Godless heathen, who used her man to try to blackmail me and, when that failed, to rob me. It had taken quite some ingenuity to get all my money back, but it had been a good warning, and I had made sure that the door and walls were reinforced.

'Very well. You will need to speak to old Thatcher about the walls, have him replaster all the damage and whitewash the lot. Go to James the carpenter and tell him I want another seat like the one he made before. See if he can mend my table and look at the handrail on the staircase . . . and anything else that needs mending.'

'Yes, Master.'

'Have the woman come and help you clean up in here. This is a mess, and I cannot live in a sty like this. I will remain with Mark while the work continues. You may contact me there. But I will come and drop in every day to see how matters progress.'

'Yes, Master.' This more sullen, because he knew he wouldn't be able to visit the tavern, or sit drinking my best wine and ale. He took my orders and meandered back into the kitchen, and my whim returned to me. I walked in and took up the knife which had killed Anthony. Feeling the blade, I managed to nick my thumb. 'By the Saints! This knife is sharp as a razor!'

Raphe glanced at me, then at the knife. 'Oh, a man came the other day and offered to sharpen all the blades in the house. I had him do all the kitchen knives. They were blunt. He wasn't expensive,' he added quickly, fearing a clout about the head for wasting money.

I put the knife back on the table, sucking my thumb, and swaggered from the room. As soon as I was out of his sight, I tottered to the stairs and sat on the bottom step. So that explained why the damn knife had slipped into Anthony's leg so quickly and easily. I could remember that slippery movement all too well – how the knife slid into him as if he were as unsubstantial as butter, and then the smell of blood and . . . mostly just vomit, really.

It was no good. I had to escape the house. The memory of Anthony Seymour's death was too close. I went out, banging the door behind me. It tried to catch, but then bounced open again. I stared at it, feeling deflated.

It was good to see Mark again. I had not sought room at Master Blount's, because just now I wasn't feeling too certain of my welcome, and, with Lady Elizabeth's household and friends being arrested, it was perfectly likely and probable that Master Blount's house would be under observation, even if he had not been taken yet himself. The men who devised clever, clever plots were all too often less clever than they thought, and usually their ending was painful, whether they attempted deviousness against a man like King Henry or a woman like the Queen.

For all his faults, and no doubt he had one or two, Henry at least tended not to burn heretics very often. Life under Mary was one long sequence of bonfires with a poor fellow on top whose main crime was only ever that he had prayed to God wearing different vestments, as far as I could see. Now she was upsetting all the landowners with her decision to return all the abbeys and priories to the Church, which meant that they would have to do the same, and confusing the poor with her new ideas about priests giving up their wives and children and becoming celibate (in many cases for the first time in their lives). Not to mention that quite a lot of fellows rather liked hearing the Bible read in English. Returning to the low droning of the Catholic mass was making many get itchy feet. Not that their feelings would sway Queen Mary in any way. I met her once, and while she didn't seem to me to be the vicious harpy so many spoke of now, she did seem remarkably set in her thinking.

In any case, Blount's house seemed less appealing than Mark's with Alice inside. I strode to the door and rapped loudly. Before long I heard Jonah's shambling gait, and his wizened, sneering face was peering at me with every appearance of dislike. 'You again?'

'I must speak to your master,' I said, and stepped in before he could close the door. He never gave any indication that he disliked me more than anyone else, but that was generally a sign that he would have closed the door in my face as a matter of course.

Walking through to Mark's chamber, I found him engaged in sprightly conversation with Alice, who sat in one of his seats before the fire like a lady born to nobility. It was clear from her look when I entered that she was less than delighted to see me again. 'Oh,' she said.

'You will be glad to know that Moll is safe,' I said, taking my seat on a pile of papers resting on a stool. 'She and Ben are with her husband. I saved them from Hal, who tried to ambush them, and then managed to convince her husband that Hal was the true culprit. He was trying to take her and the boy to the Queen, in order—'

I didn't have their attention, I could see. Mark was trying to tidy a sheaf of papers, while Alice watched with the indulgent smile of a mother watching her firstborn torturing a musical instrument. Mark, for his part, was clearly besotted with her. He chuckled as she made some witticism, and both seemed keen to ignore me completely. Even Peterkin lay on his side beside Alice as though she had always been his mistress.

'My house has been greatly damaged,' I said eventually. 'And I have been stabbed again. I would be very keen on a chamber for the night?'

'There is an excellent inn at the bottom of Ludgate,' Mark said. 'I will send Jonah to show you the way.'

'What of a room here?'

'Here? Oh, no. That wouldn't do,' he said smiling. 'What

would happen if you were found here by the Queen's officers? That could implicate me, and I wouldn't want that. No, you will have to go to the inn. You will be safe enough there, I am sure.'

It was, I think you will agree, a grim end to a harsh day. I was disconsolate, and Mark had not so much as offered me a cup or two of wine. I waited hopefully, in case my presence reminded him of his manners, but I had no such fortune. Instead, with a grunt of pain, I stood, and was about to walk from the room in high dudgeon when Mark gave a cry. Looking down, I saw that the papers on which I had been seated, had fallen to the floor. I bent to pick them up, but Mark flapped at me with his hands. 'You have done enough damage! Look at them! All disordered, and a most interesting thesis, too . . .'

I think I can safely assert that I know when I am not wanted. I took a deep breath and was about to leave the chamber when there came another knock on the door.

Now, a fellow can never tell from a knock whether it is that of a friendly face or a dangerous officer of the law. Both will often ring loudly through a house, and while one may herald good cheer and happiness, the other is likely to bring terror and despair. There is one lesson which I have learned well through life, and that is that it pays a man not to take risks. If a man is walking into a house, it is best not to encounter him in a narrow passageway. Better by far to wait in a larger space, which offers a possible means of escape by, say, the large window opening on to the street, or the second door that leads out to the kitchen and yard. If these were officers, it would be too easy for them to overcome me in the hallway from the front door.

So I stood and waited, while Mark muttered rudely about incompetents and knaves with little respect for learning and no brains to be spoken of, until Jonah opened the door and announced Master Geoffrey.

He smiled on seeing me. 'Master Blackjack. I hope I see you well, sir?'

'I was just leaving, I'm afraid.'

'No, I wouldn't want that,' he said. 'Please, remain here. We have much to talk about, after all.'

'I have to find a room for the evening,' I said. I was feeling grumpy still.

'Well, wait a little,' he said, and walked in. 'I hope you don't mind, but I asked your man to fetch me a jug and some wine. I think we have much to celebrate.'

'You do?' I said.

'Yes, of course. You have been so successful with the discovery of Moll and Ben. I am very impressed.'

'Good,' I said, and if I allowed a sardonic tone in my voice, it was deserved. He sounded as though he was mocking me. 'What are you doing here?'

'I wanted to visit you before you left. Because it will be good to end things once and for all,' he said. Just then Jonah entered, walking bent over with a tray on which he had placed cups and a flagon of wine. It was all he could do to carry the weight. He placed it on a narrow gap between a helmet and a pile of paperwork, turned and made to leave the room. Before he could, Geoffrey lazily swung his fist. There was a quiet thud, and Jonah was suddenly sprawled on the floor.

'What the devil do you mean by coming into my house and disciplining my servant?' Mark roared, as loudly as he could.

'He's not disciplining anyone,' I said. 'He's going to kill us.'

Geoffrey smiled at me, pulling out a pistol and aiming it at me. 'Yes, I'm afraid so.'

'I did wonder how you kept turning up, no matter where I was going,' I said. 'You always knew where I was.'

'Yes. You were quite easy to follow. You never seemed to take any care. Foolish in one so steeped in villainy and subterfuge.'

'Me?'

'Yes, your innocent look is almost convincing. However, I must apologize and leave you shortly.'

'Why, though? I did all I could to help you find the man who prolonged your brother's suffering?'

'My brother? I have none. No, I am afraid, that was my doing. I met your friend, who called himself Hal Westmecott.

Actually, his real name is Pug: Jonathan Pug. A rather unpleasant name for a very unpleasant man. He was in the tavern after buying powder from you, and I enticed him to share a barrel of ale with me. In the process, I made sure that the powder sat in a deep puddle of ale while he chatted. It guaranteed that the powder got sodden, and couldn't fire the next day.'

'Why? I don't understand why you'd want to see the poor priest die in such a horrible way.'

Suddenly, Geoffrey's eyes were as cold as – well, very cold ice. I could imagine them hurling icicles like spears when he was angry. 'He did not help me. I asked him politely to tell me where he had been taken by the Seymours, and why, because I thought he might be able to help, but he refused. Not that it mattered. The man Hal was searching for Moll, and the priest only knew about her. Not the real boy, nor the real midwife and wet-nurse.'

'But Hal wasn't the real executioner; he wasn't Hal Westmecott,' I said.

'No, he had killed the real Hal Westmecott because he wanted to find Moll and Ben. He thought that Ben was the son of Lady Elizabeth, so he thought to hire you to find them. He managed to meet you, and purchased some powder on a pretext, hoping you would find Moll and Ben. Since he had killed the executioner, he donned the hood and took over executions as Hal Westmecott. Whereas, all along, he should have been looking to another woman. A woman called Alice, who was sent to Sir Anthony Denny and his wife Joan Champernowne in Hertfordshire.'

'What has that to do with—'

'Joan Champernowne was always a loyal, supportive sister to Kat Ashley, Lady Elizabeth's most trusted servant. When Lady Elizabeth had to leave her stepfather, Thomas Seymour, Kat Ashley knew a quiet, safe place where she could go. And when a child-nurse was needed, Joan Champernowne sought an anonymous woman from London. A woman who wished to leave London for her own reasons, a woman who wanted to leave her husband behind and find a new home: Alice.'

'You are talking nonsense,' I said. 'You think Alice could be . . . could be . . .'

I looked at her. She had that air of ownership still, a haughtiness. It was not the demeanour of a wretched street-walker. This was more the appearance of a woman who had been valued by the rich and powerful. I've seen it in courtesans before, but never to the same extent. Alice had learned her manners from a very high-born woman indeed.

'Oh, ballocks,' I said quietly.

'It is not true,' Alice said.

'Oh, it is, I think. And you will have time to reflect on truth and justice while the Queen's interrogators ask you their questions. I have no doubt that you will soon be singing like a lark to them,' Geoffrey said.

'Oh, ballocks,' I said again.

'Well done, Master Blackjack,' Geoffrey said. He waved the gun airily. 'And now, I fear, I have to remove Alice from this happy company. Please bear me no malice, my friend. After all, you are responsible for plenty of other deaths, and I wouldn't want you to appear behind me with a pistol one dark evening.'

So saying, he took up the gun and aimed it at me. The trigger was released, and I saw the sparks fly, and I knew I was going to die. It was one thing for Hal to stab at me, but I knew what a pistol could do at close range. There was a searing flash, a roar, and I felt my legs give way. Instinctively, I turned and crawled away swiftly behind a table as I heard a loud *clang*. The chamber stank of rotten eggs and burning from the black powder, and I had a horrible feeling that I had been mortally wounded. My shoulder was stinging like the devil, but it was only the place where I had been lashed. My latest stab wound smarted too, and I had a thunderous pounding in my skull, but that was only the residual effect of a number of bruises.

In short, he had missed me.

I sat upright, peering between two piles of papers. One was smouldering where the piece of wadding had been flung, and I could see through the wisps of smoke the cloud of greasy, foul smoke from the gun's barrel.

It lay about the room like that from a badly smoking chimney, starting to stratify into different layers, which swirled and danced as Geoffrey and Mark coughed and waved their hands. I mean to say, I have fired my pistol many times, but never in an enclosed space like that room, and it was impressive how the smoke filled the space. It was like a thick fog in autumn when the mists roll over from the Thames and smother the city in a filthy, smoke-ridden fug.

But Geoffrey had already realized that he had missed me. I squeaked to see him draw his sword from the scabbard, and scrabbled my way backwards. I would have gone further, were it not for the wall behind me. And then I saw my rescuer.

I have often complained about the brute, but there is no doubt that when a man is in danger of his life, the sight of a great hound coming to his aid is a wonderful thing.

Up until that moment, Peterkin had been lying amiably before the fire, but clearly the thunder of the gun had startled him from a happy dream of chasing wolves or musketeers and devouring them. Now he was fully awake and could see that his master was petrified with terror by a man with a weapon in his hand. I credit the hound with recognizing a dangerous weapon when he saw it. He rolled silently to his feet, and stalked Geoffrey even as he stalked me.

There is something quite alarming about the sight of an enormous hound creeping along silently. Peterkin's eyes were fixed on Geoffrey to the exclusion of all else, while Geoffrey was gazing at me with something like pity. 'I am sorry about this,' he said, as he stepped closer, wary of my drawing a weapon of my own.

'You don't have to kill me!' I babbled. 'I won't tell anyone! You know me! I'm reliable! I won't do anything!'

'No, you won't. And you needn't think that you can distract me by staring behind me all the while,' he said, and then a puzzled look came into his eyes, and he snatched a quick look behind him.

As he did so, with a low and truly terrifying (to me) growl, Peterkin launched himself at my assailant. Geoffrey gave one alarmed scream, and then there was a crunch as jaws like a steel trap clenched on his forearm. He cried in pain, and the sword fell from nerveless fingers, his arm crushed, and then he was on the ground, and Peterkin was at his throat.

I have tried, in these memoirs, to be as frank and open as I can be, but I confess that the scene immediately afterwards was not one I care to call to mind. There was, let us say, a lot of blood, and this time it wasn't going to be easy to wash away, since so much was scattered with abandon on documents, armour and assorted items of Mark's specialist interests. And the ceiling. I have to admit, I was quite surprised by the quantity, even when Peterkin desisted and went to have a well-deserved petting from Mark, while Jonah sat up baffled and swore at the job he would have cleaning up the place, and Alice sat back in her chair and looked about her with horror fixing her features into a rictus.

The rest of that day was spent in discussions. To be truthful, I must admit that I took little part in the talking. As far as I was concerned, after this second attempt on my life, I was aware only of a great lassitude and languorousness. I wanted a bed to sleep in, ideally with a companion who would not be too expensive. I left the various people clamouring in the hall: neighbours, the local officer, a soldier who had been passing, two whores and a baker's boy, all trying to get a good look at the body where it lay savaged on the ground. I stumbled out of the place and walked to a small inn I knew south of St Paul's, and next morning I knew I had chosen well when I woke with my purse intact.

After a good breakfast of a slice of steak, kidneys, black pudding and three eggs, all served on a wooden trencher with a slab of bread at the side, I felt considerably better. When I walked out, I had a feeling of great contentment. I had been in danger of my life, clearly, from both the man calling himself Hal and the man Geoffrey. Both wanted to find Moll – or Alice – and to do so were happy to see me punctured. And yet their determination had resulted in their own deaths. One day soon I would have to visit Mark, but it would not be *too* soon. I had an image of the hound with his jaws chomping down on Geoffrey's . . . no, it wouldn't be very soon at all. Rather than go there, I bent my steps back homeward. After all, I was safe enough there, now.

There was a racket of hammering and sawing when I reached my door, and as I stood, considering, the door behind me opened, and the busty wife of my neighbour stood and smiled at me.

She was entrancing. She had a smile that could light an alleyway at midnight, and some stray hairs escaped from her coif and gleamed in the dull daylight, and her pinafore was bound tightly enough to show the figure beneath the skirts, which was more than enough to tempt a bishop. I gave her my most passionate leer, and she lifted an eyebrow.

'My house, I fear, is in a terrible state,' I said, waving a hand airily towards the noise. 'Else I would invite you inside to partake of some wine. I have a very good barrel of sack, if you would care to try some. But it is so noisy in my home. Perhaps you would like me to bring you a flagon?'

'That would be most kind. It would be very improper, though. My husband is away, and I'm sure you would prefer to wait until he returns?' she said with a reciprocal leer.

It was all arranged. Her maids were out shopping, and she and I could perform the mattress gavotte to our hearts' content – and possibly a lusty saltarello, too. She was oozing wanton desire, and I was full of lewd anticipation as I opened my door and hurried through to the kitchen. I found a flagon and filled it, then went to the privy quickly, and back through my house.

'Master, I . . .'

'Not now, Raphe.'

'But you need . . .'

'Not now!'

I pushed the irritating fellow from my path. No doubt he was worried about the cost of all the works – well, that was something I could worry about later. Just now, I had a vision of my neighbour's wife with her chemise wide, and burying my face in her bounties. I pulled the front door open, stepped out and—

'Master Blackjack. Come with us.'

You know that feeling, when something hits you over the head, and you're momentarily bewildered and cannot think rationally? That was how I was.

'Who are you?'

Three men, all in a mixture of really not very fashionable clothing, stood about me. The man before me was wearing a faded green cloak, brown jack and brimmed hat over saturnine features.

He glanced up and down the road, and said, 'Come with us, Master.'

'No, seriously, I have this. I have to deliver this. I'll only be . . .' I ran through various scenarios in my mind, ending up with a hopeful, 'A couple of hours or so, and—'

'Leave the jug. We're going.'

And I found I was. A brawny fellow with a light brown jack and cap took the flagon from my unwilling grasp and set it by my front door. Then he and another took hold of my elbows, and I was suddenly marching with them away from my house and, more to the point, away from my neighbour's wife. They half led, half carried me all the way to the end of the street, where a carriage stood waiting. I began to explain that I was prone to vomiting in carriages, that I was urgently needed by my master, that I was quite wealthy and there could be some gold in it if they would only leave me alone, but it was all to no avail. I was taken to the carriage, the door was opened, and I was bundled inside.

The door slammed, and the carriage began to clatter off, before I could even rise to a seat.

'You survived. That is good.'

In the darkness of the carriage, I had not made out the man sitting opposite. Now I could make out the features of Master Blount.

'No thanks to you!' I said hotly. 'I could have been—'

'Yes, but you weren't, were you? And meanwhile, you have performed well.'

'Who owns this carriage?' I asked. I looked about me. It was quite opulent. 'Is it Seymour?'

'Seymour? No! His carriage has his coat of arms on the side.'

'Then, whose is it?'

'You will have to wait and learn.'

We rattled along at a smart speed. I wondered about opening

a door and leaping out, but when I pulled aside the blind, I saw that there was a man riding beside us, the man with the beige cap and jack. He looked over at me, and I let the hanging fall back. There was no point trying to escape three men on horseback. They would catch me and bring me back. I threw myself back into my seat and stared at my master.

Blount sat with his back to the horses, leaning casually against the side, and looked quite relaxed about the carriage and our destination. Well, if he could be relaxed, so could I, I thought, and settled back, pulling my cap over my eyes.

I don't know how long we were in there. The passage of time, spent in the dark, is hard to measure. All I know is that before night we arrived at a yard. The door opened, and a fresh face appeared. He glanced in at us and then motioned to us to follow him. I climbed down and gazed about me. Suddenly, I recognized the tower that stood high some little distance away – they had brought us to Whitehall.

That thought was enough to unman me. I almost lurched, but there was no escape from here. The three men and their fresh companion were too close for me to burst past them and flee along the streets. Besides, there was nothing to say that the gates to the yard would be open, and the porter there would be sure to block my path, were I to run.

Blount was watching me with a sardonic twist to his mouth. 'Come!' he said.

Whitehall. I was certain that this must be the Seymours' doing. They had changed their mind about me and had asked for my head. That was plain. I felt a shiver in my belly, and a large rock appeared to have lodged in my breast. I felt feeble and a little mazed, for I was sure that once inside the building here, I would be slaughtered like a hog. Yet my legs were too weak to attempt a bid for freedom.

I remember the rest of the journey as a series of flashes: massive doors, a series of corridors, in through a pair of doors, crossing a hallway, into a small parlour, out into a yard, up some stairs and along a passageway to a different parlour. And there I was pushed forward, shaking and wan. The doors closed behind me, and I was left standing with Blount and staring at the petite figure sitting on a good-sized knuckle chair.

Blount bowed low, and I gazed at him with some surprise, before suddenly realizing where I was and who sat before me. I instantly bent so sharply that it was a miracle I didn't butt the floor with my forehead.

It was Lady Elizabeth.

'Please, gentlemen, rise.'

The calm voice was still familiar from the days when I had known her at Woodstock. Then she had been imprisoned following the rebellion of Wyatt and his merry Kentish friends. And now, here she was, presumably waiting to learn whether she was to be arrested again.

'Master Blackjack, I am assured that you have done me a great service once more,' she said. She had astonishing eyes, and she fixed them on me without blinking. They were very dark – I'm not even sure whether they were grey, blue or brown. In that chamber they could have been almost any colour. All I knew was that they were contemplating me, and from the approving sound of her voice, they were doing so without threatening. That in itself felt good.

'I do my best to serve you, my Lady,' I said, as smarmily as a duke.

'He managed to prevent the two mercenaries from capturing either Edward Seymour's wife and his son, or Alice and her boy,' my master interrupted smoothly.

'At great personal risk, no doubt?'

'I was stabbed, shot at—'

A kick at my shin almost made me collapse, and I glared at Blount, who continued unperturbed, 'He experienced some little trouble, but he is your loyal servant. Such affairs do not matter.'

'Do not—' I began, about to declaim about the damage to my suits, my body and my house, but a second kick at my shin was enough to still my tongue. Indeed, I was forced to purse my lips to prevent myself from crying out at the pain.

The lady stood – she only came up to a little above my shoulder – and walked to me, giving me her hand. I knew the protocol. I kissed her knuckles without making too much of a meal of it. A thought flashed into my mind of my wanton neighbour stretched over her bed, and I felt a slight shudder of frustration.

'You are in pain?' she asked solicitously.

Blount drew in breath, but I ignored him and gave her my most manly, devoted smile. 'I have been shot, stabbed, lashed and beaten in your service, my Lady, but that is nothing. At least you are safe.'

'Yes,' she said, and returned to her seat. She arranged her skirts before looking across at us. 'These tales, stories of my lascivious behaviour, are all entirely untrue. They are the inventions of those who wish to do me harm. As if I could have given birth to a child! The very idea is preposterous!'

'Of course,' I said.

'People will imagine the very worst of those whom they wish to hurt,' she said. She had picked up her necklace. It held a large cross with pearls dangling, and she tapped a pearl thoughtfully, sending it swinging back and forth. Looking at me, she nodded slowly. 'They will invent many things about me. Those who wish to see me destroyed will use any rumour, create any lie. But they will not succeed.'

I saw then a glimpse of the woman she would become. A determined woman, willing to use every stratagem and tactic to protect her realm, gracious and generous when she wished, humble when she felt it prudent, and utterly ruthless when she felt it necessary.

'No, my Lady,' we both chorused.

She nodded and picked up a book. Blount turned to walk out, but when I made to do the same, she looked up and beckoned me. Blount was dismissed with a flick of her fingers, and she waited until the door had closed behind him before turning to me.

'Tell me about the boy: Alice's boy.'

'What did she want?' Blount asked, suspicious as ever.

I said nothing. Her interest in the boy was surely no more than that of a woman checking on a valued servant's child. Yes, that was all. She knew Alice well, and was keen to make sure that she was not destitute. And Alice had taken part in looking after Ben with Moll. The two adored the fellow, of course. And Edward Seymour was keen to look after the lad as well. Seymour himself was a loyal subject to Lady Elizabeth, as he proved later. And of course he was keen to protect Ben. He adopted the boy into his family with Moll, and the two had many more children, but Ben was always treated as more than an equal, so I was told, as if he was more highly regarded.

That must be it. There was no more to it than that. And speculation on such matters is not a life-enhancing exercise. Certainly Lady Elizabeth gave no clue that she might have some other, keener interest in the pair. And there was nothing for me to say to Blount, since there was nothing there. I just shrugged, and he eyed me suspiciously before leaving me to walk to his house.

He didn't invite me to join him. Not that he ever did. I was a servant to him, and nothing else. He was not gracious like a princess, and Lady Elizabeth was a lady for me. She may not have the title 'Princess' any more, because her half-sister had taken it from her – since Queen Mary had taken the throne by right of birth, clearly the declaration that her mother's marriage to King Henry was false and the annulment of that marriage were illegal; therefore, logically, the next marriage of Henry to Anne Boleyn was itself bigamous and illegal, which meant that Elizabeth was born out of wedlock and was herself illegitimate. Thus she could not be a princess. That was the reasoning, but to me she behaved in every way as a good princess should. Which was why I had a weighty mass in my purse. She had given me a pouch of coins, and they weighed down my belt in a most delicious manner.

At my house I saw my flagon still on the step. But it was empty. That was no surprise. Any number of drunken fools wandering past here would have slurped wine left out. I stared at the jug with a feeling of morose fatalism. If things were to go wrong for a man, they might as well go wrong seriously, I supposed. Still, there was one good thing: the house opposite.

The thought of the afternoon's bed-bashing came back to me, and I felt my heart beat a little harder. I was injured, but I was alive, and just now the best way to refresh myself was to enjoy bouncing with a blowsy maid. Yes, I would see her

and make up for lost time. That would be the way to calm
my spirits and relax.

Hurrying indoors, I found Raphe dozing at the fire in the
parlour, an empty pot of wine by his side. It smelled like my
best sack, and I was half tempted to wake him and demand
to know what he was doing drinking my best, but in the end
I thought it better to leave him. Better by far to go and enjoy
the sweets on offer opposite my house. I refilled the flagon,
poured myself a cup and drank it off, and then carried it over
the road.

I knocked. The door was opened, and not by my favourite
neighbour, but one of her maids. That was a blow. The servants were returned. Still, I asked whether her mistress was in,
and the girl indicated that she was. I entered the screens and
was taken into the hall, where the woman sat sedately at a
table with some needlework. I put on my best lascivious grin
and was about to speak when her husband's voice broke into
my thoughts.

'What do you want, man?'

I felt my smile shatter like a dropped glass. I caught sight
of the woman giving me a slanted glance, but that was little
help. She had a little smirk fixed to her lips, I was sure, but
that was only a further annoyance to a man with fire in his
cods.

And then the bitch smiled. 'Ah, our neighbour told me
of this earlier, husband. He has a new barrel of sack, and
offered to bring a jug round when you were home so you
could try it.'

I could have thrown it over her. It would have been satisfying, but then I reasoned that if I were to gain favour with
her husband, I would have easier access to the house and
to her.

'But of course,' I said graciously. I set the flagon near his
elbow, but then idly rattled the coins in my purse. 'But I fear
I cannot remain this evening. I have an appointment with a
small club of friends. I hope you will enjoy the sack.' And
I took my leave.

In the end, I made my way to the Cardinal's Hat, where I
sat with Piers and several jugs of ale. I had hoped that Peg

would be there, but she had apparently been called to go and help Moll with some aspect of feminine work, and had left the brothel. It was a shame – but also a relief. After she had enticed me to the Seymours' house, where I had been in danger of my life, I would never have been content to trust her. I know, I was tempted when she was in my home with Ben, but that was a while ago – to be precise, one attempted stabbing, one attempted shooting, a murderous rider trying to cut me down, and all the other things that had happened.

There are times when a man craves merely peace and an ale or two.